Books should be returned on or before the
last date stamped below.

NORTH EAST of SCOTLAND LIBRARY SERVICE
MELDRUM MEG WAY, OLDMELDRUM

ALEXANDER, WILLIAM

My Uncle the Baillie

D0229485

MY UNCLE THE BAILLIE

MY UNCLE
THE BAILLIE

William Alexander

*Edited with an Introduction
and Glossary by William Donaldson*

TUCKWELL PRESS

F
950233

First Published in 1995 by
Tuckwell Press Ltd
The Mill House
Phantassie, East Linton
East Lothian EH40 3DG
Scotland

Introduction © William Donaldson 1995

A 20926
ISBN 1 898410 15 1

British Library Cataloguing-in-Publication Data
A catalogue record for this book is available
on request from the British Library.

The publisher gratefully acknowledges subsidy
of the Scottish Arts Council for publication
of this book.

Typeset by Palimpsest Book Production Limited,
Polmont, Stirlingshire
Printed and bound by Cromwell Press,
Melksham, Wiltshire

CONTENTS

	Introduction	1
	A note on the Text	19
1	My Uncle's Warehouse: A Couple of Callers	21
2	The Election Prospect	26
3	Richard Darrell, Bookseller	30
4	My Uncle at Home	36
5	The Crofthead Ward Meeting	40
6	The Candidates	43
7	A Sabbath Day's Journey	51
8	The Kirkyard	55
9	My Uncle Sandy	58
10	My Uncle Sandy's Love Story	61
11	Contradictions and Contrasts	65
12	Connubial Counsels	70
13	Elsie Robertson's Fortune	75
14	The Kirkin' of the Council	77
15	An Apprentice Baillie	81
16	The Ethics of the Baillieship	85
17	The Police Court	90
18	My Uncle Sandy at Home	99
19	A New Caller at the Bookseller's	104
20	Country Visitors	108
21	The Last of Tammie Tamson	116
22	Genealogical Pursuits	119
23	The Tailor's Son	124
24	John Cockerill	127

25 Engaging the New Apprentice   132
26 New Points of Departure   137
27 Another Sabbath Day's Journey   141
28 The Romance of the Bookseller's Life   147
29 An Unexpected Reappearance   153
30 Francie Tamson's Errand, and What Followed   155
31 The Last of Meggie's Tes'ment   161
32 John Cockerill's Progress   167
33 The General Situation   170
34 Richie Darrell in the Great Shadow   176
35 An Old Compact Revived   180
36 Is It the Unexpected that Happens?   184
37 My Uncle the Baillie has an Aristocratic Illness 190
38 A Passage in the Family History   195
39 Changes in the Warehouse of Castock
        & Macnicol   200
40 My Uncle Sandy Wedded   202
41 The Status Quo   207
    Glossary   211

INTRODUCTION

My Uncle the Baillie was published serially in the Aberdeen *Herald and Weekly Free Press* between 2 December 1876 and 5 May 1877. It was acknowledged as being from the pen of 'The Author of Johnny Gibb of Gushetneuk' – journalist, novelist and historian Dr William Alexander.

Then, for all practical purposes, it disappeared.

And a hundred years went by, during which it was mentioned in no bibliography, literary history, biographical or critical study.

But people did not forget its author.

William Alexander was born on the 12th of June 1826, of a long line of tenant farmers in the Garioch in central Aberdeenshire. Following a serious accident in early manhood which cost him a leg, he became a journalist on the struggling radical weekly *Aberdeen Free Press*. Later on he became its editor, steered it to national prominence, and rose to be one of the most distinguished newspapermen of his time. He also wrote what has sometimes been regarded as the best novel in Victorian Scotland, *Johnny Gibb of Gushetneuk*.

Johnny Gibb was a famous book, going through many editions and seldom out of print from the time of its first publication (Aberdeen, 1871). Alexander's powerful short stories in *Life Among My Ain Folk* (Edinburgh 1875; 2nd edn, 1882) and his pioneering study *Illustrations of Northern Rural Life* (Aberdeen 1877, Finzean 1981) – the latter a social history of impressive quality which demonstrated the potential of the form while many were still wondering if this kind of thing were even possible – also enjoyed a high reputation amongst discriminating readers.

But the rest of his extensive writings including several

further novels were left to languish in the newspaper files in which they had originally appeared.

There are several reasons for this.

One is that the author was an intensely private man who shunned publicity and regarded his writing with considerable modesty.

Another was the nature of the literary market in Victorian Scotland.

Alexander had to be persuaded by his friends to publish even *Johnny Gibb* in book form.

The market for the book-novel was dominated by England and Scottish book-novelists from Scott to Barrie (and beyond) had to live with the fact that they could not present a version of Scotland seriously at variance with the caricature existing in the minds of English readers.

A distinctively Scottish audience for the novel did exist, but there was only one way to reach it: and that was through the newspapers.

After the repeal of the Stamp Act in 1855, there was dynamic growth in the Scottish press, which brought the price of a typical paper down to a penny and ushered in a new popular literature. These papers were written in Scotland, and sold in Scotland to Scottish readers. Because of this Scotland and Scottish life could be represented in realistic and innovatory ways which owed little to English stereotypes and preconceptions.

Because books were dear, people often got their recreational reading matter in newspapers, which increasingly carried non-news items such as serial novels, social history, memoirs and reminiscences, poetry, folklore and popular musicology. And this was original writing, often of considerably quality. Sometimes, like *Johnny Gibb*, it found its way between hard covers, but mostly it remained in its original format. So, preserved in this apparently ephemeral source, there is a whole subterranean culture, the real literature of Victorian Scotland, the genuine voice of the 'Scottish Democracy'.

When original full-length fiction began to be written for the Scottish press in 1855 there was little real precedent. Here, perhaps for the first time, was Scottish fiction for a Scottish public – not for guinea-spinning English circulating libraries, or for upper-crust anglophone periodicals – but for John and Jean the Common Weal, the folk, the people. The form had virtually to be re-invented; and it was William Alexander, in a whole series of bold and innovatory works, who did the inventing. He gave it a new social outlook, new subject areas, and a new approach to language.

His was a fiction which dealt squarely with the facts of urbanisation and economically-driven social change; a fiction which swept aside prevailing literary usage in favour of vital new demotic forms; a fiction which discarded conventional social perspectives and dealt with lower class life from the inside: the social novel from the bottom up – Tolstoy by the peasants.

The prevailing medium was a standardised 'book Scots' – sometimes called 'Sir Walter's Scotch' – a convention derived from the works of Burns and Scott and based upon the usage of the Central Belt. This had become familiar to generations of English and American readers (as we can see by the howls of protest when the Scots began to change the rules) and its prestige was such that it had apparently become an acceptable literary medium even for non-Scottish writers. But the old standard was growing stale, and had never corresponded in many parts of the country with the language as people actually used it. In order to meet the new commitment to realism, therefore, it had to be abandoned, and Alexander, determined at once to achieve a scientific accuracy in vocabulary and idiom, and to unleash the creative power of the living language, pioneered the literary use of a new phonographically-inspired Scots based upon actual contemporary usage.

And he used it to interpret the country in a way largely unknown in previous 'Scottish' fiction, which had typically presented Scotland either as a land of history and romance inhabited by swashbuckling banditti or as a cosy rural backwater peopled by quaint, amusing – and ultimately contemptible – local 'characters'. But Alexander focused on the contemporary life of a rapidly modernising country, and the real problems that beset it.

His early *Sketches of Rural Life in Aberdeenshire* (Aberdeen, 1853) dealt with society in the North East at a time of rapid

MY UNCLE THE BAILLIE

change, and how the revolution triggered by the 'rage for improvement' affected the lives of ordinary people who were exposed to it, submitting many fashionable assumptions – such as the inevitability of 'progress' or the degree to which education could alter deep-rooted social and cultural patterns – to sceptical examination. *The Authentic History of Peter Grundie* (Aberdeen, 1855) treated the problem of the urban poor from a similarly radical point of view, suggesting that poverty existed not because of fecklessness or vice, but because of economic forces over which ordinary people had little or no control, launching a fierce attack on the doctrines of self-help and laissez faire and presenting the dominant social philosophy as destructive and inhumane. *The Laird of Drammochdyle* (Aberdeen, 1865, and in book form, Aberdeen 1986) took as its theme one of the central issues of the period, the displacement of the traditional élite by the rising bourgeosie, and the means, usually vile, by which social power was attained and enforced. Then came the later novels and short stories, *Ravenshowe and the Residenters Therein* (1867–8), *Johnny Gibb of Gushetneuk* (1869–70) and *Life Among My Ain Folk* (1872–3) which viewed the rural North East in the light of the new sociology and gave one of the earliest expressions in literature to the concept of social evolution.

In what appears to be his last full-length novel, *My Uncle the Baillie* (Aberdeen, 1876–7), Alexander returned to city life and the problems of the contemporary urban community.

The story is set in the northern Scottish city of 'Greyness' and addresses, destructively, the central orthodoxies of Victorian public life: self-help and laissez faire, the cult of respectability, the worship of 'success', the ideal of Civic Virtue, and the insidious materialism of a business ethic which tended to convert everything, including people, into commodities.

The narrative centres on the half-brothers David and Sandy Macnicol and their very different responses to the moral pressures of city life. The elder, David, the Baillie of the title, has come to the city as a raw country boy apprenticed into the wholesale trade. He marries the boss's unlovely daughter and begins his ascent of the city hierarchy, until eventually, glutted with wealth and power, he can decline the provostship as a mere irrelevance. It is in his orbit that the characters concerned with the public life of the city move: Stephen Gudgeon, senior Baillie, an ex-cobbler transmuted by the whirlygig of 'removable inequalities' into a wealthy capitalist and party boss, but in manner and outlook a soutar still; Peter Sneevle, the lean, hard-drinking law agent, ubiquitous and obsequious Mr Fixit to the city fathers. Then there's Uncle David's wife, the former Miss Castock, with her bevy of 'daachters', who regards herself as the pinnacle of burghal chic, but whose actual shallowness and vulgarity are apparent every time she opens her mouth; and finally the slippery John Cockerill, Uncle David's secretary, whose personal pursuit of money and power shows up the shady unregulated side of the Victorian business world.

Of course, it is possible to be a businessman without being a crook, as David's half-brother Sandy Macnicol clearly shows. Sandy is younger than David, brighter too, and a lot more unassuming and straightforward. He had started life as a farmer. But his laird was a keen sportsman who would not control the game, which meant that the crops on his estate were gobbled up and his tenants could not make a living except by cheating other people further down the line. Sandy wouldn't do this because he thought it was immoral. His fellow farmers were not impressed: they thought he was a subversive, or an idiot, or both. The suspicion and disapproval attaching to Sandy eventually chilled the affections of his sweetheart Elsie Robertson, and they drifted apart. Then he became seriously ill, had to give up his farm, forsake his beloved countryside and take a job as general factotum in the warehouse of Castock and Macnicol in the city of Greyness.

We find him when the novel opens at the focal point of a coterie of intellectuals of various ages and backgrounds. This includes Benjie, his nephew, who is the actual narrator of the story and currently employed as junior clerk at the warehouse; Jamie Thomson, another clerk who eventually becomes a doctor; Annie Macnicol, the cleverest and most unconventional of David's daughters; Dominie Greig, a retired schoolmaster, and, most importantly, a bookseller called Richie Darrell, a

peppery little man of Huguenot descent whose fierce disregard of pomp and circumstance and deep-seated genealogical
preoccupations loom large in the novel.

Alexander immediately launches into the story, and we are
at once struck by his precision, his economy of eye and ear,
his ability to convey much with unobtrusive subtlety and
force. How much, for example, and how neatly we learn
about the clerk, Benjie, the narrator: that he's young, a
country boy in humble circumstances, with a (possibly)
widowed mother, and (probably) brothers and sisters of
whom he is the eldest; we learn about his relationship with
his boss and the senior clerk, his inexperience and anxiety,
the fact that he's a stranger, too, only recently arrived in
the city. While this is going on, Alexander is simultaneously
broaching one of the main themes of the novel: the importance
in Greyness of hierarchies and pecking orders. John Cockerill,
for example, has only recently been made chief clerk and he is
very conscious of his new elevation; the narrator is conscious
of it too, in a way that suggests that elevation is none too
ceremoniously enforced.

The junior clerk speaks an authentic and unpretentious
Scots, whilst his senior is slangy and anglicised. This happens
often in Alexander. People he doesn't like condemn themselves out of their own mouths by departing in varying degrees
from a pure Scots idiom (making due allowances for education
and social class) and we can see this in the talk of Gudgeon and
Sneevle in the passage which immediately follows. Alexander
also uses body language to convey implication about people.
For example one of John Cockerill's first recorded actions
is a characteristically slovenly one: he wipes his pen on his
sleeve and sticks it behind his ear. His essential dimness is
also brought out quite deftly: when Baillie Gudgeon sends
him to get his master, Cockerill is half way down the corridor
before it occurs to him that he has been insulted; and his first
premeditated act in the novel is to consider lying because he
feels himself slighted, such is his inflated notion of his dignity
and consequence as a 'man' of nineteen summers.

There are early indications that power and consequence are
all just a sham in any case. Baillie Gudgeon's major asset is

that he *looks* imposing (the implication being that there is a lot less to him than meets the eye); Cockerill claims that his master is 'vera particularly engaged' when he's probably discussing with Richie Darrell a scrap of leather not worth tuppence.

At this point, Darrell himself steps into the story. His physical compactness and energy are the first things that strike the reader, then his sarcasm, for which, judging by Gudgeon's reaction, he is notorious. The visitors are edgy and respond with an ingratiating heartiness which rings the more false, because he obviously despises the pair of them. There's a grubby lack of dignity in Gudgeon's readiness to 'borrow' a pinch of snuff, and telling pause while Richie helps himself first before offering the box. It is clear who has the whip hand. When he has finished with them, Richie simply dismisses them, casually squashing John Cockerill in passing when the latter tries to be awkward because he cannot see – and never will – what it is that makes the bookseller important.

The opening chapter sets the tone of the rest. *My Uncle the Baillie* is an essay in consequence, dominated by a character who doesn't have any, or rather whose consequence is innate and based on personal integrity, while that of the others is detachable, and depends on their position in the hierarchy. To a man like Richie Darrell, no legitimate task is beneath his dignity or unworthy of his personal attention (and it has to be done *just so*). Gudgeon and Sneevle and David Macnicol live in a murkier world where private and public standards are strictly separate and where delegation and limited personal accountability are the rule. The honest man is occupied with what seems to be a trifle; the rogues have the management of a whole city in their hands.

And the hypocrisy, venality, and incompetence with which they do it is one of the major themes of the novel. In Greyness, the public administration is virtually a spoils system. David Macnicol has already resigned from the council once before because he thought his 'loyalty' insufficiently rewarded. Now Gudgeon and Sneevle try to lure him back with the promise of minor, but no doubt remunerative, office, and we see

David's typically mercenary response: na, na, he says, 'it's a mere throwin' awa' o' siller to nae purpose. I've naething to gain by gaein' back to the Cooncil'. The discussion with his wife which follows – she is a scion of a burghal dynasty and knows all about the power of 'old money' and how things are managed in its behoof – shows the same cool self-interest: 'I'll nail them siccar aneuch till a baillieship', says David, 'afore I lift a finger for the Cooncil'.

The squalid personal motives of the ruling class in Greyness are underlined by the Ward meeting that follows. It is an undignified shambles in which cynical self promotion lurks behind a facade of public spirit and democratic account-ability. The speakers, of course, evince the highest motives of disinterestedness and public service, but these are quite at variance with their actual values and beliefs. Stephen Gudgeon declares: 'Gentlemen, none of us, whatever party we belong to, has no private or selfish en's to serve in desirin' the honour of your suffrages – we seek the welfare o' the much-loved city o' oor habitation alone . . .' David makes a great show of impartiality and detachment, stating that 'he had never been a party man, or bound by party ties and obligations', but this is utterly disingenuous. In the hothouse atmosphere of the meeting his speech has every appearance of gravity and moderation. It carries the day and easily secures his nomination. But the reader sees it for what it is: a tissue of prevarication and falsehood from start to finish. The electors get the same uncompromisingly sardonic treatment. They are a rabble. The meeting is bedlam. Any sign of intelligence or altruism is simply howled down. It is a collective snapshot of an uncouth, ignorant, and rancorously divided community. The scandalous incompetence that prevails in the burgh courts is of a piece with the rest, and it all points to the rottenness of the civic polity of Greyness.

We see here a direct attack upon one of the most hallowed Victorian precepts: the ideal of Civic Virtue. This was widely prevalent during the later nineteenth century, and held, broadly speaking, that as cities were the spearhead of 'Progress', their government should, in consequence, be pre-eminently wise and efficient.

This was all very well in theory. But as cities grew, the scope for misgovernment grew as well, and we see Richie Darrell quiz the narrator, young Benjie, about his career prospects in a much more probable-sounding public ethos: in Greyness people go on the council to get a 'share o' the scran' and rise to civic eminence 'on the principle o' the scum comin' to the tap'.

For much of the novel Darrell is the focus of integrity in the city and his shop an oasis of probity in a woefully venal environment. He regards the public administration with contempt and neither he nor any of the other decent characters will have anything to do with it. He is an upright, independent, indomitable little man and is regarded with more or less unreserved approval by his creator. Even what seem to be his weaknesses turn out to be strengths. One of the first things we see him doing, for example, is editing for publication the sermons of his former pastor, the suggestively named Dr Cleauahair. On the face of things this seems a little pointless. The minister is dead, the flock tiny, and there seems little to be gained by Darrell personally in the discharge of this toilsome, perhaps even faintly comic, duty. And yet it is the key to him: the token of his granitic incorruptibility, the laborious, dogged fulfilling of obligation to the dead with no expectation of thanks, praise or material reward. In this as much else he is the foil to Uncle David. Richie Darrell is the good businessman, somebody who does it for reasons other than consequence and power; the honest churchman, too, keeping faith with his conscience in a way that contrasts tellingly with the sophistry of Uncle David at the Kirking of the Council (a thing compromising to a Free Churchman because it means attending a service in the Established Kirk). Of course to David public obligation overrides private scruple: the public man must adhere to different moral standards from the private citizen, painful though that may sometimes be. And so Mrs Macnicol has the pleasure, as we were sure she would, of seeing her supple spouse parade in the full panoply of a Baillie of Greyness, having pocketed his principles, without noticeable difficulty, for the sake of family ambition and worldly show.

Richie Darrell's main act in the novel is a very private one. It is to free his cousin Mary from the imputation of suicide and have her properly re-interred. This is a complex motif which draws several thematic strands together. Darrell is an enthusiastic genealogist who devotes considerable time and effort to researching his family tree. At a period when most educated people believed in the transmission of acquired characteristics, (i.e. as your ancestors did, so they passed on to you; as they sowed, you reaped), this is an intelligible, even praiseworthy, act. The idea descends from the school of evolutionary theory associated with the French biologist Jean Baptiste Lamarck (1744–1829), and it formed a powerful strand in contemporary Scottish positivist thinking. Alexander would have been familiar with, for example, George Combe's *Constitution of Man* (1828, and numerous later editions), which was required reading in mutual improvement circles in the North East in the middle years of the century. Combe insisted that man was part of the natural order. Bloodlines in people were much like those amongst the higher animals, and personality types, traits and dispositions reappeared in families generation after generation. Under this system, inherited predisposition becomes a decisive element in social causation. It also makes the present stand in a particularly intimate relationship with the past, because it is out of the past that most behaviour comes. Understanding one's family background is more than a pastime, then, it is a solemn duty (Alexander himself certainly seems to have treated it as such), a covenant with one's own nature, a voyage of self-discovery. And since the past has overriding importance in our understanding of ourselves as moral beings, enormous weight is placed upon its correct interpretation. Hence Richie Darrell's tireless efforts to find out the truth about his cousin Mary.

The exercise costs him half his bank balance, and this is approved of. Both Dominie Greig and Uncle Sandy echo the phrase 'money well spent', and we are implicitly reminded what some other people in this novel spend their money on. Perhaps using such dross to discharge an obligation to the dead is the least offensive use to which it can be put.

Of the two main groups of characters, Darrell is at the centre of those who, in some way or other, keep faith with the past while the others repudiate it by trying to change who they are and deny what they have been. In making him a seceder Alexander identifies him with the traditional core of Scottish religious radicalism and worth; the Huguenot strain makes him heir also of the Auld Alliance, symbol of wider European horizons, and political as well as religious independence. It is tempting, but probably superficial, to see him as representing what Scotland was, with Uncle David as the counter-symbol of what it has become, just as it would be to talk about the betrayal of the past by a corrupt and venal present, because although these strains are undoubtedly there, they are not in tune with the basically optimistic thrust of the novel.

Darrell's most important action is a dramatic one: he literally raises the dead.

And he is not the only character during this period to do so: nineteenth-century Scottish fiction positively teems with resurrectionists.

As the great medical schools expanded and demand for cadavers outstripped supply, grave-robbing (or 'resurrectionism' as it was grimly called) became a major public scandal; it also supplied the central device for many contemporary stories. It was one of the commonest 'codes' for speaking about continuity and change: the plundering of the tomb being a powerful symbol for the repudiation of the past and unnatural breach between it and the present. By the time Alexander came to write *My Uncle the Baillie* it was one of the hardest-worked conventions in Scottish fiction. As a good positivist with a keen eye for deterministic patterning it was natural for Alexander to be interested in this idea, just as it was typical of him to see entirely fresh possibilities in it. He turned the notion on its head, reversing its usual implication and considerably extending its reach. Richie does not plunder, he endows. By changing the past he changes the present; by cancelling an old wrong, he makes the future more sane and clean.

The essence of the argument is that what he represents reproduces itself into the next generation and the generation after that through Sandy, Benjie, Annie Macnicol, Jamie Thomson, and that a society which can do that is not, and cannot be, given over, wholly, to the worship of false gods.

Sandy Macnicol moves in a much more 'modern' world, but he has the same kind of stature, the same painful concern for truth, the same detestation of hypocrisy in all its forms and he is at least Richie's equal in dialectics. When the latter deplores the irreverent demeanour of the congregation at Bieldside Kirk, for example, Sandy retorts: 'Ye hae the real an' natural, at least, siclike as it is; an' that's surely better than a mere semblance . . . as regairds even a good thing, better that its absence sud be seen than its presence sugestit by a counterfeit'. A little later we hear Sandy denounce landlord-tenant relations under the so-called 'paternal system': 'the vera foundation's false, an' ostensible benevolence in the relationship o' lan'lord an' tenan' can but demoralise the giver an' degrade the recipient'. It is not the relationship itself, which is as remote and exploitative as well could be, but the pretence of cruel and selfish power that it is benign and philanthropic that provokes his wrath.

Not only has Sandy got principles, but he frames his conduct in accordance with them. This causes consternation amongst his brother farmers. To hold forth about moral principles is perfectly fine: everybody does that. But actually to act upon them . . . why, only a fool would do that. And for much of the novel it seems they may be right. By the time Sandy emerges as the dominant character, many of the relationships in the novel have been shown as mercenary and venal, but *working* – i.e. they are *successful* relationships as the world would see it, however opportunistic and cynical the assumptions upon which they are based. But look what happens to Sandy: he loses his health, and his farm, and his girl, and seems doomed to a drudging occupation in an environment he detests. Not only is the heroine wooed and lost, but she actually goes and marries somebody else, and a not very prepossessing somebody else at that. The implication seems to be that sincerity and honesty may be major virtues but they are hazardous to their possessor: integrity does not come cheap.

Years later, Elsie Robertson's son, Jamie Thomson, applies for a job as clerk with Castock and Macnicol where Sandy is now in charge. It is obvious that there is some kind of crisis at home, otherwise the bright upwardly-mobile Jamie would not be looking for a job. If Sandy hires him, his education stops. If he doesn't, then Jamie's hard-pressed mother may go to the wall. And anyway there are other boys as well qualified as he . . . so the apparently trivial act of hiring a junior clerk becomes loaded for Uncle Sandy with acute significance. He is forced to intervene in morally repugnant ways in the lives of Elsie Robertson and her son whether he wants to or not. If he does hire Jamie, he intrudes into a relationship from which he had long ago – with considerable tact and self-denial – deliberately withdrawn; and if he doesn't, he not only possibly acts unjustly, but deprives somebody, the least hair of whose head he would not harm, of perhaps desperately needed support. Sandy swithers. He could get Uncle David to decide the thing. But wouldn't that be the most abject moral cowardice? He looks at the applications again, decides that Jamie Thomson really is the strongest candidate, and, drawing a deep breath, hires him. It is an ingeniously constructed situation. Nothing really good can come, to all appearances, out of any of Sandy's choices. Everything is fraught with moral difficulty. And at the risk of subtle compromise to himself, Sandy does what seems to him the objectively 'right' thing to do.

This episode is coupled with the affair of Meggie's Tes'ment where once again he renders Elsie Robertson major service behind the scenes. When a grasping relative tries to cheat Elsie out of a small legacy we see Sandy as the energetic and resourceful man of affairs, and it's made very clear that he's not just a refined and basically passive moralist.

The mutual tact of Uncle Sandy and Elsie Robertson keep them largely apart during the following two years, and their outward manner to each other when they meet is cordial but formal. But several things are working towards their eventual rapprochement: Sandy is paying Jamie Thomson's fees at the Grammar School for one thing; for another, a mysterious female (who turns out to be Elsie Robertson) is unobtrusively caring for the ailing Richie Darrell in a way that provokes the admiration of everybody, including Sandy; then Annie Macnicol makes friends with Elsie's daughter Jeannie, a lively and attractive girl of ten or eleven, the image of her mother, who as a chum of Annie's is in and out of Sandy's company a dozen times a day and quickly becomes a favourite. Anyway, one lovely spring evening Sandy goes for a walk and encounters Elsie Robertson. He quietly adjusts his intended route so that he can escort her nearly home. They walk in silence for a while, then as she turns to thank him for all his kindness their eyes meet. Silently he draws her arm within his and they go for a real proper walk, together. A grave and sober love scene, this, and handled with delicacy: much is implied rather than stated and a quiet sympathetic humour bubbles beneath the surface. Various respectable citizens are also out for their evening stroll, and of course Sandy is a prominent citizen himself, so from time to time Elsie Robertson offers tactfully to withdraw her arm. Sandy retains it, 'with a comical glance into his companion's face, as who should ask, "They have said; what say they? Lat them say".' Eventually they land at Elsie Robertson's front door. To her delight and surprise Sandy asks if he may come in. And the long-anticipated reconciliation takes place.

Although it is difficult to assign this spacious and complex novel to any single genre, in one important sense *My Uncle the Baillie* is a love story: a deliberately realist love story which sets out to challenge most of the usual conventions. The characters are serious, sober, erring people, affected by their environment, sometimes negatively, and there is nothing of the high passion or general contrivance usually to be found in this form. There is no flirtation, coquetry or intrigue, just a serious and sober business deeply affecting the lives of the people involved. Love, Alexander seems to suggest, is a weightier, subtler more two-edged thing when it happens to real people, and it has all kinds of psychological and social consequences. Anyway, folk of Elsie and Sandy's age and experience (thirty-nine and forty-one respectively) should be more interesting and consequential than they were as mere kids twenty years before.

The garish 'society' match of John Cockerill and Amelia Macnicol which is mockingly linked to this emphasises the intricate pattern of contrasting and complementing relationships which lies at the novel's heart: Sandy and Elsie, Uncle David and Mrs Macnicol, Richie Darrell and his cousin, John Cockerill and his witless Amelia Matilda (not to mention the juvenile characters) combine to make as formidable a study of love and the institution of marriage as can be found in nineteenth-century Scottish fiction.

Concern for pattern and design is evident throughout, appearing, typically, in pairings of opposites: the 'good' businessman vs. the 'bad'; spiritual probity vs. slippery materialism; good language (Scots) vs. bad (English); real learning (like that possessed by Annie Macnicol) vs. false (such as the fashionable 'accomplishments' of her sisters or, at a higher level, the luminous humanity of Dominie Greig vs. the withering austerity of Miss Spinnet); real 'sibness' (Richie Darrell and his cousin) vs. false (Francie Thomson after Elsie's money); the true 'loon o' pairts' vs. the false (Jamie Thomson and John Cockerill, two very different loons with very different pairts, pursuing two very different kinds of career); 'good' marriage (based on mutual esteem, trust and affection) vs. 'bad' marriage (as a means of furthering careers and getting money and power).

The rediscovery of this novel means that another missing piece in the jigsaw of Scottish culture is back in place. *My Uncle the Baillie* is important because it shows the tradition behaving in ways we had said it couldn't. It shows us a writer who had been considered purely agricultural, and therefore marginal, writing about city life and doing so with authority. It shows us the existence of a strand of literary realism that until recently had been wholly unsuspected in Victorian Scottish writing which had been declared to be wistful, idyllic, backward-looking and escapist. It shows us that the Victorian literary scene in Scotland was more complex and interesting than we had suspected – even if we had been disposed to accept that there was such a thing in the first place. It shows us that in the end perhaps we ought not to be too complacent, even in our despair.

And despair has, very often, been the perspective from which Scottish culture has been viewed by the native intelligentsia during the present century. Reflecting a feeling of instinctive insecurity and pessimism still widely current, they have presented Scotland, broadly speaking, as the *locus classicus* of the missed opportunity and the second-rate. They have invited us to accept the period in which Scotland was transformed into one of the top four or five industrial nations in the world in its own right – namely the second two thirds of the nineteenth century – as one essentially of decline, witnessing the virtual collapse of Scottish literary culture. Since they regarded Scotland and its literary tradition as interchangeable concepts, the 'extinction' of the tradition implied the 'extinction' of Scotland along with it. Since 'traditions' were by definition continuous, there had to be something seriously wrong with one that wasn't. And so the foundations were laid for the 'sham bards of a sham nation' thesis and the pernicious effects that flowed from it.

These are fundamental assumptions, and just how deeply entrenched they are can be seen from the references to cultural sickness, disease and death which strew the pages of the standard modern guide to the period: volume three of *The History of Scottish Literature* – (Cairns Craig *et al.*, eds. 4 vols., Aberdeen, 1987–8) which represents the conclusions of about two dozen of our mainly younger scholars.

Now it is true that until recently we did have relatively little idea of what was happening in Scottish writing between the death of Scott and the coming of MacDiarmid. But this was because we did not go and look. And we did not go and look because we had already persuaded ourselves that there was nothing there to see. Thus intellectual superstition became self-perpetuating, having effectively immunised itself against the test of fact.

A cultural historiography which casually assumes that the recent Scottish past is a smoking hole and proceeds to junk the country on the basis of that assumption, is not worthy of the name.

A single new piece of evidence, however important, can hardly be expected to transform this perspective. But if the rediscovery of *My Uncle the Baillie* adds one more novel of quality to the precious stock of good Scottish fiction, and makes Scotland itself as a country of the mind, in however slight a degree, a less haunted and unquiet place, then it will have enlarged significantly the already substantial title of its author, William Alexander, to the regard of posterity.

William Donaldson

NOTE ON THE TEXT

I have silently corrected a number of minor spelling and punctuation slips, standardised spelling of character and placenames, rationalised chapter numbers and deleted one phrase present in the original text, namely in chapter 16, 'The Ethics of the Baillieship', where Francie Tamson is first introduced to the story as a 'good simple soul': I have excised this in view of his later misconduct – obviously Alexander had not finally decided what to do with him at this stage. I have also removed quotation marks around a number of Scots words and phrases to square practice here with that of the 1880 edition of *Johnny Gibb of Gushetneuk* which represents the author's considered position on this subject. All editorial comments are enclosed in square brackets.

CHAPTER ONE

My Uncle's Warehouse: A Couple of Callers

'IS yer maister aboot the place, laddie?'

'I think he is.'

'Will ye tell 'im that we wud like twa words o' 'im my birkie?'

'Ay wul aw.'

My Uncle's office boy, a youth of fourteen, dressed in a short jacket of blue cloth and green corduroy trousers, and whose whole aspect, no doubt, spoke of his recent translation from rural scenes, and the struggle of a fond mother to furnish forth the hope of her family decently for the important change that had just taken place in his life-prospects, was employed sticking letters into a big, unshapely skeleton book that lay on a strip of desk before him. The desk was inside the counter, and the boy sat on a high stool in front of it. On being accosted thus, he dismounted from his perch, and, with due circumspection, pushed open the door that let into the inner compartment of the front office. This compartment was occupied by my Uncle's chief clerk, a lanky youth of nineteen, or thereby, who had vacated the stool which his rustic minor now occupied, only a few weeks previously, and naturally was very far from unconscious of the advance that had taken place in his position. On hearing the voice of some one asking for his master, the chief clerk had allowed his curiosity to get the better of him so far that he had suspended operations on his ledger to listen and peep past the edge of the door. At the call of the office boy he now appeared bodily.

'Mr Macnicol, is't?' said the chief clerk. 'I think he's engaged, sir; jist wait a minute an' I'll see.'

'Tell him it's buzness that winna keep fresh nae time, will ye?'

'Wha'll I say wants 'im?'

'Baillie Gudgeon, an' anither gentleman.'

The Baillie had been the first and chief speaker, but it was the other gentleman who had interjected the words last spoken.

My Uncle, David Macnicol's principal clerk, had laid down his ruler and was about to turn into a passage that led from the front office toward a somewhat dingy-looking back region, amid a miscellaneous assortment of packages of diverse shapes and sizes half blocking the way, in a corner of which region the head of the establishment had his private room, when Baillie Gudgeon added—

'Say it's Mister Sneevle, the solicitor, an' me, laddie, an' that we're unco scant o' time.'

'Yes, sir,' said the clerk as he proceeded on his mission in an orderly way, first wiping his pen on his sleeve, and then putting it up behind his ear.

'Luik sharp noo, will ye, chappie?' urged the Baillie, in a half urgent, half free-and-easy tone, as the clerk completed these operations.

The two visitors, who were evidently charged with what they deemed business of some importance and urgency, stood up half facing each other with that air of impatient expectancy which men assume in such circumstances. In personal appearance they presented something of a contrast. Baillie Gudgeon, whose social position was that of an opulent shoe-maker, who many years ago had ceased handling the awl and lapstone, and now contended himself with his 'interest' in the tannery and a few similar concerns, was a large-breasted rubicund man of sixty or thereby; a man whose 'presence' formed an undeniable *prima facie* recommendation to the important office he held. Mr Sneevle, the solicitor, was thin and slightly cadaverous in complexion, with the exception of his nose, which had somehow borrowed a purple tint. His features were prominent and his face spare of flesh, with mouth of ample width, and eyes of a very dull grey, over-looked by dark straggling eyebrows.

My Uncle's principal clerk had got some way along the passage toward the back rooms, when it occurred to him strongly that he did not like to be spoken to in the way Baillie Gudgeon had done; and that a man of his experience and position was entitled to resent familiarities, especially if they happened to assume the form of insinuations implying that he did not make sufficient speed in what he was about. He had half made up his mind to act on general principles which he had at certain times seen exemplified, and without calling at his master's door to ascertain the actual state of the facts, turn and have his revenge by announcing to the two visitors, in set terms, that 'Mr Macnicol's vera particularly engaged; wud ye call back again?' But just as the clerk was shaping his thoughts into a distinct resolution of that sort, a stir as of someone leaving was heard. The door of my Uncle's own room immediately opened from inside, and a rather thick-set middle-aged man of low stature, with short neck, broad clean-shaven face, and very thick crop of light-brown hair, sprinkled with grey, and closely cut, tripped quickly along the passage to the front office, when, observing Baillie Gudgeon and Mr Sneevle, he accosted them with a sort of brusque familiarity.

'Yer wantin' Mister Macnicol? – Step in, step in, gentlemen! He'll be glaid to see twa sic high dignitaries;' and the little man who uttered himself in that particular tone which renders it difficult to make out whether the speaker's humour is bantering or serious, made a slight bow and waved the two gentlemen forward with his hand with an air that amid the due surroundings might have been called courtly.

'Hoot, noo, Richie; yer aye shavin' or sharpin' yer leems. Lat's see yer sneeshin,' said Baillie Gudgeon, extending his hand with the forefinger doubled in anticipation of the expected pinch.

'Sneeshin! Ye'll dee some gweed wi' sneeshin. If ye're gaen to leave the bench that's been so lang honour't wi' your presence, it wud set ye better to say yer catechis to yer neebour there; an' think aboot squarin' up your accoonts ance for a'. The like o' 'im's aye ready for a job.'

The lawyer exhibited a kind of uncouth willingness to

enter freely into the spirit of the observation. His smile at best conveyed only a faint suggestion of mirth; but if he did not actually laugh now the corners of his mouth got stretched outward at least, until the deep wrinkles at either end retreated toward his ears, and his lips tightened on his gums in a corresponding degree.

'I'll gie the Baillie snuff,' said Mr Sneevle, who was also addicted to the fragrant herb, putting up his hand for the purpose and speaking in a tone of express cheerfulness.

'Ye'se dee naething o' the kin',' replied the stubbly-headed little man, who up to that moment had not overtly indicated any intention of acceding to Baillie Gudgeon's request. He now took from his waistcoat pocket an oval snuff-box formed from a buffalo's horn, and flat at top and bottom, and, raising the lid, first supplied himself liberally through the medium of a tiny shovel of bone before he handed the box to Baillie Gudgeon, who accepted it with the remark—

'Ou, we a' ken Richie. But he cairries aye a starn gweed rappee – the lawyer, there, has naething like it.'

'Ye may ken weel ye haena prov't it sae seldom,' said Richie.

'I suppose ye keep him in snuff, Mr Darrell,' said the lawyer. 'Ye should chairge him for his supply.'

'Deed, Mister Sneevle, the advice does ye credit; but the like o' me hasna a scale o' chairges shapit to my han' to help me to fleece fowk wi' a show o' custom, if no o' decency.'

'Weel done, Richie; ye hae 'im o' the hip there ony wye,' exclaimed Baillie Gudgeon with a loud chuckle, and rubbing his chin with his two forefingers, as was his wont when he felt particularly pleased.

'Gae wa; gae wa to the ither en' an' sattle the toon's affairs, an' nae stan' here wastin' yer time in frivolous blether,' said Richie, who, turning to the clerk as he spoke, while his two interlocutors passed inward, asked – 'Is the Deacon in?'

'No,' said the clerk. 'Was ye wantin' 'im?'

'Ye wud like to ken, I daursay. Is't likely I wud speer aifter 'im if I didna want 'im – Faur is he?'

'He's oot on buzness; but if it's onything ye're needin' I cud—'

'Ye cud dee't yersel', nae doot. Na, na. Tell 'im that I'm
wantin' a strip o' the vera best lamb's-skin i' yer warhoose –
like that, or a sizie bigger'; and the sharp little man exhibited
a piece of stout brown paper some eight to ten inches in length
by about half that measure in width.

'Hah! I can gie you that mysel' as weel as he cud dee – lat's
see't,' said the clerk, stretching over the counter for the paper
pattern.

'Ye're a vera smairt young man, Maister Cockerill; but ye'll
jist alloo me to dee my business in my ain fashion,' answered
Richie, as he folded the paper and thrust it into one of the big
outside tail pockets of his brown coat. 'Tell Deacon Sandy to
call in at my chop as he gaes hame i' the gloamin'.'

As Richie Darrell uttered the last words he was moving
toward the door through which he quickly passed into the
outer world, leaving my Uncle's chief clerk, John Cockerill,
to solace himself for the slight cast on his sense of self-
importance, by uttering cynical remarks to his junior, who,
it may be here candidly stated, was the compiler of this true
history, concerning the impracticable and senseless nature of
some people.

'He wud need it! Makin' a fuss aboot tippence worth o'
sheepskin leather; first at the maister aboot it, an' syne wud
hae nane but the man 't's neist to the maister to sair 'im. It
wud be fat he deserves to tell 'im to gae to the nearest cobbler's
an get some o's au' cuttins. – Fat wud Baillie Gudgeon an' the
lawyer be in sic a chase aboot,' continued Mr Cockerill, whose
temper had been slightly ruffled on both sides. 'I'se wauger
they'll be in nae hurry oot again though; but if ony ither body
calls, faever it be, jist rap an' gae in to the maister at ance; or
at ony rate lat me ken.'

So saying the irate principal clerk returned to his desk, and
the office boy mounted his stool again, and resumed his work
of filing business correspondence.

CHAPTER TWO

The Election Prospect

I T is right at this stage to explain that my Uncle, Mr David Macnicol, whose elevation to the dignity of a municipal magistrate it is proposed to record, was well known throughout the city of his habitation, and even beyond it, as a careful and prosperous trader. His business, as described by himself, was that of a merchant. He held shares in shipping, he dealt in leather, and he transacted as principal or agent in a variety of drysaltery and other goods. His warehouse, which was situated in a second-rate street, and wore a dull and miscellaneous aspect in the interior of it, was one of those places about which there never appears to be anything in the nature of stir, but in which men nevertheless contrive to amass money. There was reason to believe that my Uncle – himself originally a poor lad from the Glentons of Strathtocher – had done fairly well in that way long before he became known as a public man. But it was now a full half-dozen years since he had been first elected to the Town Council; and from that date onward his standing in the community had been greatly more definite and potential. Nor amongst his own relatives was the effect less marked. These were generally of the class who can afford to feel virtuously on the subject of wealth and position because they possess neither, but who, if they at times discussed their kinsman a little severely amongst themselves, were on the whole rather fain to be known as connected with the rising merchant who had also figured in the Town Council of Greyness. My Uncle's marriage to the only surviving child of his employer, the late Baillie Castock, whom, in due course, he succeeded in business, inasmuch as it lifted him at once into the society of the place, had been a subject of mingled censure and glorification amongst those to whom he stood related by blood and marriage. It was clear that plain Dawvid Macnicol, the erstwhile clerk, had the ambition to be something, and he was achieving his purpose by means open to diverse interpretations. Yet when he sought and obtained the imprimatur of Town Councillor, who could deny that the responsible voice of the community was on his side, and in token thereof had, in a constitutional way, conferred upon him a distinctive character among his fellow-citizens?

In my own case, it may as well be said at once that my Uncle's patronage had been exercised to the effect of setting me on the stool in his front office; a position which, as already indicated, I had occupied but a very few weeks when my story opens. His act in this might be described, no doubt, as placing my feet on the lowest rung of the ladder leading up to fortune; and I was bound to be grateful accordingly. In addition to my Uncle David, there was his brother Alexander, familiarly styled Sandy, whom Richie Darrell had asked after under the name of the Deacon. Sandy, as my widowed mother's twin brother – both being several years younger than the central figure in my story – seemed to stand in a peculiarly near relation to myself, even as compared with the individual of whom I have felt it incumbent upon me chiefly to write; but though he occupied the position of a kind of factotum on the business, and one way and another came to bulk rather largely in my poor personal history, he was necessarily a much less considerable personage than the head of the house, and it may suffice to let his character develop itself as we go on.

'We took a luik in to see you, Mr Macnicol – aboot the election, ye ken,' said Baillie Gudgeon, addressing my Uncle, David, when salutations had been exchanged, and the two visitors had got seated in my Uncle's own room, 'Ye'll need to gie's a hitch this time.'

'I fear there's naething in my poo'er Baillie,' was my Uncle's guarded reply. 'No; I fear there's naething in my poo'er.'

'We're vera anxious to get good men,' suggested Mr Sneevle.

'Men o' expaireince,' interposed the Baillie.

'There's so much important business comin' afore the Cooncil that it's a positive duty for men that the electors can hae confidence in; an' men that hae a lairge stake i' the toon, to offer themsel's,' pursued the lawyer.

'True, true,' said my Uncle, meditatively, 'an' I've nae doot, though it's a thankless job, that men'll be forthcomin'.'

'Weel,' said Baillie Gudgeon, coming to the point at last, 'there's a vera strong wush to get you back to your aul' ward at the Craftheid; an' in fac' Maister Sneevle an' me, as twa aul' freens, an' him yer nain awgent forby, cam' here to get your consent.'

'I cudna think o' sic a thing!' answered my Uncle with a decision that seemed greatly to shock and stagger his friends, who simultaneously exclaimed—

'Hoot! hoot! Maister Macnicol.'

'No; no. It'll be a close fecht – a mere throwin' awa' o' siller to nae purpose. I've naething to gain by gaein' back to the Cooncil.'

'Oh, but Mr Macnicol ye've aye stood by the pairty ye ken,' urged Mr Sneevle.

'Ay ay; as weel's the pairty's stood by me,' replied my Uncle firmly.

Baillie Gudgeon and Mr Sneevle looked at each other with a knowing glance, as the former cautiously said—

'The cast's nae a' thegither sattl't yet, ye ken; there'll be a bit office or twa free, siclike's the Hospital convenership.'

'I dinna want the Hospital convenership. It's a thankless job sairin' the public, I tell ye. Hooever, ye'll get men ready an' willin' to be cooncillors nae doot; an' it seems ye hae plenty luikin' for onything else 't's a-gaein – providin' ye cairry yer men.'

'Ou, we canna but cairry ye ken,' said Baillie Gudgeon. 'The tither side's fairly pitten their fit in't by proposin' a bawbee tax for the drainin' o' the Stinkin' Lochie; the public will not stan' mair taxes; an' there's ither things that we a' ken aboot that'll craw i' their craps.'

'Weel, weel,' said my Uncle, with a touch of dryness in his manner. 'There micht be waur things nor drainin' the Lochie.'

'Eh, but ye cudna speak o' a tax,' said the Baillie earnestly.

'I'm nae sayin't I wud,' was my Uncle's reply; 'It's nae lickly I'll hae to express mysel' ae wye or the ither.'

'Weel, we jist cam up to you in a frien'ly wye first, Mr Macnicol, kennin' that the Provost has a vera great regard for you,' said Baillie Gudgeon, after a pause.

'Ye needna lat on that we've been in i' the meantime,' added Mr Sneevle. 'I've nae doot things'll come a' till a proper bearin'. This meetin's quite an informal ane, ye ken. There's nobody committit. But I do think raelly that it's your duty to come forward at this time, whan we've sae mony questions o' public importance comin' up. As the Baillie was jist sayin' afore we cam' in, there's nane mair capable, an' fyou likely to be mair willin' to yield private feelin's for the general good than you. Ye'll think fawvourably o't, Maister Macnicol; an' min' the Ward meetin's 'll be upon's in a fyou days' time.'

With this flattering speech, and a sufficiently distinct understanding of how the land lay, my Uncle's visitors took their leave and proceeded to call on the next possible candidate for municipal honours.

CHAPTER THREE

Richard Darrell, Bookseller

AULD Hallowgate, the thoroughfare that contained my Uncle's warehouse, was entitled to be described as one of the main arteries of the town of Greyness. At its lower and wider end it touched the very heart of the town, and there the traffic was considerable. Proceeding outward, and after passing the intersection of two or three tributary streets, it got narrower of itself, its course became slightly devious, and the current of traffic thinned away to right and left till it got reduced to something like half its original volume. It was at its wider end that my Uncle had his place of business. A furlong northward along the street, where the houses were old-fashioned and irregular in size and style, a quaint-looking structure, with crow-stepped gable toward the street, came curiously in between two groups of more modern houses. The gable, narrow as it was, had been made to give space for a door and ground-floor window as well; and over the door was a small signboard, on which were dimly painted the words—

R. DARRELL,
BOOKSELLER

The window of the shop that fronted the street, and which was necessarily of limited size, was rather inconveniently packed with books. These, as one could see at a glance, were mainly theological in character, with a sprinkling of the commoner school classics and a few historical books. The greater part, though not the whole of them, were second-hand too; and in the case of a few large tomes the prices were 'marked in plain figures,' evidently 'done' by the hand of the proprietor. The shop door, which opened with a latch, there being a big keyhole a little below, was painted green, and its upper half was filled with glass. On pressing the latch open, it was found that one step had to be made down from the pavement to the shop floor. And even then, if a tall customer stood quite erect within the shop, the crown of his hat came within two or three inches of the whitewashed ceiling. A narrow counter intersected the shop laterally, a passage round being left open at the end, opposite which there was a door that let into a small back shop or inner apartment. Along the two sides, and all within arm's length, the walls were covered with shelves filled with books much of the character of those in the window. A modest glass case, underneath which were sheaves of quills, boxes of steel pens and wafers, note paper, sealing wax, and other stationery, extended from the door nearly half-way along the counter, inside of which the prominent features were the fire-place, with its high and narrow old-fashioned grate, and a deal chair, on which the bookseller took his seat as occasion served.

The aspect of the place as a whole rather suggested the idea that bookselling had not been the craft to which the owner of the shop had been bred. And it was not. Yet that might be said of him which could hardly be said of sundry of the more pretentious booksellers in Greyness – he was read up in, and prepared with a definite opinion concerning, all the chief works in the class of books in which he dealt. They knew just what the publishers' catalogues told them; he knew his books on the footing of having assimilated their contents, and formed his judgment of their authors. And he had even ventured on independent publication too. When the Rev. Dr Cleavahair, who had so long occupied the Burgher pulpit with acceptance, had died, leaving a void theologically that could not be filled, in so far as Richie Darrell and various others that had drunk deeply into the spirit of his ministry were concerned, he had in the interest of the community in general, and the Burgher congregation in particular, edited as well as brought out a volume of the doctor's sermons as they could be patched together from notes laboriously taken, during delivery, by himself, and by other admirers, male and female, of that justly esteemed divine; who, to the general regret of an appreciative circle, had left no decipherable MSS. of his chief discourses behind him. And it was remarkable how many keen and prolonged discussions on high topics took place in the little shop among the varied group of characteristically-intelligent companions, whom the bookseller contrived to attract thither. Probably such discussions did not tend greatly to promote business; and it was not with an eye to business that Richie Darrell's cronies ordinarily called or were by him desired to call. Nevertheless, it seemed very evident that in the bookseller's scheme of life, such mental exercitations were in the nature of an absolute necessity; and he was far from regarding the time occupied in them as mis-spent.

For the rest of it, Richie Darrell's business did not require, nor indeed admit, of assistants being kept. And thus it was that when he had occasion to go on needful errands, as also daily, when he went to his home, three-fourths of a mile distant in the suburbs, for dinner, he shut the door, and having turned the big old-fashioned key in the lock, dropped it with a plump into the outside right tail pocket of his brown coat, and so left the shop shut till his return. The bookseller was a bachelor, with neither wife nor child, and he did not encourage close intimacies at his home. Perhaps the man who knew him better than any other was Ebenezer Greig, retired schoolmaster, who, alike in physique and temperament, was very much of a contrast to the bookseller. His figure, which was tall and stooping, was invariably set off in a rusty black coat with narrow tails; and though he had known vicissitudes and sorrows not a few, the one thing that stood out most conspicuously in his character was his uniformly placid temper. He too had been an esteemed elder in Dr Cleavahair's congregation, and being now out of active occupation his visits to Richie Darrell's shop were somewhat frequent. And it would occasionally happen that when the bookseller's temporary absence from his post threatened to be longer than usual, Dominie Greig would be pressed into taking his place behind the counter, where he could at least converse with the customers that dropped in, till the master of the shop returned.

My first acquaintance with Richie Darrell's shop was made when sent thither as errand boy in fulfilment of the order about which he had called at my Uncle's warehouse. It was not without a considerable amount of sneering, and a very distinct indication of the low esteem in which he held customers of his type, that, on my Uncle Sandy's return, John Cockerill had condescended to deliver Richie's message concerning the bit of lamb's-skin he wanted.

'Benjie!' exclaimed my Uncle Sandy, who, to John Cockerill's mortification, at once proceeded to pick out the article specified, entirely ignoring that young gentleman's very cutting sarcasms: – 'Benjie! Ye'll rin up the street wi' that bit parcel to Mr Darrell. Ye ken's shop, or ye can fin't oot.'

'Yes, Uncle,' said I, dropping from my stool, and gathering up my bonnet.

'He has the choice o' twa bits, an' I think the ane or the ither'll suit 'im.'

'An will I say the price?'

'Weel, if he asks't,' said my Uncle, to whom the idea had apparently not occurred. 'A mere trifle, nae worth puttin' a price upon. Hooever, he'll insist on payin' though it were but the half o' a farthin'. Say three bawbees the piece.'

The queer little shop of which Richie Darrell was master, and in which he did business, now, when I think of it, must even in its day have seemed a poor and antiquated concern compared with the principal book shops of the town. To my unsophisticated gaze, however, it bore no such character; but seemed rather a place where the desire for knowledge and learning might find large means of satisfaction. And after all the experience that comes between boyhood and mid life, I do not know that on a close and impartial view I should be disposed greatly to qualify my first impressions of Richie and his shop.

'An' ye've brocht my order, sir,' said Richie Darrell, as he opened the parcel and carefully scrutinised the lamb's-skin to which he applied the paper pattern, for which my Uncle had not waited to call as desired.

'H – m –, he's no sae far fae't aifter a',' said Richie, in a sort of half soliloquy.

Then stepping into the back shop, which was lighted by a small square window in the far end, and contained a working bench and some binder's and other tools, he brought out a rather bulky old tome that was half-way on in the process of re-binding. To the back of it he deliberately applied the pieces in succession, fitting them carefully on with both hands.

'Three an' a bawbee, said ye, young gentleman?'

'Na, three bawbees,' said I.

'Weel here's your cash,' continued Richie, putting aside the bit he preferred, and opening his till – 'An' so ye're come down a' the wye fae Strathtocher to be Provost o' oor toon?' he added, suddenly changing the subject, and addressing myself in a more directly personal fashion.

'Na, nae to be Provost,' was my slightly sheepish reply to the bantering observation of the queer little man, whose particular manner seemed to compel a sort of interest, not unmixed with apprehension.

'An' fat for no, lad? We're jist settin' on to hatch a new brodmil o' toon cooncillors. They're the raw material o' baillies and siclike, ye ken – the baillies bein' seleckit wi' due regaird to the size o' a man's painch, an' a' that; though we've aiven seen them win to the bench on the principle o' the scum comin' to the tap. An' fat better stuff hae ye to mak a Provost o' than a weel trackit Baillie? Wudna ye like to be a toon cooncillor than; as something within the limits o' your modesty?'

'No I wudna,' was my answer, blurted out in a state of mind, half of amazement half of amusement, at the dimly understood observations of my interrogator.

'Wow, man, but ye've nae public spirit ava; fat greater object o' ambition can be set afore an aspirin' youth than to busy 'imsel' i' the toon's affairs, win into the Coonicil, takin' fat share he can get o' the scran, an' feenally sit doon wi' a baillie's chyne aneth's chowks; or maybe step into the muckle cheir itsel' – Fat wud your schaime o' life be, if it's a fair question?'

'I want to learn business, an syne gyang abroad,' said I,

with that air of raw confidence and consequence, which har-
monises so well with utter lack of knowledge and experience
of the world.

'H – m!' said Richie Darrell, in a changed tone, and with his
thoughts apparently half abstracted from the subject in hand
'H – m. I daursay ye're nae the first that has startit wi' ideas
o' that kin' at fourteen, an' foun' oot that though the warld's
a big place maist ot's inhabitants maun be content to be gey
little bookit by the time they're fifty – Hooever, ye ken fa it
is that said "the hand o' the dilligent maketh rich;" an' that
"the man who is diligent in his business shall stand before
kings, he shall not stand before mean men." Ye'll aiven tak'
tent an' gie heed to siclike coonsels as ye get i' the Proverbs o'
Solomon, as ye've nae doot learn't them at yer mither's knee,
an' lat the oonkent that comes aifterhin' tak' care o' itsel', as
far as wardle's gear an' the wardle's honours gae. An', i' the
meantime, here's a gweed bawbee pencil to ye for your ain use
fan ye're studyin' at even – Min' to tell the Deacon, wi' my
compliments, that I'll expec' to see 'im at the Craftheid Ward
meetin' on Monday nicht. If he winna come forrat 'imsel', it's
little aneuch that he sud tak' the trouble o' catecheesin' the
candidates that offer themsel's to the suffrages o' the free an'
independent electors o' the Ward.'

Whether the 'Deacon,' as Richie Darrell, for some reason
best known to himself, persisted in calling my Uncle Sandy,
should obey this particular behest, and attend the Craftheid
ward meeting or not, I had made up my mind, as I marched
back to my stool that, Providence favouring, I would certainly
take care to be there if only to gain some needed light on
the process of manufacturing members of the municipality,
a process concerning which I had hitherto got only dark and
mysterious hints, but these in such profusion as to be not a
little perplexing to an ignorant mind.

CHAPTER FOUR

My Uncle at Home

AT the time of which I presently write my Uncle, David Macnicol, was, as has been already indicated, a man not quite fifty years of age. In person he was a little over middle height, and pretty strongly built. The fresh complexion that distinguished his full whiskerless cheeks rather contrasted with the hair of his head, which was already sprinkled with grey, and had begun to fall off, the general effect being to give him all the advantages in point of gravity of presence which should naturally have come to him had he been ten years older. The general solidity of his manner, too, and the total absence of any tendency to exuberance or imaginative lightness in his mental habitudes, which impressed me much, as I well recollect, from the very first time I saw him when he visited Strathtocher as the great man of our family, conspired to support the suggestion of a very matured and responsible character. When I reflect upon it, he must at an early age, as these things go, have seemed a man unmistakably destined to wear the chain of a Baillie in due course. At the time he first entered the Town Council he was not quite forty, and but a few years married to Miss Castock; and having been patriotic enough to oblige his municipal chief – the head of the Safe-and-Slow party with which he had allied himself – by taking on a second term of simple councillorship before retiring, it can well be understood how the fact that no higher office whatever rewarded his conscientious loyalty was the occasion of some sharp comment alike in the seclusion of connubial confidence and in favoured circles of private friendship. As the daughter of one who himself had worn the insignia of office, Mrs Macnicol *née* Castock was not ignorant of the way in which such things were ruled; and wherefore then should she refrain from giving expression to her sense of the ill usage to which her husband had been subjected at the hands of those he had served so well?

That was several years ago, however, and my Uncle when he first became councillor Macnicol was only a young man, with the very oldest of his children merely toddling by his knee. He was now the father of a family of six daughters, the two elder of whom, aged fifteen and thirteen respectively, might be held to be verging on the region of young ladyhood. It need not be wondered at then if the claims and exigencies of his position had come to be viewed with a yet more jealous regard to the honour and dignity of those whose interests were involved. To say that my Uncle's conduct in receiving the deputation that had called upon him in the way he had done met his wife's approval would not perhaps quite cover the whole case. It might come fully nearer it to say that his entire family connection, as well as his entire conception of life on its upper side, forbade his doing otherwise than he had done.

'I hope ye left them in nae doot aboot what ye consider due to yoursel' an' them that ye're conneckit wi'?' observed Mrs Macnicol, when my Uncle had told her the occurrences of the day.

'No,' said my Uncle, 'No. They're weel aware I'll only stan' if I'm to be alloo't the chance o' takin' office.'

'The chance! I would put it at naething less nor the certainty.'

'Ou weel, ou weel; it comes a' to the same thing; only ye maun seem to leave a mairgin, my dear.'

'I'se warrant Peter Sneevle would be seekin' nae mairgins, but tryin' to get you pledg't secure aneuch. It's nae a vera frien'ly turn o' the man that's gotten so mony a weel-payin' job aff o' ye to come on sic an' erran'.'

'Wheels within wheels, my dear. Depen' ye upon't, Peter ken's what it's a' for; only he's nae in a position to disobleege me i' the maitter in the meantime; an' that's aboot aneuch as far's he's concern't.'

'Ah weel, I'm glad to hear't. But I am surpris't that Stephen Gudgeon would 'a had the face to come to ony gentleman that was marriet to my father's daachter to ask

him to tak' a bare cooncillorship to obleege him an' his set.
If he would min' fa it was that gae him a helpin' han' upo'
the bench first he micht think shame. My father was a weel
edicatit man, but I'm sure I've heard him say that "o' a' the
probationers that ever he took in han', Stephen Gudgeon was
the weel warst"; an' aifter his 'prentice month was owre, he
had to gae to the bench wi' im for weeks an' weeks every ither
day whan ony case likely to be defen'it by Gabbin' Gibbie was
comin' up, to help him through the hedge, and keep 'im fae
makin' Her Maijesty's court o' justice ridiculous.'

'Aye aye, but folk shortly forget things o' that kin',' said
my Uncle.

'But they sudna be alloo't to forget them!' said Mrs
Macnicol with some vehemence. 'It's little enough respect
to my father's faimily when he had nae son o's ain left to
succeed 'im; a man that did sae muckle for the place o's
nateevity – Ye'll even lat the Provost 'imsel' ken as muckle.'
'We'll see. It's like enough they'll come back again wi' the
Ward meetins so close at han', an' them only arrangin' yet.
If no I can wait my time.'

'Ye've waitet your time but owre lang already, my dear.
Min' ye've a great responsibility i' the maitter. Though it
werena fat's due to the memory o' them that's awa – ye've
– a young – faimily to dee joostice till! There's Rachel'll hae
to be sent awa for twa quarters to some superior school to
finish; an 'er sister Jeannie 'ill be followin' 'er shortly; hoo
sudna oor girls gae oot to the wordle wi' a' the advantages
that their father's family's enteetl't till; the same as their
mither did when she was sent to Miss Primgait's seminary
– the vera best boordin' school i' the quarter at the time –
along wi' Provost Doddawa's daachters.'

'As for a boordin' school, if the fees are paid it comes a'
to much the same thing as far as that goes, I daresay,' said
my Uncle dryly, and as feeling himself pressed a little more
closely than he cared about.

'The same thing!' gasped Mrs Macnicol, getting suddenly
hysterical, as her manner occasionally was when questions
affecting the name and reputation of her venerated parent
came up – and the association of ideas in the matter seemed

at times not a little odd – 'Mr Macnicol, what can ye mean? Are we to sit still an' hae the finger o' scorn pointet at's by them whase forbears were never heard o' i' the toon's affairs? Oh, David! David – little did I think it would – ever come to that wi' the faimily o' my father's daachter! Nae 't I'm carin',' said Mrs Macnicol, wiping her eyes – 'Gweed forbid it; but think o' the memory o' them that's awa – think o' your innocent faimily, an' your duty to them.'

'Oh weel, my dear, jist hae patience,' said my Uncle, finding that he had rather put his foot in it; 'the thing's a' in the richt aneuch train. Only we mauna seem to be owre anxious aboot it. But fearna ye; I'll nail them siccar aneuch till a baillieship afore I lift a finger for the Cooncil.'

With this assurance Mrs Macnicol at once regained her cheerfulness, and proceeded to speculate on the probabilities of the approaching election.

CHAPTER FIVE

The Crofthead Ward Meeting

HOW far it would have spontaneously entered the mind of my Uncle Sandy to attend the meeting of the electors of the Crofthead Ward, in the local politics of which he had no legal standing as a voter, and in which to my knowledge he took little interest otherwise except an interest of the mildly cynical sort, I do not know. It was at anyrate one of the characteristics of this particular Uncle of mine that in things indifferent, and which did not involve any question of principle, he was usually ready to yield any tastes or predilections of his own somewhat easily to the preferences of others; especially if these were urged with any degree of persistency. It was an axiom of my Uncle Sandy's that by much the greater part of the extraneous friction of life in civilised society, as it existed in the town of Greyness, at least, resulted from men and women holding tenaciously by personal opinions on points of no essential importance; and insisting on trifles that turned purely upon personal taste and feeling, the taste not being always the most correct nor the feeling the most unselfish, as rigidly and with as little regard for the tastes and feelings of others as if they had been matters involving vital principles or the convictions of the moral conscience. And accordingly it was a part of his philosophy of life that the vastly greater portion of this friction was purely gratuitous, an outcome virtually of hard and thoughtless selfishness; and that a man's duty rather was to leave himself open to the insinuation of weakness in character, and simply to walk on as he might in silence, than by an unconscious but not less real arrogance carry his point (which very likely was not worth carrying) at the cost of probable laceration on one side, and still more probable exasperation, unworthily caused, on both.

His belief in a man's character ultimately taking care of itself, was implicit; and he held that the seeming weakness might in the long run be found to be a far greater power than the apparent strength that was believed to have conquered it.

In his ideas concerning the avoidable friction of life, my Uncle Sandy had no claim to originality. Far from it. Philosophers of admitted profundity had previously propounded exactly the same kind of notion, and with much greater 'insight' and eloquence than he could command. The singularity of his case was that in his own life and practice he was really guided by his avowed belief. It was probably the sort of half instinctive knowledge of this I had promptly acquired during the few weeks I had lived in somewhat intimate communion with my Uncle Sandy in his bachelor lodgings, that gave me confidence in expecting that whatever his own particular feeling on the subject might be, he would concede that feeling to the desire of his friend Richie Darrell, and so give me the opportunity of witnessing the proceedings of an election Ward meeting, concerning which my ignorance was complete, while my curiosity had been fully awakened by what I had incidentally heard. I naturally delivered the bookseller's injunction with all the impressiveness I could command; and despite certain observations in the way of characterising the whole business as a 'mere farce,' and a deplorable piece of nonsense, the result was that in due course I found myself at the Crofthead Ward meeting by my Uncle Sandy's guidance and under his wing.

The electors of the Crofthead Ward were by old repute the most vivacious and outspoken section of the electors of the town; and when the annual Ward meeting came round, they invariably made it a point to exhibit their vivacity and outspokenness pretty much at the expense of the gentlemen who aspired to the honour of representing them at the chief public board of the town. Their place of meeting was the Burgh School-room, where, in his more active days, Dominie Greig had borne efficient sway as senior teacher. It was a quaint old building the Burgh School; and in its structure conformed to none of the new-fangled ideas concerning 'cubic feet of air space per pupil,' that run so much in the brains of modern school inspectors and teachers, to the affliction of the ratepayers, who must bear the cost of providing buildings adapted to the ideas of people who profess to be more enlightened than their forefathers. It was long and narrow, and the coved ceiling, at its centre, which was hardly higher than that a man of medium height, standing on the floor, might have touched it with the point of an ordinary walking stick, had in it two or three circular indentations which were understood to be ventilators, only it was doubtful how far they performed any service whatever in that way. I can well believe that when the place was crammed with a hundred and eighty or two hundred boys, under Dominie Greig and his learned and laborious colleagues, it had been occasionally rather hot. At anyrate, when the Ward meeting had assembled, it certainly was so.

The understood order was that the cross benches, fronting the main door, and rising by an easy slope to the back wall, were reserved for the principal personages in the drama; the common pews on both sides of the longitudinal passage along the school were always early crammed with the body of the electors, and those who came later stood in the passage surging backward into dim space toward the ends of the school as the house gradually filled. A certain small knot of characters who figured at every meeting of the Ward took care betimes to have themselves ensconced on the more conspicuously convenient and comfortable seats, and then awaited the opening scene with every disposition to enjoy and stimulate its humours.

CHAPTER SIX

The Candidates

THE hour of meeting was seven; and it was three minutes past that time when some small ebullitions of preliminary 'chaff' gave place to a vigorous 'ruff' anticipatory on the part of the expectant audience; then a pause, and again for the second and third time a fresh 'ruff,' as some noted character entered. At last, just as the minute hand of the old clock pointed to five minutes past the hour, Baillie Gudgeon, followed by half-a-dozen others, including my Uncle David, entered 'amid general cheering,' and took their places on the cross benches. They had just taken their seats and assumed an unconcerned look, when a little bald-headed man in a front side seat stood up, took off his hat, and, elevating his face to a nearly horizontal position, as if to prevent the big spectacles he wore falling over his nose, said – 'I muv that Baillie Gudgeon, the sainior representative o' the Ward tak' the cheer.' 'I sec-ond that,' said a voice in the rear.

'Vera much obleeg't t' ye, gentlemen, for the honour you have done me in callin' me to preside over such a numerous and influential meetin',' said Baillie Gudgeon, when he had got moved out of the front pew into the arm-chair that stood in the centre before it. 'The electors o' the Craftheid Ward, I am sure, will mainteen their character on the present occasion, an' give every ane o' the candidates an impartial hearin'. Gentlemen, we may differ on many subjects, but we are all at one in seekin' the public good – (cheers, and hear hear). Gentlemen, none of us, whatever party we belong to, has no private or selfish en's to serve in desirin' the honour of your suffrages – we seek the welfare o' the much-loved city o' oor habitation alone – (renewed cheering). But I will not deteen you; the gentlemen will explain their own views, and it will be for you to exercise your time-honour't priveleege o' catecheesin' each candidate to find out their opinions on the vera important public questions that will engage the attention of the Cooncil – (hear hear). Gentlemen, you requare men o' expairience – ('Shut up Baillie,' and laughter) – at the present creesis – (continued interruption). But I will not deteen you. The first business is to appoint a clerk to the meetin'. Mr Peter Sneevle, solicitor, has usually given his vera efficient services in that capacity. Is it your pleesure, gentlemen, that Mr Sneevle be appointed clerk to the meetin'? – (cheers). Is Mr Sneevle present?' added the Chairman, glancing round as if he needed assurance of the fact.

At that moment Mr Sneevle, who was by no means far off, rose, and moving up to the small table that stood alongside the chair, took up his clerkly attitude amid the approbation of the audience.

'Has any gentleman a candidate to propose?' asked the chairman.

The vacancies were two, and it was well enough known that the candidates would number four, each of whom had to be formally nominated and seconded. The eight speeches which accompanied this process were just a little dreary. Several of them had been carefully elaborated beforehand, and written out on scraps of paper for the security of the speaker and the convenience of the Greyness newspaper reporters; each of the speakers touched on his candidate biographically, and announced with a sort of startling seriousness his sense of the importance of getting a man of his singular ability into the Town Council. The specialty of the plea on one side – that to which my Uncle belonged – was the absolute necessity for electing 'men of experience,' if the town was to be saved from disaster; on the other it was the crying need for 'new blood' to keep things from utter stagnation.

'We'll hear the candidates noo,' said the chairman when the nominations were finished. 'Alloo me to call first upo' my excellent frien', Mr Macnicol. Mr Macnicol needs no introduction to you. He has serv't the Ward afore noo, in a vera efficient and disinterestit mainner – (hear, hear).'

When my Uncle David stood up to address the electors,

the novelty of the situation made me turn involuntarily in the direction of his brother, only to find that Sandy had either slipped out of the schoolroom or retreated to the obscurely lighted back region. I was able, however, to perceive that Richie Darrell, who stood in the front of the crowd that occupied the centre part of the floor, with his hat in his hand, was looking on with a keen and scrutinising look. And I may here observe that one of the things that particularly struck me, was the kind of fascination that the proceedings seemed to have for Richie, and a small group of kindred spirits, who, I felt certain regarded the whole ongoings with a sort of quiet contempt, which utterly forbad their taking any active part; yet they would at all risks be present, and duly see the whole affair gone through. My Uncle David remarked that as his nominators had, in a manner all too flattering to him, said, and as their respected chairman knew, he had never been a party man, nor bound by party ties and obligations. He had had too much experience of public life not to know the responsibilities it involved, and the sacrifice of private feeling, and private comfort to which the man who would really do his duty must make up his mind. Still as there were undoubtedly questions coming up in which he flattered himself the little experience he had had would enable him to be of some use, he could not in the face of a desire so widely expressed among an influential section of the electors refuse to put himself at their service. If it was their pleasure to elect him they might depend upon his acting with thorough independence, while his watchwords would ever be – economy and efficiency.

My Uncle's address was by general consent admitted to be the speech of the evening. That of the other candidate on the same side was merely a weak and ill-delivered echo of it. The two opposition men launched out into criticisms of the reigning municipal dynasty, and urged the necessity for various reforms, which could be had only by poking it up severely, as they were prepared to do. Their oratory obtained the larger share of the cheering, some of their hardest hits being applauded to the echo; but then it was observable that the part of the audience that used their lungs most freely in cheering belonged to the unenfranchised mass, and not to the responsible electorate.

When the speeches had ended, and the clerk of the meeting having written up his minute to that point in the business, had elevated his spectacles to the top of his brow, and lain back on his chair to await the next act in the drama, the chairman tentatively asked –

'Noo, gentlemen, are ye satisfeet wi' the candidates' views; or wud ye like to pit some questions?'

'Satisfeet! nae vera lickly,' exclaimed a heavy shouldered man, with a short neck and double chin, who had got himself stuck into an elevated corner seat at the wall, fronting the chair, and commanding a good view of the audience. 'We've hed little to be satisfeet wi' yet – lat them be pitten throu' their catechis.' 'Fire awa', than;' and 'Go on wi' yer barrow, Tam,' were the cries that greeted this exclamation, to which Tam replied by a grunt and a choleric 'Time aneuch; hurry nae man's cattle.' By and by a politically disposed person, in the guise of a towsy headed working man, with a surly cast of countenance, and an equally surly tone in his voice, desired to know whether the candidates were in favour of triennial Parliaments; whether they would support an extension of the franchise; and whether they were prepared to vote for the Ballot Bill? The replies to the first two questions conflicted somewhat, but were all of a temporising character, though this was less apparent than it might have been, from the fact that some of the candidates were not quite certain what the queries meant, and so made their answers conveniently vague. To the third question, which had probably been anticipated, being of yearly occurrence, my Uncle replied in a well-rounded sentence that 'the ballot was against the spirit of British institutions,' and even the opposition candidates were fain to declare that 'Mr Macnicol had expressed their sentiments about the ballot.' On this the political working man got incensed and declared that the candidates had better go home and read up William Cobbett. The audience cheered and laughed, while some sympathising spirits cried 'Pitch into them,' and the noise grew till the chairman interfered and ruled that they 'could only hae questions – nae speeches.'

'I want – to put a question to –,' exclaimed a thin-faced nervous-looking man, rising up in one of the middle seats.

'Haud yer jaw, min, till ither fowk be throu,' interposed the first querist, and the man sat down again suddenly. – 'Will ye use your influence wi' the Government than to obtain a grant for the purpose o' levellin' the Castlehill an' gi'en employment to the workin' men o' Greyness at fix't waages?' asked the working man in a tone of increased severity. This safe and sweeping question was promptly and unanimously answered, amid many 'hear, hears' and much cheering, with a 'certainly,' 'certainly,' 'with much pleasure,' and 'delighted – a vera proper proposal.' The querist seemed satisfied and threw himself back in his seat without uttering another word, whereupon the man in the back seat who had spoken first demanded to know – 'Fat aboot the drainin' o' the Stinkin' Lochie?' 'Hear, hear,' exclaimed the two opposition candidates. 'That's it noo, Tam,' exclaimed the occupants of the rear benches, stamping the floor with their feet emphatically. My Uncle looked wise; and the chairman looked perplexed, till, having stooped over and consulted the Clerk, he rose and declared himself at a loss to understand the gentleman – 'Come noo Baillie, nane o' yer gammon,' exclaimed some anonymous elector. 'A' humbug ye ken' – 'Weel, if ye wull hae't plainer,' cried another – 'Fat are the candidates prepar't to dee aboot drainin' the Lochie? pit that to them.' 'Oh, I un'erstan'. But, gentlemen, I doot if that's a constitutional question. Oor excellent Clerk, Mr Sneevle, than whom no one knows better, will tell you that that's a question surroun'it wi' vera, vera sairous dif –' 'Buff an' nonsense, Baillie, lat them answer the question!' broke in the man wi' the double chin. 'Order, order! cheer, cheer!' cried Mr Sneevle; 'hear, hear, hear,' shouted others, while many laughed uproariously and stamped upon the floor. The chairman, who, in the endeavour to make himself audible, had got red in the face, was heard to utter some disjointed words about 'vestit interests that aiven the Cooncil daurna meddle wi',' and 'mair taxation.' He had no choice, however, but put the question which was the crucial one of the time, in a party sense. My Uncle made a politic reply. The sheet of water in question, originally a natural lakelet in whose shallow waters wild geese and sea gulls had been wont to feed, had in process of time been impinged upon by the eastern suburbs of Greyness; and necessarily the birds had fled, while the water of the Loch had become less pure, and the vegetation in and around it less fresh. He admitted the growing obnoxiousness of the Loch in a sanitary point of view – though it was really wonderful how remarkably healthy residents in its neighbourhood were – but dwelt on the great engineering difficulties attending the draining of a sheet of water an acre and a-half in extent and only twenty feet above sea level, and still more the formidable business involved in meddling with those who, as the chairman had reminded them, had vested rights in the Loch. Still it was a question for the inhabitants to consider at the right time. For his own part it was no new question to him; far from it; he had carefully looked at it in all its bearings – antiquarian and social – and if the state of trade were such as to warrant it and other burdens reduced to a proper point, he would consider it – he certainly would consider it carefully. My Uncle's companion candidate, of course, gave a similar opinion; and the two men on the other side, amid much noise, chiefly meant for their encouragement, stigmatised the apathy of the dominant party in the Council in not having drained the Loch long ago, ridiculed the idea of vested rights in a stagnant and unwholesome puddle, and declared that if they were returned at the top of the poll the electors would see the Stinkin' Lochie drained in twelve-months time, and the general health of the town improved without anybody feeling himself a six-pence the poorer.

The question of the Loch warmed up the meeting in a wonderful way, and the rounds of cheering accorded to the opposition candidates had hardly begun to abate, when a well-conditioned little man with a round good-humoured face, pushed forward to the front of those standing in the middle area, and proceeded to expound his ideas of what should be done with the disputed Loch. 'Questions, questions – nae speeches,' cried numerous voices. 'Well, I want to know if the candidates will support a bill in Parliament for getting the Loch converted into a pond for the rearing of fish to supply the inhabitants with food?' cried the round-faced little man. 'Oh, oh,' loudly responded several voices, while peals of laughter resounded on all sides, and even the chairman and candidates smiled. But the questioner was in too dead earnest to be thus put aside, and he accordingly went on to argue out his case. His first view had been to get it converted into a swimming pond, and impose a small capitation tax for the maintenance of a swimming master to instruct the youth of the town in that noble art. But further consideration had given his thoughts a still more utilitarian form; and he was prepared to prove that with a somewhat more liberal dilution of fresh water, fish of divers sorts – pike, perch, and eels – would thrive and fatten amazingly on the sewage that found its way into the Loch, furnishing a source of internal food supply sufficient to reduce the taxation of the town by at least one-half.

When the audience had toned down a little, the nervous man again got on his legs, and rapidly put the queries that burdened his mind, which had relation to the attitude of the candidates toward international disarmament in the first place, and toward a decimal coinage and the metrical system in the second. He had got but the scantiest possible satisfaction in the way of response, when a sallow, sleek-haired man, who affected the role of the social reformer, stood up with a determined air and a long string of written questions in his hand, which he desired to put *seriatim*, and for which it was becoming very evident he would get but an impatient hearing. The first was – 'What are the candidates' opinions of the liquor trade generally; of the Forbes Mackenzie Act in particular; and of the Maine Liquor law, both hypothetically and practically?' As the querist went on to explain and sub-divide his questions, the temper of the meeting gave out more and more; and the cry to 'Pit him oot' became urgent. The sleek-haired man stood his ground resolutely for a time, bearding both the candidates and the audience, and reiterating his opinions in a hoarse shout, but he was finally snuffed out by persistently-continued 'ruffing,' amid which somebody moved thanks to Baillie Gudgeon for his able and impartial conduct in the chair, and the meeting of the Crofthead Ward, which was declared to have been an

eminently successful and satisfactory one, immediately came
to an end.

   The days that passed after the Ward meeting were devoted
to canvassing and other electioneering operations. My Uncle
David called personally on each of four hundred electors,
ordinarily in the company of a member of his committee,
chosen for his special knowledge of the people about to be
visited. My Uncle's cue, as is wont in such circumstances, was
to be affable and jocular all round, and the attendant member
plied the electors on their weak points. Mr Sneevle was a very
assiduous and skilful election agent, and my Uncle being a
good client of his, as well as a strong candidate on general
grounds, it was almost a matter of course that he should put
him in, as he did, at the top of the poll.

CHAPTER SEVEN

A Sabbath Day's Journey

ON a sharp frosty morning of a Sunday in mid-spring – it was about ten years prior to the date of which I have been writing – before the mass of the inhabitants of Greyness, gentle or simple, had begun to stir out of doors, or indeed to furnish much tangible evidence of being yet out of bed, a couple of pedestrians might have been seen wending their way by separate routes toward the outskirts of the town. The hour was not so very early, it being only a little before eight o'clock, but even the most frequented streets of Greyness were so deserted that the desultory tread of some heavy-footed police constable, as he daun'ert along the pavement, was sufficiently notable to arouse the attention of wakeful people who occupied front rooms toward the street, as well as of the few who from various causes had been prompted to peep out of doors; and the thoroughfares of the place were still practically in possession of incidental groups of pigeons, which flitted hither and thither, lighting in twos and threes on the causeway to pick up what they could find, and croodle threateningly at each other as they tramped round tail-ward in the vicinity of edible treasures, the ownership of which was undetermined. Of the two pedestrians, one was a man about mid-life, rather short in stature, and whose person was enveloped in a blue camlet cloak, with big brass clasp and links fastening the stiff upright collar about his throat. As he walked briskly along toward the northern suburb he kept the front of his cloak together with one hand, and actively plied an old fashioned walking stick with a carved bone top in the other. The other wayfarer, who was also directing his steps northward, was a young man, seemingly of about thirty, rather thin of flesh as from recent ill-health, and who, if his

mood was not an abstracted one, looked at least as if he would
not have thought of anything but pursuing his morning walk
alone, had not the man in the cloak, a little way beyond the
point where their separate routes to the outside converged into
the broad highway leading straight over the hill and away into
the country, stopped short on first observing the prospect of
companionship, and as the other approached accosted him
with a prompt and courteous

'Good morning, sir.'

'Good mornin',' said the young man in reply.

'Ye're astir betimes. The snell mornin' air hasna made you
prefer the inside o' your bed closet to the open canopy o'
heaven?'

'I don't see why it should; an' your presence here leads me
to conclude that your taste an' mine mayna differ so far on
that point.'

'An' may I have the pleasure o' your company for a Sabbath
day's journey than, or say pairt o't?'

'Pairt o't, certainly; I'll be only owre glaid. Only I'm nae
so sure either o' the length o' my walk or the direction it may
lead me.'

'An' ye dinna coont it Sabbath desecration to tak' an
aimless stroll for your nain idle gratification an' pleasure
on the Lord's Day mornin'?' asked the man in the cloak as
the two walked on.

'If it war for my nain pleasure,' said the young man, 'even
that would prevent its bein' a'thegither aimless; an' quite
conceivably, if my idea of gratification war a richt ane, micht
gae far to sanctify the act. But nae doot a nearer road to the
same en' wud be to start wi' the object o' takin' a formal
Sabbath Day's journey, forbiddin' the idea o' pleasure an'
luikin' neither to the richt nor left on ootward objects by
the way.'

'Come, come, noo, my free-an'-easy frien'; dinna begin wi'
your latitudinarian notions. Michtna the object o' a man's
early Sabbath walk be the commendable ane o' visitin the
churches?'

'An' yet there's abundance o' churches to visit without
gaein' ootside the area o' the hard causeway stanes by a

single furlong; or for that maitter without leavin' your bed
for a couple o' hours later in the day than this.'

'I see ye're a man o' loose opinions, sir. It'll need some
wise an' soun' heid to set you richt. I' the meantime we'll
tak' a snuff, an' ye please,' said the man with the camlet cloak
pausing in his rather nimble walk, as the two travellers reached
the top of the slight eminence over which the road they were
travelling led, and suiting the action to the word, after which
he offered his snuff-box to his companion.

Behind the two pedestrians lay the town in true Sabbath
stillness, its every-day industries all at rest, the few tall
chimneys to be seen pointing skyward without sign of life
or movement near them, and only scanty wreaths of smoke
from the domestic hearth circling up here and there. The
level sun had partly struggled through a bank of grey cloud
on the eastern horizon, but the hoar frost still lay white and
thick on the hedges and grass fields, and the frozen roadway
rang beneath the feet of the wayfarer. As they stood and gazed
over the still landscape the sound of the first bells of the town
was answered, now by the faint tinkle of the old chapel bell
three-quarters of a mile to eastward, and again by the fuller
tones of the parish kirk bell of Bieldside, a mile or more to
northward in front of them.

'Unmeasured music! Weel; there's something for mair
senses nor ane,' said the elder of the two pedestrians after
pausing to gaze and listen. 'The simple process o' comin'
here on the twa legs that Nature has provided for's, gies
a man the upper han' o' the pinchin' elements, an' instead
o' oorlich pine, lats 'im feel the glow o' health at ilka pore
o's body. He may feast his een on the sober livery o' the
grey-broon lan'scape; an' his lugs maun be made o' sauchen
tree if he dinna get his thochts carriet oot o' 'imsel' by the
soothin' unsecular jangle o' the steeple bells, big an' little,
floatin' awa for miles and miles upo' the crisp air, leadin'
back to the time o' the pure an' primitive monks that kent nor
Bishop nor Paip, callin' to their mornin' an' evenin' devotions;
suggestin' ideas o' the solemn joy that was felt as the Christian
Covenanters o' this lan' – alas for their brethren elsewhere,
sic as the Huguenots o' France – won their freedom to meet

in the general congregation for a pure worship; an' not less
remindin' us that alike when a King is born into the earth, as
whan the meanest o' his subjects passes into the deep unseen,
the bell has fittin' tones o' glaidness an' o' grief.'

The speaker forthwith moved sharply on again without
encouraging any reply or exhibiting the least inclination
further to prolong the strain in which, to the surprise of his
companion, who felt his interest in and curiosity concerning
him sensibly roused, he had unexpectedly indulged. His
manner was to walk right on for a space, and then when
the humour seized him call a halt, to take snuff or indulge
in a dissertation on something that had interested him, it
might be a distant feature in the landscape, it might be a
spring of water by the wayside, or it might be the aspect and
promise of some early budding plant in the ditch at their feet.
These were interludes; the main thread of discourse suddenly
taken up, when the travellers had gone on for a minute or
two in silence after the subject of bells had been dropt, had
relation to theology more or less. It seemed as if each of the
two interlocutors would have been pleased to discover the
exact whereabouts of the other in that region, but without
perfect success on either side. If the senior had indicated
to the junior that he considered his views somewhat lax, he
had not succeeded in gaining a precise notion of how far that
laxity went, and on the other hand, though the junior had
had principles of undoubted orthodoxy expounded to him, he
found, on pressing a little closer, that his elder companion's
idea of a sound theologian was not fully met in any living man
he could name – and certainly not among the neighbouring
clergy on whom his criticisms were wonderfully severe –
though one or two deceased divines to whom his earlier
recollections carried him back were spoken of in terms of
nearly unqualified approval.

CHAPTER EIGHT

The Kirkyard

THE route taken by the pedestrians carried them northward and then eastward. They had, in their intermittent way, walked four good miles when a couple of hours had elapsed; and then turning into a winding road which led upward to a quaint-looking old kirk of limited size, that stood on the brow of a considerable elevation, they found themselves among the gravestones in the Churchyard, almost an hour before the time for commencement of the service.

That a careful, not to say reverential, examination of certain of the gravestones contained in the crowded and ill-kept churchyard constituted an important part in what our friend in the camlet cloak had described as his visitation of the churches was clearly apparent. In so far as anything else connected with the church and its services was concerned, there was not much indeed to justify his Sabbath day's journey. The one service of the day began at twelve o'clock. A quarter of an hour previous to that time the bell commenced to ring, but though the parishioners, male and female, had before then grouped themselves, *in cumulo*, about the kirkyard gate, under the trees, and about the kirk gable (when it happened to rain they gathered in the kirk porch, to the extent of its capacity), to discuss the weather, the crops, the markets, and the general gossip of the parish, not a soul would fairly enter the kirk itself till the minister was seen marching up the kirkyard walk in his gown and bands. Then they entered in a body, pell mell, and with no little noise, and took their seats to submit, with what liveliness they could muster, to the formal repetition of the well-known first and second prayers, and the interjection between of a not less formal and hardly less familiar sermon. And then, with the bawbees gathered in the old wooden ladles, and the blessing pronounced, not a second was lost in making for the door for a regular stampede homeward.

'Reverence an' unction!' exclaimed our friend in the camlet cloak, in reply to a remark of his companion, as they followed the fugitive congregation out of the church. 'The first's wantin' i' the pews, because baith second an' first are wantin' i' the poopit. I've kent a parson that cud compel an air o' ootward devoutness in his congregation, such as hed nae place in 'imsel' in reality, simply by the force o' sonorous speech; but we haena won aiven that length here.'

'An' perhaps we're better without it. Ye hae the real an' natural, at least, siclike as it is; an' that's surely better than a mere semblance, even if it's devoutness that's counterfeitit.'

'Young man, your knowledge o' life can be but sma' as yet, an' that may excuse the crudeness o' your remarks. Wait till a score o' winters hae queel't your pow an' sober't your expectations a little, an' ye'll be content wi' sma' mercies.'

'Truth to say, the course o' my uneventfu' history, brief as it may hae been, hasna been o' a kin' to foster extravagant expectations; but that's hardly the point. I was only sayin', as regairds even a good thing, better that its absence sud be seen than its presence suggestit by a counterfeit.'

'Vera learn't, but raither young mannish. Hooever, we'll eat a biscuit for the refreshment o' the body i' the meanwhile,' said the little man, as he stept along outside the kirkyard gate, and then turned slowly backward munching as he went.

Again he wandered round the old churchyard, and again stayed his steps and took off his hat at a grey old 'lair'-stone covering the grave of some whose memories, to outward seeming, he deeply revered. The odd thing about it all, as it seemed to his companion, was that the grave-stone which, old as it was, appeared to be better kept than most of the others, bore no inscription of a more recent date than sixty years ago, so that it could scarcely be the remains of very near relatives even that lay below. The observation, indeed, was offered that the dust of his parents and grandparents lay elsewhere. One additional remark the speaker volunteered, pointing to a section of the lair-stone left plain and unlettered below the last of the names upon it:—

'That blank tells a mair pathetic story to me than a' the letterin' that gaes afore.'

'A story o' a life prematurely endit, maybe?'

'A what!' exclaimed the little man, looking sharply at the other for a moment. 'No – I crave your pardon, sir, you didn't mean that. We'se let the subject drop wi' a single remark – ae brainch o' a faimily tree en's there; an' the en' is unrecordit in brass or stone. But – hoo sud I fret mysel'? Fan the shears o' fate clips anither vital thread, if anither unmarkit grave fin's place within the kirk-yard good an' weel; if it maun be ootside God's acre lat it be fae nae deed o' oor ain. – We'll be goin', by yer leave.'

In turning to quit the place the eye of the man of the camlet garment lighted on the inscription which some fond husband, presumably, had put over the grave of his departed wife, and in which, as the manner was, that husband went on to speak of 'the unselfishness of woman's love, and the constancy of woman's affection,' as exemplified in her of whom he had been bereaved.

'He's been an uncommonly fortunate or an extremely credulous man that,' curtly remarked the little man. 'Dinna ye put your trust in the unselfishness or constancy o' woman, my good sir, or ye're likely to fin' your feet upo' slippery places in due time, an' your fondest hopes made the sport o' the ficklest fancy. It may be aiven that allegiance to the blackest o' black-guards may be your undoin', but in ony case pit ye oot your fit nae farrer than ye can weel draw it in again ere your taes be aneth ony ane's tackets. So rins the philosophy o' experience.'

With this utterance, the wearer of the camlet cloak, as his wont was, passed from the subject, and having refreshed himself with another pinch of snuff the two left the churchyard, and pursued their way townward again. They walked more steadily and a little more rapidly than they had done in coming outward from Greyness, and in due course arrived at their 'respective places of abode' in that well-known town, as the minister to whom they had listened had duly prayed they might 'in peace and safety.'

CHAPTER NINE

My Uncle Sandy

IN the two preceding chapters the reader was made privy to the particulars of the incidental *rencontre*, which, if he is an acute person, he will hardly need to be told formed the first and quite informal introduction to each other of Richard Darrell, bookseller, Auld Hallowgate, Greyness, and my Uncle Sandy. At the time my Uncle Sandy was very much of a stranger in Greyness. For that matter, poor man, his feeling was a good deal that of one who was a stranger in the earth itself. My Uncle Sandy's breeding till past his twenty-fifth year had been that of the free open life of the country; and whatever his aspirations otherwise might have been, he had never once thought of exchanging that kind of life in favour of the dull routine of ordinary commerce in its indoor shopkeeping aspect, even should the ultimate prospect be that of thereby realising a fortune. His day-dreams had all been of the kind of life that implies breathing the free air of heaven, and witnessing the varied aspects of nature, as the inseparable accompaniments of active avocations, exercising the physical as well as the mental powers. But circumstances occasionally prove too strong for us all; and so it was with my Uncle Sandy.

As responsible tenant in a small farm, whose naturally sterile soil even good cultivation would not make profitably fertile, under the not quite exceptional conditions of high rent and the burden of feeding the unlimited hordes of wild animals which his landlord assiduously fostered for his own exclusive advantage, Sandy had come to the conclusion that change in some shape was necessary. That his landlord should exhibit as large a sense of justice as to admit the manifest truth that the creatures he killed week by week, and sold to the wholesale rabbit-dealers, represented crops on which his tenant had expended money and skill, transmuted in the most wasteful way into about the least valuable of marketable carcases; and, so admitting, should have ceased to maintain a staff of savage bipeds to aid him in rearing and slaughtering the creatures for his and their behoof, was to have been expected only if his landlord had been sufficiently civilised on the 'wild-beast' side of him to be able to distinguish between vulgar butchery and skilled 'sport,' and sufficiently cultivated as a morally responsible being to be able to realise the idea that certain primary duties, not of the selfish sort, are always involved in possession and privilege, and that there are principles of absolute equity by which a high-minded man would desire to be bound, even when, in the technical law sense, it might be in his power to violate them. My Uncle Sandy's landlord was not of this sort. And so, although by his carefully-nursed rabbits he had eaten off my Uncle's crops year by year, he pronounced him to be 'a troublesome fellow,' because he had sufficient courage to maintain that it was not for such use that those crops were grown. And he finally took credit for treating my Uncle Sandy with uncommon leniency when he declared his readiness to allow him to sever the lease of his farm, without exacting a pecuniary fine for granting such permission.

The estate on which my Uncle Sandy had been a tenant was one of those on which the relations of landlord and tenant were spoken of as being on a paternal footing; the idea of its being a commercial relationship was strongly resented and declared to be the suggestion of radicals of a very red type, only fitted, if not designed, to excite prejudice against the landlord class, whose instinctive benevolence forbad their ever going farther than to take all they wanted, and proclaim the grand old doctrine of 'LIVE and let live.' 'Aye truly,' thought my Uncle, 'live as you wish, and then let others live as they may! that's aboot it. But gie me the chance o' honestly haudin' my ain, to saw an' to reap, to dig upo' the earth an' ding doon again, to howk in o't an' fill up again, an' a' wi' as siccar a haud ower a' that's mine as the laird thinks needfu' to hae owre a' that's his; an' syne the paternal may hae scope free an' ungrudg't to dee its beneficent wark. Till than, the vera foundation's false, an' ostensible benevolence in the relationship o' lan'lord an' tenan', can but demoralise the giver an' degrade the recipient.'

CHAPTER TEN

My Uncle Sandy's Love Story

IN the time when things seemed more prosperous, and hope was strong within him, my Uncle Sandy had wooed, and, as he believed, won the love of the bright-eyed, merry hearted Elsie Robertson. Elsie had been his school companion indeed, and it would have puzzled my Uncle Sandy to say when the idea first dawned on him that she was his sweetheart; rather, perhaps, it would have puzzled him to recall the time when he did not, in a more or less definite way, associate that idea with Elsie; and in such circumstances the transition from the idea of sweetheart to that of wife is natural and easy; as natural and easy, as in this case it seemed to be, for the laughing, flaxen-haired lassie of sixteen, with her wealth of natural ringlets falling over her shoulders, to develop into the sedate and somewhat reserved maiden, who at twenty-one carried with her an air of womanly maturity. Sandy's purpose, latterly, had been to emigrate to some other country, where the conditions of life for such as he seemed more encouraging. But when it became known that he had renounced his lease, honestly avowing as his reason for so doing that he felt the conditions degrading to his sense of self-respect; and that he had made up his mind, come what might, that he would not go on ignominiously sacrificing the legitimate fruits of his industry and skill, in order that the depraved love of slaughter in another might be gratified, and his blunted moral perception remain unruffled, the very men who had exclaimed quite as loudly as he about their sufferings and losses, under the same grievance, began gravely to doubt his prudence. That he had not farmed well and carefully they could not say; neither could they aver that his allegations of essential injustice and loss were unfounded; but then they hinted that if instead of entertaining high-flown notions about abstract principles of right and wrong, and the sense of honour and manly independence, he had exerted greater effort in hard and dexterous bargain-making in the markets – turning over cattle and horses for a profit to be got off somebody – in place of 'makin' naething o't' or even 'sinkin' money,' he might at least have continued to struggle on as others did; and if fortune favoured, even to have improved his capital. To admit that his ideas ran counter to all this, and to affirm that if the honest cultivation of the soil was not to be allowed to proceed on a footing that would reward the legitimate toil of the cultivator, it was no occupation for him, and that accordingly he was about to seek another sphere, was held to argue an unsettled and flighty disposition. My Uncle Sandy would probably have set little store by all this; but when his plans for change were all but completed, and it turned out that one of his neighbours – a man who had done greatly more in 'bannin' the laird doon the avenue' than he – had quietly gone and bargained for his farm, accepting all the laird's terms with ready servility, and even offering a small advance of rent, he found to his intense mortification that the public estimate of his character had not been without its influence upon the bright and blooming Elsie Robertson. How it is that distrust is so in such cases, and how that misunderstandings arise, no one may well say. That Elsie's feeling of absolute confidence in my Uncle Sandy had been at least temporarily disturbed was evident; and that my Uncle, on his side, was deeply disappointed, and even angry, was certain. But in his circumstances, and with the prospect that seemed to lie before him, an explicit understanding, one way or the other, was necessary.

'An' dee you want to insist that we're engag't?' asked Elsie in a tone of piteous pleading.

'I've never even said we war engag't, Elsie; an' ye're as free to follow your ain wish as if we were the merest acquaintances,' said my Uncle. 'I haud you to nae promise; an' ye may bid me good-bye the day an' forget me the morn if ye care.'

'I canna forget ye,' sobbed Elsie. 'I'll aye think o' you as my freen – the best freen I hae on earth.'

'Elsie! spare yoursel' as weel's me. There's but ae word to describe fat ye wish noo; an' that word's – separation – the sin'erin o' a' that heeld you an' me in a bond clean ootside o' which aiven the dearest freens on earth, baith yours an' mine, hed to stan'. To ca' me your freen aifter that's only keepin' up a feelin' that can never bring to you the comfort o' aiven the commonest frien'ship; an' may weel be the cause o' positive pain.'

'But you *are* my dearest freen; an' I canna forget you,' exclaimed Elsie, in tones of passionate helplessness.

'Better far to forget me. To be ca'd your freen aifter a' that's come an' gane Elsie – the thocht's maddenin'; it's the suggestion o' hope never to be fulfillt, the incitement to despair wilfully dangl't afore a man's een,' replied my Uncle Sandy with vehemence.

'Dinna, oh dinna say that.'

'I maun say't, Elsie; it's true; an' I say't mair for your sake than for mine,' said my Uncle.

Then there was a silence for a space, as they stood side by side in the loan where they had often met before; and again there were passionate pleadings; but all to no purpose. Elsie's wish still was to be free and unpledged. That granted, she clung tenaciously to the idea of retaining a special interest in her 'friend,' and would even go the length of communicating with him, when absent, indirectly at least, as such. To my Uncle Sandy all this seemed utter madness, or worse; and he once more declared that if Elsie did not feel that they could part as pledged lovers, 'twas better for her to turn her thoughts entirely away from one of whose character she of all others had had ample means of judging, and whom she could never know better than she did at that hour, and in due course let them rest on another whom she might find worthier of her heart's affections.

And they parted thus. Soon thereafter a long and severe illness upset all my Uncle Sandy's plans. In the first place the pecuniary costs of this illness bore somewhat hardly in on the small capital, by means of which he had trusted to carry out his scheme of emigration hopefully; and in the second place, though the illness under which he suffered had gone off, he had recovered his health but partially, and consequently felt himself unfit to encounter the hazards and hardships that might be counted upon in essaying life in a new country. It was in these circumstances that my Uncle Sandy, after sundry vain efforts to find a sphere elsewhere, first became a resident in the town of Greyness by thankfully accepting the office of shop porter to Baillie Castock, in whose service his elder brother, the chief personage in this story, had risen through the various grades from apprentice to junior partner, his elevation to the latter position corresponding with the date of his entering the Castock family in the capacity of son-in-law. It was to the well-known magistrate just named that my Uncle Sandy, too, was indebted for this first step in commercial life. It was the opinion of Baillie Castock, when he had fully weighed the whole matter, that though no doubt a little green Sandy 'mith mak' 'imsel' vera eesfu' i' the warhoose in coorse o' time;' and that being so, the senior and junior partners after due deliberation, fixed my Uncle Sandy's salary at fourteen shillings a week.

It was barely twelve months after the date of his entering the warehouse of Baillie Castock that my Uncle Sandy came first in contact with the book-seller as already narrated. I have reason to believe that the wound inflicted by the unfortunate termination of his correspondence with Elsie Robertson, whom up to that date he had never seen again, and only knew that she had gone to a southern town in the capacity of lady's maid in a family, still rankled rather keenly at times. How far he had become prepared to accept Richie Darrell's advice to refuse further credence to the doctrine of the unselfishness of woman's love, and the constancy of her affection, is another question on which no opinion need here be pronounced.

CHAPTER ELEVEN

Contradictions and Contrasts

'AN' has he too kent what disappointment in love means?' mused my Uncle Sandy, as he thought over the incidents of his Sunday excursion with his new-made acquaintance, Richard Darrell, bookseller. 'What the meanin' o' his remark aboot the blank on the lair-stane may be, he kens best 'imsel'. Maybe ane that he had thocht to tak by the han' as his bride and to lay her banes by his in that grave has gane and left him. Maybe no – but nane excep' a man that had "lov'd and lost" would speak like yon. "Never believe in a woman's constancy or her unselfishness" – but' – and my Uncle Sandy shut his eyes and mused more slowly and soberly still – '*I* winna say that. I daurna think it in my inmost thocht; an' I'll lat nae ane say't wi' reference to ony experience o' mine at least.'

Whatever else might come of it such cogitations as these led my Uncle Sandy to a prompt fulfilment of the promise he had made to find out the old bookseller in his shop, a place that has been already described, and which during many years thereafter was destined to be with him a frequent howff. Very likely the limited range of his acquaintanceship in the town of Greyness at the time had made him willing to fall in with such companionship as seemed in any respect congenial. Yet of this there could be no doubt that the thought that most frequently came uppermost in his mind and floated about there in a vague way was the notion that somehow or other Richie Darrell would be moved to go back again, and it might be reveal himself further upon this old and ever new subject of the love of man to woman, and the blighted hopes and agonising endurance that to many spring therefrom. To my Uncle Sandy, as he felt, it would have been the greatest relief to have had the opportunity of articulately resisting,

and in the most emphatic way he could protesting against
the hard and harsh doctrine to which the bookseller had
given utterance. I do not know that he at all saw his way
through the gloomy puzzle in which he felt himself involved
concerning Elsie Robertson's unlooked-for and perplexing
treatment of himself, ever present though the subject was,
giving a sombre colour to his whole life. Likely enough it
was only the instincts of his own sincere nature that then kept
him right under the sense of a disappointment such as he felt
no man could experience twice in his lifetime, and which had
come while he was true to all the best impulses of his nature.
But in the long run, when years thereafter he could look at the
whole matter calmly, I know that my Uncle Sandy's settled
conviction was this – that if a right-hearted man has once
loved a woman truly, whatever disappointment to his hopes
may ensue, even should it go the length of her caprice leading
her to break outright the express or tacit bond she had allowed
him to make between them, he can never to the end of time
find rest and satisfaction in the thought that that woman was
false and only false nor do otherwise than feel that, deep as
the impassable breach between them may have become, he has
the right to know the certainty of what he speaks, and feels,
in a way that others who might think to gratify his ears by
detraction of one who has been to him unsteadfast cannot.

If my Uncle Sandy's philosophy erred on the side of charity,
I daresay Richie Darrell's did not. It was not easy, however,
as my Uncle found to lead him into any prolonged talk on the
subject. A stinging remark or two concerning the weaknesses
and follies of the female sex in general came commonly enough
but little more. Richie would then fly off from the subject
to another for which he had more favour. As my Uncle by
and bye found, the worthy man's antipathy to the sex led
him to exclude them entirely from any permanent place in
his domicile, a matron, who with her family lived under the
same roof and across the common lobby from his parlour door
being simply engaged to cook his meals and do his housemaid
work, as far as possible in his absence at his shop, the woman
retreating to her own apartments at his approach; but along
with this there was the seeming incongruity that in a few

rare instances in which the idea of sexual attachment was utterly excluded, Richie appeared to recognise the very ideal of womanhood in all its excellencies.

'Can I serve you to-day, ma'am?' he would say in his blandest tones and with his most elaborate bow, as Miss Spinnet, the stately and reserved maiden lady who occasionally favoured him with a call stepped down into his shop. Miss Spinnet was three score and five, hard featured, and wore very ponderous dark-coloured preserves on her eyes. She was taciturn for a women, moveover, and not easily served.

'You'll have none of the best old divinity cheap?' asked Miss Spinnet one day in my Uncle's hearing.

'Oh yes, ma'am – Owen – Baxter—'

'I want Barrow and Chillingworth, or Charnock.'

'Sorry, ma'am; but they're seldom in the market. I've a good copy of Hooker – only title page chafed'—

'Don't trouble,' said Miss Spinnet, as Richie moved to get the volume from the shelf, 'You don't know where I can find these?'

'I really do not. I'm afraid not in town,' added the bookseller, as he politely let his stiff visitor out into the street again. 'Good day, ma'am.'

'Admirable woman that,' resumed Richie, with a grave impressiveness, as he returned to his place behind his small counter. 'She's a business woman; she never wastes time in frivolous gossip or said-sae chatter.'

It was the first time my Uncle had seen Miss Spinnet, and as he had failed thus far to discover her charms and virtues, he, in reply, contented himself with clearing his throat, and casting a half-amused half-puzzled look toward the bookseller.

'What!' exclaimed Richie, fully comprehending the significance of my Uncle's glance. 'Ye wud prefer the attractions o' some saft-tongued witless hizzie, wi' 'er smirkin' face an' 'er slippery wyes. But, lat me tell you, my young man, that Miss Spinnet kens as muckle o' the vera marrow o' our best theology as ony half-dizzen o' yer evangelical divines o' the present day.'

'I dinna doot it,' said my Uncle somewhat irreverently, 'for I've heard it alleg't that some o' the books she name't are stan'in quarries for certain divines to dig the materials o' their sermons fae. But kennin' so little o' formal theology mysel', I freely confess my inability to do justice to the lady's merits in that licht.'

'An' ye may think shame to say't, man,' replied the bookseller. 'Ye'll men' or ye'll dee waur. Hooever, there's little profit fechtin' wi' a perverse generation that consider themsel's wiser nor the wisest o' their forefathers; the fruits o' their conceit'll be seen time aneuch.'

When the memorial discourses of Dr Cleavahair were passing through the press the happy thought had occurred of asking Miss Spinnet, who had been in the circle of that learned divine's attached hearers, to revise the proof sheets, and the astute and searching way in which she had corrected certain lapses in doctrinal sentiment, and filled in various blanks in the applications, had no doubt made a marked impression on the Editor of the volume.

But while Miss Spinnet, with her austere manners and theological bent, was an ideal of her sex to one side in the bookseller's eyes, my Uncle – whose mood at the time in relation to such matters was very likely somewhat abnormal – was a good deal surprised, and a little perplexed to find that his other female divinity, for the time, existed in the shape of a soft, rosy-cheeked, chattering country school girl of fourteen, who visited the shop to supply herself with pens, paper, and similar requisites. Nancy Darling was in every way as completely at the antipodes of Miss Spinnet as it was possible to imagine. In her frequent, and not very necessary errands into the shop as she passed, she staid long and occupied the bookseller's time with much inconsiderable talk, and many unimportant questions; yet did his patience never give out nor his gallant courtesy desert him.

'Excellent girl – she's a lassie that her parents an' teachers may be prood o',' said Richie Darrell, with an emphasis fairly rivalling that with which he was wont to speak of the admirable Miss Spinnet.

'Human nature is a singular combination,' thought my Uncle Sandy. 'I have had my own perplexities about it, but clearly I have not yet seen any way far into its windings.'

CHAPTER TWELVE

Connubial Counsels

A period of three to four years had elapsed when the
lamented decease of Charles Castock, senior partner of the
well-known firm of Castock & Macnicol, merchants, Auld
Hallowgate, Greyness, and recently senior magistrate of the
burgh, occurred. The mournful event was duly announced in
the local newspapers; and the leading facts of the deceased's
life, with his various services as a public man, and his numerous virtues as a private citizen, set forth in a paragraph of
some length. The natural effect of Baillie Castock's death was
to improve the social standing of my Uncle David. As his son-
in-law, the husband of his only daughter, my Uncle succeeded
to the share that Mr Castock had retained in the business, and
as the worthy man had been a widower he succeeded to the
chief residue of his estate as well. I do not in the least doubt
that my Uncle sincerely mourned the old man's decease;
but, of course, like other people in similar circumstances,
he could only submit to the mournfully satisfactory feeling
of being, in a grievous way, made substantially richer in this
world's goods. And I think his wife shared the feeling with
equal intensity, and, at least, more lugubriously. She wore
the deepest of deep mournings for her parent, and did not
spare to appear frequently in public so attired. But it would
have been in vain to deny that when the edge of her grief had
somewhat worn off, she felt it the bounden and responsible
duty of herself and her husband to let the public of Greyness
be fully aware of their precise social position as things now
stood. In this respect I daresay she only shared the feeling
common to many others who hold it vital to existence that the
world shall not underrate them socially or otherwise. To my
Uncle's wife the matter presented itself mainly in two aspects

– as it affected the general society of the place, and in relation
to the family connections. As bearing on the first of these she
could not forget the claims and responsibilities of those who
represented one that in his time had worn the golden chain of
the burgh baillie, and had departed in the undimmed lustre of
that high office. The scheme was even then afoot of pushing
my Uncle into the Town Council; the full outcome of his
wife's aspirations in that direction we already know in effect.
In the matter of family relationship, curious to say, my Uncle
Sandy threatened to be the sorest perplexity. Not but that
there were hosts of poor relations on both sides who would
have been troublesome by their vulgarities, and so on, if they
had only got the chance. But my Uncle's wife was an adept
in the modern system of dealing with such people; namely,
by patronising in a cheap way those of their number who
were docile and lived gratefully at a distance, and absolutely,
and very resolutely ignoring such of them as chose to be at
any time inconveniently in the way, and without the merit
of social equality were imprudent enough to look for an
unvarying recognition on the basis of mere consanguinity.
Such people, in point of fact, presented hardly any greater
difficulty than if they had had no existence. With my Uncle
Sandy it was different. He had now been for a space of five
years in the warehouse and, as my Uncle David's wife knew,
had in that position gained very fully the confidence even of
her own father as a useful and trusted auxiliary in business
matters. Still Sandy's manner of life and conversation were
far from satisfactory to her.

'Mithna ye try an' persuaad yer brither to gie up some
o's countra haibits, my dear, an' keep mair amo' the kin' o'
company 't we wud like to see 'im ta'en oot wi'?' said my
Uncle's wife.

'His countra haibits?' answered my Uncle David inquir-
ingly. 'I'm nae aware that's haibits are waur nor ither folks.'

'Tut man; what's mair common nor to see 'im stan'
up i' the braidest street o' the toon, be wi' 'im fa may,
an' speak wi' some roch half heilan' creature in a grey
plaid an' clatterin' tacketie sheen; or some sma' fairmer's
wife wi' 'er butter basket on 'er airm. An' to see 'im

wi' a glove on's han's Sunday or Saturday, is neist to a ferlie.'

'Folk canna help speakin' to a countra body at a time,' said my Uncle, evidently not desirous of pursuing the subject, the truth being that he did not much relish the idea of admonishing the uncircumspect Sandy.

'Weel, ye k-now perfectly that it's not becomin' in his position noo; an' fa wud speak till 'im if his nown brither wudna dee't? There's the like o' that bodie Darrell noo. It may be a' vera weel to buy a triffle fae the creatur at a time – he's respectable aneuch in's ain place, an' nae doot has muckle adee to mak' a sober livin'. But it is not seemly to mak' maist a companion o' 'im. He's gotten a lead o' comin' aboot the warehouse tee, an' I've aiven heard 'im sayin' things to yersel' that war vera unbecomin' an' vera improper for the young men oonder you to hear.'

'Noo, my dear,' exclaimed my Uncle half-impatiently, 'Richie Darrell never comes aboot the place but fan he has an erran'; an' Sandy has nae blame in that.'

'Dinna tak' me up that gate noo Dawvid. I was only wussin' 't ye sudna forget that fan fowk's nae born intill a position, it taks ef-fort till acquire a richt idea o' what's necessar an' due to themsel's as weel as to them that's been ordeen't till a lower station. Ye sudna forget them that's – a-wa!' gasped my Uncle's wife, who here became suddenly hysterical at the thought of her deceased father.

'Oh, my dear, your father didna tribble 'imsel' aboot the like o' that,' said my Uncle tenderly and truly, the late Baillie, about whose transmitted dignity his wife was so deeply concerned, having been one of the most unsophisticated of men when left to his own devices. My Uncle's wife, after sobbing on in silence for a time, continued—

'An' Sandy wud need to be mair prudent. Didna ye tell me yersel' noo that he had been insnorlt wi' some witless countra quaen as his sweetheart?'

'The girl Elsie Robertson? Hoot, my dear, that's an aul' story; lat that pass,' said my Uncle.

'An aul' story! Maybe,' replied my Uncle's wife, 'an' a new story as weel; for lat me tell you that it's only a month ago that the gipsy gaed aff wi' some half crazy tailor creatur for gweed an' a'.'

'What! She's marriet Tammie Tamson, the tailor, has she!' exclaimed my Uncle, with unaffected surprise. 'Fair fa' Tammie; he's waitit lang an' patiently; but perseverance has brocht its ain reward at last than. He's my brither's senior by a dizzen o' years; but that's nae mark; he'll be the better able to put the needed restraint on's wife's giddiness.'

'It's not a fit subject for jeestin' aboot, my dear,' said my Uncle's wife seriously. 'Ye may weel see hoo nairrow an escape yer brither made wi' ony sic orra, ill-wylt kitty.'

'H—m, well,' quoth my Uncle, who did not quite see it, 'she's a vera comely lass, to say naething mair. An' she's come o' respectable pawrents.'

'Comely! an' respectable! The daachter o' a countra cottar!' said my Uncle's wife, whose own style of beauty was of the sort that is best described by negatives. 'At onyrate she had care't little aneuch for him; an' he may thank's stars that he wan by 'er; though I daresay *she* wudna 'a been likely to fash him nor nae ither body aboot her parents' position; nor their pelf either for that maitter.'

'Weel, weel, my dear. It'll be jist as wise nae to meddle wi' Sandy aboot that maitter at ony-rate,' said my Uncle. He was too much accustomed to observations of the kind to dwell particularly upon the circumstance that the statement just made might possibly be meant to have a reflex reference to his own case, in the way of reminding him that *his* connubial connections had brought him something more substantial than mere personal attractions.

'Aye, but it's a maitter that concerns mair nor 'imsel'. Fan people's ain position's weel k-nown i' the place, an' ithers near conneckit by bleed come to be conneckit in business as weel, it's vera necessary that they sud hae regaird to the feelin's an' influence o' them that's helpit them on. Far be't fae me to say't Sandy's nae a clever lad an' a deservin', but that's nae a'; ye sud bear in min' that it's nae for them't's at the heid o' an establishment, an' wi' ither prospects afore them, to forget their responsibilities; or lat this an' the tither person bear in upo' them's they war enteetl't to be regairdit as their equals.'

Thus exhorted, not once but frequently, it was my Uncle David's own blame if he did not rise to the responsibilities of his position. It somehow happened that though he at times recognised the expediency of talking seriously to Sandy about what seemed his too easy familiarity with all ranks and conditions of men at inconvenient times, he could never find the fitting terms in which he might couch his admonitions; and thus Sandy was after all left very much to follow the devices of his own heart in this as in other respects.

CHAPTER THIRTEEN

Elsie Robertson's Fortune

IT was quite a common-place course that events had taken thus far as the reader will see. In the byegone years it had been perfectly well known to my Uncle Sandy that Tammie Tamson, the tailor of Trotterburn, had been frantically in love with Elsie Robertson. But the bare idea of regarding him in the light of a rival suitor had not so much as occurred to my Uncle, much less that of viewing any attentions he chose to pay to Elsie with a lover's jealousy. Tammie, a rather watery-faced, weak-kneed little man, as became his craft, was a clever workman enough in his way, and well patronised by the bucks of Trotterburn, (they were not very numerous), among whom he failed not always to shine as chief in the cut and quality of his own garments. But what the wiser heads there, and indeed through the Strath generally, said about him was that he wanted 'soliteed'; and their opinion got confirmed when Tammie all of a sudden declared that he would not waste his time longer fashioning plush waistcoats, corduroy breeks and fear-nothing spats for the rustic dwellers in Strathtocher; and throwing up his thriving business in Trotterburn, went off to achieve the fortune his talents merited in some fashionable emporium in the south.

How it came I know not, but beyond doubt the feeling of Elsie Robertson toward the tailor fraternity had been distinguished by its full share of the sort of half contemptuous regard too often directed against that useful craft; and she had, in her own merry and light-hearted way, been wont to look upon and speak of Tammie Tamson as the very *beau ideal* of all that was fit subject for mirth or mockery in the typical tailor. The ideals on which her mind or affections could rest were all of a more robust and manly sort.

74

Thus it stood up to the time that Tammie Tamson left Trotterburn for the south. As we know Elsie Robertson went to the south too. I can well believe their surprise was mutual when in a certain kirk on a certain Sunday they found themselves incredulously staring at each other over the space intervening between two cross galleries. The thoughts that then arose in Tammie Tamson's mind are to me unknown, beyond this that he deemed it incumbent upon him without loss of time to re-introduce himself to the woman who had excited his admiration and his equally hopeless despair. Tammie was not revengeful, had indeed many good qualities in him, and though he had in the bye-gone time been subjected to rebuffs in such form as is least grateful to a man's vanity as well as his deeper feelings, I don't know that the experiences of the past had left any very deep or permanent impression upon him. It was with an unmistakeable cordiality therefore that he now greeted Elsie Robertson. Elsie's own feeling was probably less unembarassed; possibly she had come suddenly to a sort of dim conclusion that there was such a thing as Fate; possibly also that in her case Fate and Tammie Tamson the tailor were not widely dissociated. Certainly she was not long left in doubt about the tailor's intention to renew his suit with all his old ardour.

To say that my Uncle Sandy had hoped that Elsie Robertson would not marry another than he would be doing him an injustice. Yet, when on the express authority of one of the parties directly concerned, triumphantly transmitted to his old cronies at Trotterburn and then indirectly to my Uncle's ears, the marriage of Elsie to Tammie Tamson had come to be an immediately impending event, he unquestionably had within him somewhat of the feeling of a man who strongly desired to be alienated in body, soul, and spirit from the whole human race, and from Tammie Tamson, the tailor, in particular.

And after all Elsie Robertson had not yielded even to Fate without a struggle. A couple of years had elapsed since the tailor and she had again met; and, the conclusion at which the gossips, with the intuitive knowledge that belongs to them in such circumstances, had arrived, was that even then she had in part at least repented of her unhappy break off from my Uncle

Sandy, and might have been again approached by him with all hopefulness. But how? Who was to take the first step? If my Uncle Sandy believed that he might, he also felt that he could not. It might be that the old feeling had not died out in his heart; yet he had, through influences external to himself, and beyond his control, been set in a different attitude toward the object of it. And the very thought of seeking to regain the old attitude, without an express indication that the way thereto was open, seemed in his sight in the nature of an endeavour to reassert his own position at the cost of humiliation to her at whose will the altered relations had come about. No doubt my Uncle Sandy was unduly sensitive as things go in this rough world; but so it was. It might be that Elsie Robertson, on her side, would gladly enough have recalled what had passed in the time when she knew her own heart and its yearnings and needs less than she now did. The only thing certain is, that though she delayed and was troubled, she did not do what she might have done toward that end.

And meanwhile, as opportunity offered, Tammie Tamson, the tailor, wooed as ardently as ever, and was happily as impervious as ever to such tokens as there might be that his suit was not a cause of unmixed pleasure to the object of his devotion. And he had his reward. Elsie Robertson at last gave in. She shed floods of tears ere she did so, and after; but she now felt that the time was past – that life to her, whether by the power of Fate or her own shaping, could never be what she had dreamt it would be – though the marriage came upon the community of Trotterburn and the dwellers in the Strath with much of the feeling of a sudden surprise.

Of course, like any other event of the kind, it just had its time as a nine day's wonder; gossip in Trotterburn found the subject stale by and bye; things resumed their wonted quiet, and Time silently pursued his steady march till something else occurred, the next heard of Elsie Robertson in due course being that she had presented the tailor with his first born son.

CHAPTER FOURTEEN

The Kirkin' of the Council

WHEN the Town Council of Greyness met for the annual election of office-bearers and the swearing in of the ordinary rank and file of the body, the ancient Town Hall of the place wore an air of more than usual state. On that day fixedly of all days in the year, the two halves of the main door were opened to their full width, the Town Clerk donned his official gown, and his subordinates were all at their appointed posts. It was not much of a spectacle to be sure and, except when 'feeling ran high,' the main bulk of the audience, apart from the Council membership, invariably consisted of some dozen of *quid nuncs* and gossips who had witnessed the election year by year for quarter of a century. There were always to be found the component parts of the small coterie of loungers who assembled daily at the corner shop for a chat and an exchange of snuff boxes, including the superannuated weaver, with his keen sharp eyes and his asthmatic cough, the burly old coach-guard, the half-idle sheriff-officer, with his 'concurrent', and their quondam associate the town's drummer. There, too, was the rubicund, bald-headed barber, from the Crofthead Ward, with two or three others of his neighbours who, at his call, had deserted their shop counters for an hour to enable them once more to carry away a fresh impression of the scene. These, with two or three middle-aged men with the aspect of broken-down lawyers, or meagrely paid and fed clerks, a few half-grown lads, with political tendencies early developed, and a mysterious-looking man in rusty black, who carried a green umbrella, and grimly surveyed the whole business in a self-contained way, constituted the representatives of the public when the Baillies were solemnly invested with their chains of office.

77

The fact of my Uncle David's election to the Town Council of Greyness, under the circumstances already described, implied his election to the office of youngest Baillie; and he had the distinction of being nominated in a laudatory speech by the Provost of the burgh, Baillie Gudgeon, as seconder, emphatically endorsing, and voluminously paraphrasing what the Provost had said.

'It's a big shame,' said my Uncle David's wife when he returned to his home for the first time as Baillie Macnicol, 'to think that sic an impressive ceremony sud be clean thrown awa. Fat for sudna't be arrang't differently, an' lat the general commoonity see't?'

'It's quite open to the community,' said my Uncle with an air of firmness becoming his new position, 'but they don't take advantage o't.'

'An' little won'er, answered Mrs Macnicol, 'what respectable person cud go there an' expect to sit doon side by side, maybe wi' some questionable character?'

'Hoot-toot, my dear; the folk are perfectly respectable though maybe nae movin' in the highest circles; an', from the point o' view o' a public man, we maun use a lairge discretion.'

'I see nae reason why ladies sudna be invitet,' continued my Uncle's wife, who, after all, was in great spirits, and disposed to be talkative over the matter. 'The admission cud be by ticket. But far be't fae me to seek to exclude the meanest in the lan' or aiven them that's fa'en into error oonder the laws o' their countra. We a' ken that the magistracy's set for "a terror to evil-doers" as weel's "a praise an' protection to such as do well." I wud be the last to deprive the vera laps't masses o' a sicht sae weel fittet to produce a solemneesin' effect; lat alane the prayer for the pooers that be, an' the oath o' allegiance that my father keepit in prent for mony a day amon's Cooncil papers. — Is the Cooncil to be kirkit o' the Sabbath, said ye?'

'Of coorse — they'll gae to the High Kirk as usual.'

'An' will a' the dissenters an' Free Kirk men amo' them gae?'

'That's nae likely. In fact I doot if ony but them that belangs to the Establish't Kirk'll gae.'

'Weel, I canna blame them. Only there's a difference atween a mere Toon Cooncillor an' a Magistrate. An' of coorse ye're the only Baillie that doesna belang to the Establish't Kirk.'

'Oh, I ken it'll be ill ta'en my bidin' awa. Still an' on, I dinna see hoo I cud consistently enter the door o' an Erastian kirk. – Fat think ye?' asked my Uncle, whose denominational position was that of a keen Free Churchman, though he nevertheless felt that absence from the grand kirking ceremony was too like wanting a part of what he had bargained for to be pleasant.

'Of course the question hadna come up in my father's time,' said Mrs Macnicol. 'But ye ken, my dear, ye've ta'en the responsibilities o' the State upo' ye – a judge o' the lan' in a mainner.'

'It's a vera perplexin' question – vera perplexin',' continued my Uncle. '"The Kirk o' Scotland Free" has deen wi' Erastianism an' a' its fruits; but o' the ither han' the Free Kirk stan's by the principle o' an estaiblishment. We've always upheld the duty o' the civil magistrate.'

'Weel, my dear, bein' i' the position o' the civil magistrate, I canna but think it vera possible for the dischairgin' o a duty to the Queen's maijesty, as it were, to tak' yer pairt i' the procession, and even hear the sermon, wi' a clear conscience, keepin' only the principle afore ye, an' disregairdin' ootward things.'

Thus fortified, my Uncle made up his mind to think as favourably of the procession as he could during the two days that would yet elapse ere the Sunday arrived.

The Council procession was a rather imposing affair. A couple of questionably reverent toon sergeants, in red coats and white cotton gloves, carrying halberts (as the long stick with a tin knife on its head was called) stalked along the main street, from the Town Hall to the High Church, with the Provost and four Baillies gravely following, their gowd chynes fully displayed on their ample bosoms. The general body of Councillors, or such of them as would consent to go, walked behind, and a considerable bevy of idle youth accompanied them most of the way, passing church-goers also slackening their steps for a moment to gaze upon the procession and offer criticisms on the style and gait of the chief figures composing it. In church, the Council sat enclosed under a ponderous canopy, in what was known as the Magistrates' Gallery, trying to look wise in the eyes of the inquisitive congregation as they listened to a sermon which, being meant to be special, was more likely than otherwise above average dull. At the end of the service the procession repeated itself the reverse way and then broke up.

The idea of my Uncle forfeiting his part in all this grand display, was something not to be readily entertained. He was entirely satisfied that personal vanity had no sway in the matter, and he thought he doubted whether after all his influence as a magistrate would not be diminished by his failing to appear in company with what was the nearest approach to 'the sword' known in Greyness. The stout casuistical exercise through which his mind went in reconciling general fealty to his Church, with his very particular duty to the State, was all in the line of thought indicated in his remarks to his wife, to whose complete satisfaction he was able to announce on Saturday:—

'It's a duty I canna shirk, my dear; it may be onerous, but I'm not like a private citizen or a plain cooncillor. I maun tak' the responsibilities o' public office.'

Though my Uncle's wife could not, of course, have the advantage of seeing him in the Magistrates' Gallery, she took the opportunity on the Sunday morning of carefully watching the procession as it passed, from a second storey window, their house happening, luckily, to be on the line of route. As the brave and solemn pageant moved on its stately way she peered cautiously over the heads of her three eldest girls, who were there to enjoy the spectacle with her. That over, she went her way well satisfied to worship in her own church; the events of the day suggesting one or two appropriate reflections and illustrations which she carefully stored up for the lesson she was wont to impart to the Misses Macnicol before evening sermon.

CHAPTER FIFTEEN

An Apprentice Baillie

WHEN from the ranks of simple citizenship a man has got elevated into the serene and lofty region of magisterial dignity the feeling must, in certain respects, be not unlike that of the æronaut, who has suddenly ascended to that height in the physical atmosphere where breathing becomes difficult from the rarified state of the air. Nor was my Uncle David exempt from a feeling of this sort. In his movements out and into his office, in the arbitrary way in which he would and would not do this and the other thing about the warehouse; and in his style of address to his subordinates as well, he gave token of a certain light-headedness, which was not unobserved of John Cockerill and myself.

'Did ye see the chyne hingin' oot aneth's weskit fan he cam' ben?' asked John, on the first morning of my Uncle's appearance at the warehouse as the Baillie.

'Ay; does ilka baillie wear a chyne?'

'Of coorse. Is that a' that ye ken aboot it! There would be little fun in't if they hedna their chynes, ye geese.'

'Weel, they're unco little eese, for they dinna sae muckle's gar them dee for watch guards.'

'Watch guards! Man there's nae mony o' oor baillies won by the aul' fashion't watch strap wi' a dunshoch o' keys an' seals hingin' doon their leg. But the chyne's inten'it for honour; same's the gilt heid on the muckle weather-cock – dinna ye ken that?'

'Ou ay,' replied I, in an indefinite way, rather floored at anyrate for the time, by my companion's rapid eloquence.

'It's a gweed thing, ony wye, that the maister's been made a baillie, for it was easy kent that he was richt ill aboot it,' said John Cockerill. 'An' it soun's fine aboot a place. There'll be lots o' fowk comin' in aboot the warehouse wantin' the Baillie to sign papers an' things; and syne the coorts – I would like richt to see 'im tryin' a thief or twa. Wudna ye?'

Naturally enough my feelings and desires entirely corresponded with those of John Cockerill on this point; and being in the capacity of errand-boy it was easier for me to gratify my wishes in that particular in a furtive way than it was for him.

My Uncle had never in all his life previously given ten minutes attention to any question affecting legal forms or the principles or details of criminal law; but in view of his approaching elevation to the bench his mind had got engrossed with the whole range of subjects connected with the jurisprudence of the country. He had possessed himself of a copy of 'Bell's Principles,' and had quietly obtained for private use a bunch of single statutes, which seemingly had served the like purpose with some one else before. It is not for me to speak of the extent of his profiting by his legal studies; although it might hardly be a breach of charity to believe that at his highest point of attainment his zeal remained fully commensurate with his knowledge. In the matter of judicial training, however, my Uncle had during his initiatory stage the benefit of attending the sittings of the Police Court under his experienced friend Baillie Gudgeon, whose manner on the bench and general magisterial procedure, if they did not form a model for all beginners, were such as while specifically characteristic of himself in externals, might be regarded as in a general way typical of the whole magisterial bench of Greyness in essence. When his court had been duly 'fenced,' and the prisoner at the bar solemnly interrogated as to his admission or denial of guilt, the Baillie would lift his quill pen and adjusting his silver spectacles on his nose, set very earnestly on to take notes of evidence. Mr Branks, the public prosecutor, who was also the police superintendent of the burgh, and an abrupt, slightly cranky sort of man, had it all pretty much his own way in that particular court. His habit, naturally enough, was to assume rather peremptorily the guilt of every person he saw fit to charge with an offence, and if the accused happened to be undefended, do his best to obtain a speedy conviction by putting what the lawyers call 'leading questions' to the witnesses. The Baillie, to whom, of course, it never occurred that this practice was unfair, went steadily on with his notes, staying now and again to put a question himself, which the prosecutor heard occasionally with tokens of impatience. The Baillie's interjected questions it must be admitted had usually a considerable spice of irrelevancy about them; and it is to be feared that his notes of evidence were not always over lucid or logical. They went in this wise: – 'Duffy – drunk and disorderly – plead not guilty – proof – two gills–1 bot. porter – another man came in – witness went out – woman – other man drunk too – witness heard noise – witness came in after other man – not drunk – witness paid own share of drink – accused fell over form – broke glasses – cursing and swearing – not sure if other man struck accused – sure not more than three gills, one Donald, and two bots.,' and so on; and so on.

The Baillie was always perfectly satisfied with the value of his record; and in passing sentence he seldom failed to remind the prisoner of what he had in his 'notes' against him. He was strong in admonitions too, and even where the case was clearly not proven it was with much reluctance that he would allow himself to be deprived of the privilege of exhorting the accused to take better care next time. Occasionally there were perplexing cases; and while Baillie Gudgeon could go on gravely and steadily, where a rough rule of thumb process led up to the statutory 'five shillings or ten days,' it was alleged by cynical people that when there were any unusual features in evidence, or otherwise, he was entirely at the mercy of the public prosecutor who practically dictated the findings of the Court. If the bench happened to show a tendency toward acting contrary to his ideas the prosecutor would rattle through his case, offering as little of commentary at the tail of it as might be; and then swash down in his seat with the exclamation, 'Noo, Baillie, that's my case!'

When things had come to this pass the Baillie first looked over his notes; he then, with upturned face and shut eyes, deliberately stroked his chin with an air of the severest judicial gravity.

'Prisoner at the bar – hae ye onything to say for yoursel'?'

'No, sir.'

'Nothing?'

'No.'

Then came another pause during which the Baillie went through the same movements as before. His resources in that way being exhausted, he had recourse to his snuff-box, cautiously peering over the front of the bench, most likely only to find no part of the prosecutor visible but the top of his bald head. If that important official had sufficiently got over his temporary heat the sound of snuffing might haply rouse him, seeing he dearly loved a borrowed pinch, and the sight of the friendly box extended in his direction would induce him to get on his feet once more for a whispered confab with the bench, when the sentence would incontinently be pronounced. Otherwise, as the Baillie hung his sneeshin mull over the front of the bench, or even ventured on a magisterial hoast as a signal of capitulation, the prosecutor, without turning his head, would simply repeat, 'I'm done, Baillie – the Coort's waitin' you,' and continue to nurse his huff. In this case the Baillie would resume his look of profound judicial wisdom, and after a glance or two further at his notes would say – 'There's some pints o' law in this case not a'thegither clear. It's a case o' some importance, in fact, an' vera interestin' to the prisoner at the bar. An' as the assessor's no here the day, it'll stan' adjourn 't till the morn's mornin'! The Coort's over.'

During his probationary month my Uncle sat assiduously by the side of Baillie Gudgeon day after day; and, as I have reason to know, that in addition to the large amount of example and precept given in public, the Baillie spared not to ply him with ample counsel, clinched by apt 'instances' in private, it could not but be that he would have himself alone to blame if he did not take his place upon the bench a fully-equipped Baillie, in so far as judicial ideas and the due administration of justice, in the Greyness fashion, were concerned.

CHAPTER SIXTEEN

The Ethics of the Baillieship

'YE'LL better nae lat that gowd chyne turn your heid a'thegither, merchan',' said Richie Darrell, when the spirit had moved him to call at my Uncle's warehouse after he had been elevated to the dignity of Baillie.

'Turn my heid! Fat dee ye mean, Richie?' said my Uncle affably.

'Ye dinna ken, I suppose. Tak' it as a general question than – Cud ye tell me hoo it happens that there was never yet a man made a Baillie in this toon but he got blawn up wi'a kin' o' pompous conceit till he was near unkenable?'

'Hoot, fie, Richie; ye dinna believe that.'

'Maybe no. Hooever, my belief's nae the point, Baillie Macnicol,' said the bookseller, emphasizing the last two words. 'We've a' kent men that hed the ambition to achieve distinction o' different kin's, an' succeedit mair or less; but in nae walk o' life, in nae stratum o' society, does't happen 't the men that get to the upper platform at which they've been aimin' hae so uniformly been impress't wi' an overpooerin' sense o' the abstract dignity o' their new position, as in the case o' the men that have succeedit in bein' made Baillies.'

'Oh, ye're jokin' noo, Mister Darrell,' said my Uncle.

'An' its nae dependant in the vera least on their qualifications for the duties they're suppos't to dischairge – we a' ken weel they may be, as they af'en are, *nil*,' continued the bookseller; 'but that neither diminishes the eagerness o' the aspirant as lang as he is an aspirant, nor sobereezes the pomposity o's mainner aifter he gets the chance o' makin' imsel' a spectacle for petty evil doers, to face wi' counterfeit penitence the ae day, an' ban wi' hearty gweed will the neist.'

'Well, well, ye know, Richie, we can hardly expect their benediction,' said my Uncle, fencing a little wildly, but still talking with persistent affability.

'Ye're but a sookin' Baillie yet ony wye, and ken little aboot it,' replied the bookseller. 'Wait till ye've hed it het an' heavy fae some o' yon draigl't carlines and brazen-fac't cutties fae the Nether Port fan ye're o' the tae bench, an' them o' the tither frontin' you. An' i' the meantime see an' nae lat your new-come dignity rin awa' wi' yer common sense,' he added abruptly, as he finished the topic.

'No fear o' that Richie,' said my Uncle. 'We get aye providences anew to keep's sober fatever oor station.'

Though my Uncle spoke with even more than his usual familiarity I don't think that he could entertain at all gratefully the idea of Richie Darrell despising dignities, or even talking of them lightly; and to this latter, in so far as the office of Baillie in Greyness was concerned, Richie was, it must be owned, a little prone; one of his favourite traditions being that concerning a browster woman of questionable repute, whom the magistracy in the previous generation had been ill-advised enough to sentence to a day's incarceration in the public jougs for selling ale on Sunday, and other illicit doings, and who, in addition to much unsavoury speech during her trial, whiled away the time of her punishment with repeating ever and anon in the ears of the eagerly attendant mob the names of the various living baillies of Greyness who had patronised her house at all hours of Sunday and Saturday, and the consequent ingratitude implied in their present treatment of the very person by whom they had been 'aye ceevilly enterteen't.'

'It michtna be handy for some fowk if ill doers war alloot to shak' their crap the same gate noo-a-days,' was the bookseller's usual finish to the story when related in the hearing of any of his magisterial acquaintances.

It was probably the case that my Uncle wished to avert everything in the nature of a home thrust from Richie Darrell, without, as may be supposed, being entirely successful. And very evidently he was quite desirous to let my Uncle Sandy feel that the fact of his being now a Baillie had not in the least turned his head or made him deem it any more a condescension to ask and act upon his advice than hitherto. I don't think it had in the least occurred to Sandy that any indication of the sort was needed. He had been sufficiently grovelling to entertain the notion that the desire to be a Baillie was a rather petty kind of ambition, and had been bold enough to tell his brother so. But, seeing that brother thought otherwise, and had acted upon his ideas in the matter, Sandy, in his usual unsuspicious way, had then dismissed the thought and was only recalled to it by my Uncle the Baillie gravely commencing a formal explanation in the words—

'There'll be no difference in business maitters, excep'in that ye'll need to be aye aboot the office 'fan I'm i' the Coort, an' sic like ye ken; an' to keep your han' free ye'll jist haud at that loons.'

'Oh that's a' richt,' said Sandy. 'The loons 'll be easy aneuch to manage; 'if they're nae ower muckle meddl't wi'.'

'In fac' I'll lippen mair to you than I've been deein' aiven,' continued my Uncle the Baillie with a distinct emphasis that was meant to give Sandy full assurance on the point.

Towards John Cockerill and myself it was really the case that our master in the comparative publicity of the warehouse now assumed a little more of the stiffness and reserve that became his altered position. Master Cockerill did not by any means dislike this. He had imbibed something of the notion that an accession to his master's dignity added more or less to his own importance; and in the case of callers at the warehouse he was not slow to exhibit this when opportunity offered.

'Ye was wantin' the Baillie was ye? Weel he's not in; ye'll jist need to call back. Fan'll he be here? Depen's on circumstances entirely. The Coort may be over in half-an-hour; or it may sit till twal o'clock, or langer. I'll be glad to gie the Baillie ony message if ye prefer't. No, I cudna fix the exact time't he'll be in nor hoo lang he may stay. His time's nae his ain ye know.'

The chance of an occasional display of this sort when both the Baillie and my Uncle Sandy happened to be out together was exceedingly satisfactory to John Cockerill, and amply made up for any feeling of increased distance between the Baillie and him in the ordinary intercourse of the warehouse;

let alone the fact of its giving John opportunity for ministering in various ways to his master's desires and needs as a magistrate. And for myself it must be admitted that the balance of considerations led me from the outset to entertain a kind of vaguely pleased feeling that I had an uncle who was a real live Baillie; and there were many reasons why this feeling should grow in strength and substance.

The winter had passed and the spring was gone, when on a bonnie July day I took coach with the buoyant sense of life and freedom, of which the man who has been battered all round by the blows of circumstance can recall but a sober shadow, to spend my first formal holiday in my native Glen at the home of my mother. And I found that the high official name of my Uncle the Baillie had penetrated even there. That a man born in our parish should hold the distinguished position of a Baillie in Greyness was felt to be much in itself; and that that man should be my mother's half-brother was a fact that, amid a sparse and primitive population, helped to make even the utterly obscure nephew who did his miscellaneous work a sort of conspicuous character.

'He's neist thing till a shirra noo, isin' he Benjie?' asked old Francie Tamson, addressing myself.

'A shirra!' exclaimed the stubbly-headed souter of Strathtocher with a sneer, ere I could frame my reply in any sort. 'Fa wud compare a toon's Baillie wi' a shirra? The shirra's a mere lethal official, answerable to the authorities; but the Baillie's an oondependent functionar', wi' naebody but the Provost atweesh him an' the Queen's Maijesty.'

'But the Provost *has* mair poo'er?' asked Francie, seriously.

'Seerly,' answered the souter, in a vague yet decisive tone.

'Dear be here; isna't byous noo,' continued Francie Tamson. 'I min' sae weel fan your uncle was only a little fite-heidit laddie, rinnin' aboot barfit in a grey wincey kiltie. Mony's the day that he trottit aifter me to the peat moss; an' was as prood's a king fan he could get a ride upo' my aul' grey shaltie. Dear be here: an' he's a Baillie noo; the laddikie that red upo' oor Donal'.'

Francie Tamson was not the only dweller in the Glen that

could call up early reminiscences of the man who was now shedding such lustre upon the obscure region of his nativity; and I should surely have been more than human if I had not, after all, returned to Greyness with an enhanced sense of the honourable distinction achieved by my Uncle the Baillie.

And then, to do my Uncle the barest justice, when I again returned to my wonted round of duties, however formal he might be in the presence of others, he failed not when an opportunity occurred, to take me into his inner sanctum, and there, in his own proper tones, as a mere man, ask me, 'Weel Benjie, laddie, ye've won back. An hoo's your mither an' a' the lave? Some tribbl't wi' a sair heid noo an' than, aye, is she? An' hoo's the crap luikin'? Fine. Nae word o' hairst yet? They wud be glaid to see ye at hame again, I suppose. Did they think ye he'd grown ony sin' ye cam to the toon? Oh, weel, it's a gweed thing't they're nae fear't for's shargarin' ye, man.'

This was my Uncle David in his natural manner, and that manner at its best, I had never, save once or twice before, seen him unbend so; and the chances of seeing it again, now that he had got so much farther above the common level than before, had clearly become diminished. Nevertheless, as has been said, and notwithstanding the severer notions of my Uncle Sandy, I had a sort of inward feeling of pleasure at the idea of the honour shed on the whole family connection through my Uncle David having attained the status and dignity of a Baillie.

CHAPTER SEVENTEEN

The Police Court

I T was no doubt with a certain feeling of enhanced responsibility that my Uncle took his seat on the bench on a particular day during his third month, as a fully-developed magistrate. The Baillies of Greyness performed the duties of the Police Court in rotation, each man his month till all the four had been gone over, from senior to junior, when the same round began again. When peculiarly difficult cases had to be tried it was the practice for the sitting Baillie to call to his aid one of his colleagues – usually the senior magistrate for the time, whose stock of judicial experience could be drawn upon as the occasion might demand. They had 'the legal assessor' to be sure; but then the legal assessor was an effete old bodie of some eighty winters, who never stirred beyond the doors of his own chambers, which were under the same roof as his dwelling-house, and merely across the lobby from the parlour; and thus the function of the legal assessor came to be a very shadowy one in face of the more energetic Mr Branks, who was always at hand and active; and as the bench had a lingering suspicion, could retaliate when too openly crossed. But when a couple of Baillies stalked solemnly into the Court-room and took their places on the seat of judgment in face of the motley assemblage that crowded the narrow space behind the pumphel seat, occupied by the Clerk, Prosecutor, and legal Bar, when such happened to be present, it impressed the public with a sense of the power of the Greyness judicial machinery, apart from legal assessors and people of that sort.

On the morning to which reference has been made, my Uncle, now quite familiar with the modes of the place, mounted the steps with an air of sober dignity, and, giving the pass to Baillie Gudgeon, who moved on to the further side of the bench, took his seat with more than his usual gravity. He had scarcely got his papers arranged, and Mr Branks was glancing over his summonses, when Gabbin' Gibbie, the solicitor, with a law book or two under one arm, came hirplin' up the stair, and pushing his way through the crowd that filled lobby, took his place on the three-legged stool that stood at the further side of the desk.

The *cause célèbre* about to be tried was a charge of theft of books, in which several boys had been concerned, some of them, at least, being of what is known as 'respectable parentage.' When Mr Branks had called his case, a couple of lads of thirteen or fourteen were placed in the dock as the culprits. They denied the charge and stared about, evidently feeling the novelty of their situation, but not particularly alarmed nor the reverse. The customary story of the police who had hunted up the *corpus delicti* in the shape of two or three school books, and one or two other volumes which the accused had disposed of to a dealer of slightly shady reputation, was got over with merely a sharp snarl or two during cross-examination for the defence by Gabbin' Gibbie, whose theory concerning that useful force – consistently maintained on every occasion – was that they were always greater malefactors than the persons against whom they testified. Each several sneer from Gibbie in this way Mr Branks endeavoured to repay by a distinct snub administered to Gibbie personally, and the bench could only look on or utter a mild and fruitless objurgation, in favour of peace and amity.

Next came a schoolboy companion who had turned Queen's evidence, and necessarily had not particularly clean hands himself. Him Gabbin' Gibbie subjected to a severe twisting, and at this point the interest and excitement of the scene began to grow.

'So ye helpit to mak' awa' wi' the buiks, an' syne hen't it – gaed awa' an' peach't upo' them't ye hed helpit to lead astray! Eh? Hoo muckle o' the spoil micht ye 'a gotten yoursel', noo?' asked Gibbie, addressing the witness very directly.

'Yer honours,' interposed Mr Branks indignantly, 'that's a style o' interrogation canna be alloo't'—

'An' fat for no? Is this Coort to be dictatit till by you, I

wud like to ken! I'll pit my questions i' my nain gate in spite
o' you.'

'I protest against any witness bein' bullied an' drawn on
by leadin' questions;' and Mr Branks flung himself back on
his seat.

'Your ain daily practice, Mr Branks,' retorted Gabbin'
Gibbie. 'But I'm deein' nothing o' the sort. I'm perfectly
entitl't to press my question in ony Coort o' law i' the three
kingdoms; an' I mean to deet – By the leave o' the Coort,'
added Gibbie, glancing upward at Baillie Gudgeon, who was
more in his view than my Uncle.

'What was the exact wordin' o' the question?' asked my
Uncle after a short consultation with his senior colleague.

'How much of the spoil might you have got?' answered the
clerk, 'Isn't that it, Mister Gilchrist?'

'Yes; an I'm quite prepared to argue the point on grounds
of legal formality' said Gibbie.

'Of coorse it's a legal point entirely,' said Baillie Gudgeon.

'If your honour think so,' said Mr Branks a little tartly. 'But
I've prosecuted in this coort for a score o' years; and I never
heard an objection on the same ground that wasna sustain't
at once.'

'Excep' ta'en frae the ither side,' answered Gibbie.

The bench again conferred, and then endeavoured to get
the prosecutor and defending counsel to arrange the matter
between them. That being in vain, they said they would hear
the arguments of counsel on the legal point. Mr Branks, who
spoke first, was curt and snappish; and his pleading consisted
of little more than a strenuous insistence on the habit and
practice in Geyness Police Court during the past twenty
years. Gabbin' Gibbie's manner was the very opposite of
this. Gibbie was one of those pert little men who carry
a remarkably small quantity of brains in a not very big
skull, but who yet have all the wits they possess well at
command; and above all never lose the power of fluent
talking. He commenced his address to their honours in a
very formal style; and then applying himself to his law
books, which he had marked at the proper pages by slips of
paper, he read long passages bearing on general principles,

which he fortified by citing numerous decided cases. This in addition to his own running commentary, in the course of which various Latin law phrases were quoted copiously and miscellaneously, such as the *jus deliberandi* and the *lex taliones*, could not fail of producing an impression, inasmuch as if Gibbie but dimly understood his own learned utterances, the Bench were probably still more in a fog about them. When Mr Branks had replied, the bench conferred again, and longer than before. It was clearly a difficult question they had had presented to them. They made as if they were about to retire; but again settled down on their seats, and after a half-longing, half-enquiring glance or two from Baillie Gudgeon towards the sternly-silent Prosecutor, the Clerk was beckoned to, and stood up accordingly to receive the suggestions of the bench – or to give them his own. My Uncle then wrote a little in his notes-of-evidence book, and, clearing his throat, announced the finding:—

'The Court allows the question, but in a more unobjectionable and legal form, viz: – To what extent did you participate in the price got?'

'That's worse, in place of better!' exclaimed Mr Branks, sharply.

'Dinna address the bench in that fashion, Sir; that's neither mair nor less than contempt o' coort,' said Gibbie, elated at his own apparent triumph, and feeling he might venture on the strong step of reproving the public prosecutor, his whole action calling forth a burst of applause from the more unwashed part of the audience.

Mr Branks did not deign to reply, but uttered himself with some asperity concerning the 'disgraceful conduct' of persons who, by their behaviour, apparently desired to frustrate the ends of justice.

'Seelence! Noo we maun hae seelence; or the coort'll be clear't by the offisher this moment,' said Baillie Gudgeon in a voice of authority.

Then Mr Branks renewed his protest against the improved version of his opponent's question, and further debate occurred with the net result that it was again amended by inserting the words 'if any' after 'extent.' From this 'recension' the bench –

practically Baillie Gudgeon, to whom my Uncle evidently felt bound in the circumstances to defer – would not budge. It was in vain for Mr Branks to insist that the question was an unfair one to the witness, and had no proper bearing on the guilt of the accused. The senior Baillie was quite satisfied after the able pleading on the side of the defence – and he was sure his frien' the sittin' magistrate concurr't – that the question was a proper one legally; and that the latest emendation had left an ample loophole 'on grun's o' equity.'

'I can only say then that no person is bound to criminate himself; and I warn the witness that he does not need to answer the question at all,' said Mr Branks.

'Surely, surely; that's your duty Mr Branks; tell the laddie to be as mim's a May puddock gin he likes,' replied the senior magistrate. 'Noo, go on – I'm interferin' owre muckle.'

The assault by Gabbin' Gibbie was then renewed with no very definite result as regarded his crucial question, except that he contrived to make the witnesses's statements obviously inconsistent with each other. Only the little man having got headway to some extent was, by the indulgence allowed him, very free in casting about insinuations against all and sundry whom he could in any way connect, however innocently, with the transaction in which the two youths he defended were involved.

The evidence for the prosecution was to be closed by proving ownership in certain of the books and other particulars. 'Next witness,' said the Clerk; whereupon the bar officer pushed his way through the crowd till he reached the door, and opening it with some difficulty succeeded in dragging the person wanted in from amid the disappointed persons waiting outside who crowded the stair-head lobby, that being the only enclosure available for witnesses.

'Richard Darrell, bookseller' said the bar officer when he had conveyed the witness to his proper place.

Baillie Gudgeon and my Uncle in succession recognised the witness by a grave nod, 'who being fully sworn and interrogated, deponed' that the two accused lads had called at his shop offering sundry school books to sell, under colour of being allowed by their parents so to do, seeing the books were not longer required by them. This they had done once without success, so far as sale was concerned; and a second visit on a similar errand, after a too brief interval, had directly aroused his suspicions and led him to retain the books, asking his would-be customers to call next day for their final answer.

'An' you have no doubt these are the books, Mr Darrell?'

'Nane, Mr Branks. That's to say pairt o' them; ye've fish't up a few't I ken naething aboot,' said the witness, looking over the small heap of books put down before him.

'Have you seen any of the others before?'

'Here's a volume that was in my shop only a few weeks ago – a copy of Boston' – said the bookseller in an animated and decisive tone.

'Was it sold by you, and to whom?'

'It was sold by me; to a lady, into whose possession it never cam'.'

'Will you explain to the court how?'

'To mak' a lang story short, the book was to be deliver't; an' nae bein' bless't wi' a staff o' assistants it was sent wi' a bit witless nackit o'a laddie that never gat the en' o's erran', but cam' back blebberin' and greetin' aboot bein' dung owre b' some muckler loons, an' gettin' the buik ta'en fae 'm. It bein' in a mainner gloam't ere he gaed awa' I took blame to mysel' for sen'in' the loonie at that time o' nicht; an' thocht little mair aboot it – but if ye can bring that buik hame to the nickums ye'll dee a service nae in ony respect to be measur't by its value.'

'We've brocht that point hame beyond dispute already,' said Mr Branks, with a satisfied air, as he resumed his seat.

'An' fat micht she be this woman't ye sent the book till?' asked Gibbie, commencing his cross-examination.

'She's a lady, sir,' said the witness

'Oh, nae doot; they're a' ladies noo a days – Mairriet or single?'

'I daursay ye wud be wiser nor ye are if I taul you; wudna ye? but that has unco little adee wi' your case.'

'No insolence here, sir,' exclaimed the counsel for the defence in an angry tone. 'Answer my questions.'

'Certainly; but ye dinna seem owre thankfu' for my sma'
attempts in that direction.'

'Nane o' your impertinence, sir, I tell you – Give a plain
answer to a plain question, or I'll appeal to the bench.'

'To Caesar thou shalt go then; for I claim the protection
o' the Coort against the sma' insolence o' ony pettifogger,'
answered the incorrigible witness.

The ruling of the bench was that Gibbie must be a little
less vehement in his manner of accosting the witness, who
in his turn would answer with all the affability and openness
he could command, at which suggestion the witness made
a significant bow to the bench. Then the cross-examination
continued pretty much in the previous style, till the defending
counsel evidently began to flag. In point of fact Gabbin'
Gibbie, with all his pertness and persistency got very speedily
tired of interrogating the bookseller, from whom at every turn
he was receiving a harder snub than he found it possible to
repay in kind.

It then degenerated into a sort of crack between the bench
and witness, whose sneeshin mull, through the agency of the
bar officer, actually found its way across to Baillie Gudgeon's
fingers in a furtive way, unobserved by Gabbin' Gibbie –
who would not have spared to denounce such tampering with
the fountain of justice – but not unaccompanied by a caustic
hint to the Baillie to 'mind his mainners' when on the bench.
Mr Branks had his replication of evidence; and took care to
treat the witness with special consideration, while he set down
Gabbin' Gibbie in the most remorseless way when he tried
once and again to interrupt by interrogatories or objections.
Mr Branks felt himself once more master of the situation,
indeed; and went on swimmingly and easily, stimulating
familiar remarks from the bench, or for that matter from
any other quarter except the tongue of his learned opponent,
over which he deemed it his duty to keep a very strict watch.
It was in the course of this re-examination that Richie Darrell,
getting for the moment confidential, voluntarily offered the
remark that the lady for whom the now derelict copy of Boston
had been entered was Miss Spinnet, whose high qualities
and generous intentions, in promoting the study of sound

theology, by lending such valuable and instructive books to people who were too thoughtless to possess themselves of copies, he extolled with strong emphasis. At this point Gabbin' Gibbie looked round quickly for a moment with a smirking face, and then turned to the desk to make a note. His purpose, which he duly did his best to carry into effect, was to seize the opportunity afforded by his closing speech of roasting the bookseller concerning 'this Miss Spinnet – this pious vestal – hm-h – that the witness Darrell has a fancy for.' Gibbie's ideas of wit and sarcasm were met by repetition, once and again, of any remark that he fancied touched an opponent on the raw, and accordingly the pious vestal was kept well in the foreground of his address; the other strong point of which was abuse of the lad who had given evidence against his companions. The suggestion of favouritism in 'certain quarters' – the counsel for the defence looked pointedly toward Mr Branks – was also thrown out; and the utter meanness and dishonesty of one who could be guilty of an offence, and then 'peach upon others not more guilty – nay, in all the circumstances, not so guilty as himself' – were broadly asserted.

Thus fully instructed the bench conferred shortly as they sat; but clearly it was a case for a more deliberate *avizandum* business. They hinted at deferring judgement till the morrow; but at this the expectant audience murmured, while the prosecutor and counsel for the defence deprecated the proceeding: of course on totally opposite grounds – Mr Branks suggesting that the case was as clear for sentence as case could be, and Gabbin' Gibbie not indistinctly hinting that influences adverse to his clients and in the interests of the favoured few might be found operative before the court could be again formally constituted. So the two baillies retired to the magistrates' room, where they remained for a half hour, in the company of my Uncle's notes of evidence which he carried with him; and doubtless carefully weighing and digesting the able technical arguments of counsel for the defence. Very evidently my Uncle was perplexed, even with the advantage of the assistance and advice of the senior magistrate; as his face showed when he returned into Court to announce the judgment, which was that the charge was proven; 'but in consideration of the youth of accused, and their not being alone concerned in the felony, the sentence of the Court is that they be conveyed furth of the court-room to the precincts of the House of Detention, and there-after incarcerated in one or other of the cells of the common lock-up for the space of five hours.'

The prisoners looked a little aghast at the formidably worded sentence; but their counsel gave them heartening by the remark that it was 'only hoors, whaur he had expeckit days;' and as the Court was breaking up they had the further comfort of hearing Baillie Gudgeon remark to the bar-officer, who was also turnkey, 'Ye'll lat the loons oot i' the gloamin' min'.'

Such was the method of procedure on 'field days' in the Police Court of Greyness, in which my Uncle was now a leading figure.

CHAPTER EIGHTEEN

My Uncle Sandy at Home

TIME had passed on, as it is the habit of time to do, till my Uncle David had fulfilled his full term of service as a Baillie, that term being limited by the duration of his period of office as a councillor. The community of Greyness had in the meanwhile been given to understand that he had filled the position of a magistrate so ably that his re-election for a further term, if not in the nature of a foregone conclusion, was a thing absolutely demanded in the interests of the town. He had at the preceding election been promoted from the position of junior baillie to that of wearer of the third chain of office; and in prospect of the retirement into private life of his ripely experienced colleague, Baillie Gudgeon, the choice of senior magistrate lay between him and another. That other was Tammas Souter, who in point of years and Town Council and Parochial experience was by much my Uncle's senior. Still, though Tammas had a kind of trembling anxiety to fill the office of eldest Baillie, and so have the opportunity of taking the place of Preses when, as Baillie Gudgeon phrased it, 'the Provost's fae hame or oonweel,' there was clearly no chance for him. Why, nobody could well say; except that he was too thin in flesh, and in cold weather, in addition to getting blue and watery about the tip of the nose, had frequently to wear a couple of thick waistcoats to bulk out his person and give him needed warmth; and a senior Baillie in Greyness was never seen to be thin in flesh and carrying a drop at his nose. At anyrate 'public feeling' in some unaccountable way was said to be entirely in favour of my Uncle. In Greyness public feeling (privately manufactured at times) was a great power; and with a faint show of resistance my Uncle had submitted to the sacrifice involved in being re-elected, under

99

a neat arrangement which enabled him to feel certain that he, and not Tammas Souter, would fill the coveted position.

My own time in the town of Greyness had now extended to about four years. The pristine verdancy of rustic life had consequently got worn off somewhat, and I had come to look upon all that which went to make up my surroundings with that kind of stereotyped sense of fitness which stands very much in the way of every one of us in respect of our being able sufficiently to note and appreciate the things that are ludicrous, as well as those that are mean and contemptible in our daily lives. As it concerns the subject of which I have just spoken, in particular, I had come to regard the office of a Baillie in Greyness as in a manner the natural function of my Uncle David; and would now have had difficulty in abstracting his fully rounded personality from the conception of Bailliehood. That he should come to be senior Baillie, consequently, seemed to me a natural, if not inevitable, event.

It was now over a dozen years since my Uncle Sandy had met what he had deemed the great disappointment of his life and had got the course of his future career entirely changed. He had pretty much worked through that peculiar coldness in feeling which is apt to environ one under such disappointments as that just referred to; and being now a man approaching middle life it is to be feared that his habits were gradually getting fixed in the particular orbit in which he had chosen for some years to move. He had, as he averred, little aptitude for the formation of new friendships – my own idea is that he had all the aptitude that was necessary or desirable – but certainly he was moved by a stable and clinging attachment to the old, even in cases where sufficient cause of severance might seem to have intervened.

It could scarcely be said that the friendship between my Uncle Sandy and Richie Darrell was an old one; it could not be plausibly averred that the two men had much of similarity in their tastes, and still less that they had it in their temperaments. But their friendship was old enough to have given it some solidity; and if they suited each other rather by sharp contrast in some things than by homogeneity of character throughout, I don't know that their intercourse had in it less of the element of permanence or less of what was fitted to make it fruitful to both on that account.

In the case of Dominie Greig, with his quiet placid ways, there certainly seemed more of congeniality. The Dominie moreover presented that somewhat rare combination of a mind stored with the goodly gatherings of one who had been a student in the technical sense, while he had in equal measure been instructed by the lessons of a varied life experience; and thus it was that, while he never by any chance obtruded himself, his power of attracting others was great in proportion to any effort he ever seemed to put forth. Toward him and his opinions my Uncle Sandy showed as much deference, perhaps, as toward any one within the range of his acquaintance. And to the quiet insight into and fullness of sympathy with the nature and tendencies of youthful humanity possessed by both, I owed it that I was saved from at least some part of the crudities and inanities into which I should otherwise have been led by the portion of vanity, self-conceit, and stupidity of which I was the natural inheritor.

In the adjustment of his domiciliary arrangements, my Uncle Sandy laboured under the pleasant delusion that he was in a very particular and stringent sense absolute master of the situation in all respects and at all seasons. His landlady, whose birthplace was also Strathtocher, was a widow of that class who, having got their faculties of management developed under circumstances of trial and difficulty, are never thereafter disposed to fold their arms and sit down in a merely self-sustaining routine of domestic duty. She had reared her family and sent them adrift to follow fortune and carve out homes for themselves, boys and girls of them, as they chose; well satisfied that if things took the wonted course they would all sooner or later desire to go permanently from under her roof-tree, and put themselves under roof-trees of their own. Nor would Mrs Geils consent to be provided with a home by any of them, when the time had come that they could offer it. No, no; she had kept her lodgers for many a day, and she would keep them still.

That my Uncle Sandy should enjoy unrestricted freedom as a dweller in the domestic establishment of a woman like Mrs Geils, was about the least likely of all conceivable things. The actual state of the facts was that she ruled over him, exactly as she would have ruled over one of her own sons; and, to the credit of the much-abused class to which she belonged, let it be said that her ruling was as much guided by a regard to his interest, comfort, and well-being as if he had actually been her own flesh and blood. Only there were rigid laws and points of domestic etiquette which my Uncle dared not to violate or disregard. Outside of these, it is true, his landlady would never have hesitated for a moment to make subsidiary things and persons bend at once to the wishes and commands of her principal lodger.

There was however ample freedom about the house, the home-like character of which had indeed made it the occasional resort of an odd variety of persons, young and old, from both town and country. Dwellers in Strathtocher, when they made their annual journeys to the city, found their way thither in force from the Stabler's to obtain Sandy's aid in seeking out places where cheap bargains could be had; they often found their way on slenderer pretences; and, in return for their heartily-expressed friendship and the latest ideas from Strathtocher, never left without a substantial meal, supplied by the hospitable Mrs Geils, at her lodger's cost or her own. Of residents in the town I have spoken of Dominie Greig and the bookseller, the latter of whom, however, was as curt and peremptory in his manner of visiting as in many other of his ways. More frequently than otherwise his call consisted of a ring at the door bell, and two minutes' talk on the door-step; it never, by any accident, exceeded a quarter of an hour in duration, and no amount of persuasion would induce him at any time to form one of the small but animated group that now and then assembled round my Uncle Sandy's tea table. It was about the date indicated that I had been admitted to the privilege of unrestricted participation in even the more formal of these gatherings, at which were occasionally to be seen a picturesque admixture of adult and juvenile humanity, the most frequent attendant in the latter category, apart from myself, perhaps, being Annie Macnicol, the third daughter of my Uncle the Baillie, now a girl of fourteen, whose unconventional tastes – which were a source of no slight vexation to her mother – probably accounted for the very strong attachment she manifested for my Uncle Sandy.

CHAPTER NINETEEN

A New Caller at the Bookseller's

IN his periodical visits to the bookseller's shop in those days, my Uncle Sandy was occasionally accompanied by myself, and quite as frequently by my cousin and his niece Annie Macnicol. Amongst my Uncle the Baillie's six daughters, Annie, as already mentioned, was the third eldest. Annie was admittedly the failure of the family. The other five Misses Macnicol, all according to their years, were most proper and promising young ladies, each taking up her education after the prescribed boarding school pattern, and gaining the due amount of *eclat* as she passed the various stages in the fashionable branches. Poor Annie alone had sufficient depravity of nature to declare that she hated music, as understood by punching away at the keyboard of a mediocre piano for a couple of hours a day, endeavouring to get up her scales or reduce the score of some weakly sentimental song, or piece of elegant dance music, to regulated sounds. And I fear she did not shine in her mastery of the technical niceties of modern languages. It was not that Annie had no taste for the arts or literature. In a furtive, unauthenticated way she delighted to pore over our own old ballads and would sing the singable part of them, as well as many other national songs, with great zest and readiness. She took to sketching in her own way with avidity; and her liking for books, of which it occasionally happened that her accomplished teachers had never even heard – much less read them – was the gravest fault of her life. Hence it was that Annie Macnicol had got into the way of being a frequent visitor both at my Uncle Sandy's comfortable old-fashioned lodging and also at Richie Darrell's shop; where, as Nancy Darling had now passed away into the regions of connubial life, she was in her way the reigning divinity.

My Uncle Sandy and Annie had dropped into the bookseller's shop on an autumn gloamin', as the former, accompanied by the girl, walked homeward after finishing his work for the day. They had entered only for a minute or two when a small boy of thirteen or so took up his place in front of the window outside, and as the waning light would allow began to spell off the titles of the books displayed there. After a little he moved toward the door, and with some hesitation in his manner, opened it and stepped in.

'Well, my little man,' said the bookseller, 'what micht it be?'

'It's a book there't I wud like.'

'Oh; a book. But which book, my laddie – a picture book?'

'No; it's Caesar.'

'Caesar!' exclaimed Richie Darrell with an air of astonishment. 'Can ye read Caesar?' he asked, looking a little more closely at the bright-eyed, but thinly clad little figure before him.

'No,' answered the boy, with half averted look.

'An' fat use wud it be to you than?'

'I wud like to try't.'

'An' ye wud like to try Caesar? I doot Caesar's gey stiff readin' for you yet, man,' continued the bookseller, proceeding to the window, out of which he lifted a second-hand copy of De Bello Gallico. 'The price is fourteenpence. Ye wudna ca' that owre muckle, wud ye?' he added, pushing the book over so as to bring it quite within reach of the would-be customer.

'No,' said the boy, who however contented himself by looking wistfully at the book without handling it. He said nothing more, though he had evidently meditated some further utterance for which his courage was not equal, and in a minute or two after began to sidle quietly toward the door.

'An' yer nae gaen to be my merchan' the nicht, are ye?' asked the bookseller.

'I'll maybe come back again to-morrow,' said the boy, who was now fairly on the way to leave.

My Uncle Sandy had either not been attending closely to the colloquy throughout, or he pretended not to be, in consequence of partial engrossment in a book that Richie

Darrell had put in his hand when he entered. It had been heard with open-eyed interest by his niece Annie, who, as the boy was leaving tugged my Uncle's sleeve, and trod on his shoe in token of her urgency.

'Fat is't, Annie?' asked my Uncle Sandy, turning full round from the counter.

'It's only fourteen pence!' exclaimed Annie, in an earnest whisper.

'Oh! the book; an' ye want me to buy't till 'im?'

'Yes uncle!' answered Annie, now in full tones, and with some vehemence, for the boy was again out on the street. 'Why wouldn't you buy't for the poor boy? I think he hasna nae money o' his ain. Poor laddie!'

'Weel Annie, ye're a romantic person. The laddie's maybe a mere rogue an' vagabond, prowlin' aboot to see fat he can lay's han's on,' said my Uncle Sandy, in a tone more than half quizzical.

'He is not!' exclaimed Annie, with honest indignation at the idea. 'He's a nice boy; ye could easily see if ye had been lookin', though he be poor.'

'Weel, rin aifter 'im an' bring 'im back,' said my Uncle Sandy, opening the shop door.

In an instant Annie had emerged in pursuit of the boy; and while my Uncle Sandy was clearly anything but uninterested in the scene, or displeased thereat as he stood by the shop counter, the keener temperament of the little bookseller had carried him outside the door bareheaded to see what would happen.

'Ah, here she comes,' said Richie, stepping briskly into the shop again, and returning to his place behind the counter.

'Come away, Sir, come away,' he continued, as Annie returned in triumph with her _protégé_. 'Now you may consider yourself a very lucky man, Sir. I have to ask your acceptance of this copy of Caesar's Gallic War, as the gift of Miss Anne Macnicol, per her uncle, the Deacon. I hope you will, like a chivalrous knight, do your best to prove yourself worthy of the favour of the lady who has thus smiled on you.'

To mitigate the confusion of mind into which the recipient of the book was evidently thrown by this eloquent speech, my

Uncle Sandy added a word or two of practical, homely advice; and the boy left, carrying with him the treasure that had so recently seemed beyond his hope of attainment. He was gone, and quite out of reach, before it occurred to my Uncle Sandy that he had completely forgot to ask his name or parentage, or the least thing about his personal history or circumstances whereby he might be able again to identify him.

CHAPTER TWENTY

Country Visitors

WHEN my Uncle Sandy had got time to reflect upon the whole circumstances connected with the appearance of the boy whom he had surprised and gratified by putting into his hands the book he strongly desired to possess, the thought of his own stupidity in not taking steps to keep him in view came forcibly home to him. All he could do now was to ask Richie Darrell to have his eyes about him for the re-appearance of the laddie, and to make sure then that he found out his name and other circumstances. But month after month passed on, and Richie was not able to report the least success in the matter. The boy had never again called at the shop, nor had he observed him passing.

'There's only ae conclusion I can come till, Deacon; the laddie's nae a Greyness bairn ava. Nae that I ken ilka man, woman, an' child i' the toon by horn or keil mark; but it's a positive fact that in a place like this, wi' its fifty, sixty thoosan' inhabitants, ye'll aiven hae sic a smatterin' o' the haill mengyie as'll lead you to recognise the Greyness idiosyncracy, as the Dominie wud say, at some point, fae the tackets upward, an' contrairiwise to detect a kin' o' foreign flawvour aboot ilka human creatur that's nae to the mainner born.'

'But,' said my Uncle, 'there was nae word o' a' this till ye had been baffl't otherwise an' had to construct a theory.'

'No, no; but mature reflections are best. The laddie was but dimly seen; an' of coorse he *mitha* been a phonomenon o' native growth in Greyness, an' so free o' the ordinary conditions; but in that case he was bound to reappear on or near the former scene. The fact that he has fail't so to do is convincin' proof that he's an alien,' argued the bookseller.

'We've been a' "aliens" in oor turn,' replied my Uncle

Sandy. 'At ony rate the boy seem't baith needy an' deservin';
an' it wud 'a been o' interest to trace his history a wee bit.'

'Dootless, dootless; an' maybe spen' some o' your hain't
bawbees deein' that for 'im that the pawrents responsible for
his existence should dee. Hooever, the laddie's evanish't, an'
we maun aiven mak' up oor min' to oor circumstances. Ye're
not a man o' romantic ideas, Deacon.'

The bookseller had about this time got strongly engrossed
in some private affairs of his own, about which he spoke to
my Uncle with a sort of mysterious reserve. They were family
affairs, but of what sort did not yet precisely appear, inasmuch
as the bookseller's allusions implied a certain amount of
knowledge on my Uncle's part which my Uncle did not
possess, though in his own sensitive fashion he had tacitly
allowed the assumption to pass, lest by a plain question he
should seem to touch on what his friend did not wish to
tell. The situation, for the time, was one which perhaps only
those endowed with an undue delicacy of feeling will either
understand or appreciate; though, unhappily for my Uncle
Sandy's comfort, it was not a solitary instance of the like kind
with him.

So the winter had gone, and spring, with the singing of
birds, the bursting of buds, and glad stirring in all nature, had
come. The 'aitseed' was mainly finished, and country bodies
from the uplands had time once again to visit Greyness. Day
by day dozens of farmers' carts were to be seen lows't, and
jammed in front of each other in strings along the narrow
street, in which the greater number of the stablers provided
accommodation for man and beast. They came in at the most
unearthly hours of the morning, off their journeys of twenty or
thirty miles; and, having disposed of their lades at the Shore,
and filled the carts with lime, or coals, with a garnishing of
sundries above, they were ready to depart homeward at hours
equally unearthly in point of earliness. It was at such times
as these that Mrs Geils, who was certainly not a sluggard in
her morning habits, was wont to be occasionally startled by a
long and loud ring at her door bell about half-past five in the
morning, when the first bell at the factory had just begun to
ring, and the early workers were passing along the street to

commence their day's labours, and all to find that it was some of her rural friends fresh from Strathtocher yap for breakfast, and under the impression that it was weel up i' the day.

It was at a later hour however, and indeed my Uncle Sandy had breakfasted, and was on the eve of leaving for the warehouse, when one morning a sound was heard outside as of somebody endeavouring, might and main, to force in the door of Mrs Geils's house.

'Preserve me, fat noo?' exclaimed Mrs Geils, making for the lobby wherein stood my Uncle Sandy preparing to go out. Sandy stepped forward and opened the door, which by that time was suffering renewed assault of a yet more determined sort.

'Gweeshtie Sandy, I'm richt glaid to see you. We thocht never to get the street; an' syne your door's that stiff, I thocht it wud bleck's to apen't; but aw think aw wud 'a made oot though ye hedna come,' exclaimed a very quaint looking elderly man of rustic aspect, dight in hodden grey with broad blue bonnet on his head, alongside of whom stood an equally quaint elderly woman, with a well worn wicker creel on her arm.

'You Francie, an' Kirsty wi' ye!' exclaimed my Uncle. 'Hoo's a' wi' you?'

'Brawly, are ye brawly Sandy? An' are ye brawly Mrs Geils?' said the figure addressed.

Of course it was Francie Tamson all the way from Strathtocher, with his wife Kirsty; and as Francie had not visited Greyness for the past ten years surprise at his present appearance was natural. Amid the conflicting emotions that beset him as he haumer't uneasily along the unaccustomed wooden flooring to Mrs Geils's kitchen the thought still uppermost in his mind was the unaccountable stiffness of the door and door handle; and it needed an elaborate explanation to make clear to Francie the difference between the style of door fastening in use in Greyness and his own sneck and wooden bar at home.

'An' fowk rings a bell fan they come to yer door, Mrs Geils?' said Francie Tamson.

'Na, sirs; but that's like the verra gentry,' added Kirsty, his wife, when Mrs Geils had replied in the affirmative. 'But is na't feerious tribblesome an' oonhandy?'

The worthy couple had a world of errands, as they soon let my Uncle Sandy know; but beyond and above these a burden of special importance seemed to lie on their minds. From the recesses of the straw-lined creel a small present of butter and eggs had been drawn for Mrs Geils, and duly handed over. Then came a half-mysterious pause. The creel was not nearly emptied of its whole contents; and manifestly Francie and Kirsty did not mean to empty it just then.

'We wus wuntin' to ken faur yer breeder the Baillie bides?' asked Francie. 'Cud fowk like huz see 'im?'

'Oh, easily,' said my Uncle.

'But to tak's advice likein'?'

'Weel, I suppose he'll gie you ony advice he can, if you wish it.'

'We've never been in tribble afore; an' thocht it wud be better, though it's a lang road, to gyang to the heid-speed at ance,' continued Francie.

'But what is't, if it's a fair question?' asked my Uncle Sandy.

At this question Francie looked toward Kirsty, and Kirsty looked toward Francie; and then they both looked at the wicker creel.

'Oh, weel, never min',' said my Uncle. 'I must be off. Mrs Geils'll gie you some breakfast; an' you can come an' see the Baillie aifter.'

'Weel, but mithnin ye wyte an' lat's see the road; it winna hin'er nae time?'

To this proposal, however, my Uncle objected, and left after giving Francie and Kirsty as explicit directions as he could how to find the Baillie.

'But ye'll maybe convoy's a bittie o' the road,' suggested Francie, addressing Mrs Geils, as the two prepared to start when, after due deliberation and multitudinous questionings, they had finished breakfast. 'I've tint ony meiths 't ever aw hed aboot streets.'

The answer of Mrs Geils, whose household operations had by that time been delayed quite as much as was good for her temper, was fully more prompt and decisive than her visitors had anticipated, and had reference to Francie having 'a gweed Scotch tongue in's heid;' but Kirsty, with a woman's ready tact, sought to find plausible grounds for her distinct negative, at which Francie had simply stared.

'Hoot, man; Mrs Geils hasna time eenoo. Pit ye a bit coal in o' yer pipe noo, an' come awa',' said she, addressing her husband. 'We'se be back in gweed time to oor denner; an' ye wud maybe gyang oot syne wi' me to the best chop for prents 't'll wash, an' yallow cotton 't'll wear weel, onbeen owre dear. See noo, man, dicht up that strae amo' yer feet; ye're skailin' as muckle oot o' that creel as wud strae yer sheen twice owre.'

And so they departed, leaving Mrs Geils to anticipate their return to dinner, with what equanimity she could command. The call upon my Uncle the Baillie had been the great point they had set before themselves in the scheme for their journey to Greyness. To get at him at his private residence was out of the question, inasmuch as my Uncle, like other prosperous people, had seen meet to move far out to the west end of the town. But, of course, their perseverance would not be baulked in seeing him at his warehouse. The extraordinarily plain hints of John Cockerill, with whom they came first in contact, suggestive of the propriety of their taking themselves off elsewhere at once, fell quite ineffectual on Francie and his partner; and when, at last, by dint of waiting and speerin', they had succeeded in getting an audience, the reception accorded by my Uncle the Baillie was hardly of a sort to encourage prolonged conference.

'Ah! oh yes, I recollect you, Francis. And is this Mrs Thomson? – Cockerill, get these letters postit, an' tell Mr Sneevle I'll be wi' 'im immediately. Now, is there anything I can do for you?'

The big wicker basket, to which Kirsty clung tenaciously, had been taken into my Uncle's sanctum and put down on the floor. Both Francie and Kirsty were a little disconcerted on being ushered into the presence of my Uncle, whom they remembered only as a plain citizen, when in former years he had been wont to visit Strathtocher periodically; and no doubt their belief that a baillie-ship implied a marked accession of dignity and authority had thus far been justified, and possibly with a more appreciable directness than they had anticipated. The eyes of both were again directed to the wicker basket, and while Kirsty pulled off the covering towel – Francie observed:

'It's twa yearocks for a present to – to – Mrs Baillie – yer wife, ye ken.'

Kirsty pulled out a couple of fowls, off which she had carefully plucked the feathers, leaving them otherwise intact, with their legs tied by a strip of cloth, and laid them out for the inspection of my Uncle, who, in the face of such tangible evidence of goodwill, felt bound, however reluctantly, to put himself in a thankful and listening attitude, though still hinting that time was precious with him. When the various preliminary topics, as the weather, and the state of health, and general well-being of divers people had been sufficiently insisted upon, Francie came at once to the gist of his errand, which was to lay before my Uncle the iniquity perpetrated by an only sister of his own, in framing her Tes'ment so as to exclude 'him' (Francie) and 'his' (Kirsty), from all share of her 'goods, gear, and effects.' And the journey to Strathtocher had been undertaken mainly for the purpose of laying the whole case before the Baillie and getting him to right it. As a Strathtocher man they had full faith in his good will, which they not indistinctly indicated they had hoped to fortify and reward by the two yearocks; and as a Baillie they had never for a moment doubted his innate authority and jurisdiction in the matter. It was doubtless with a feeling of sorrow therefore, as well as disappointment, that they heard the abrupt and emphatic declaration from my Uncle that he had neither the will nor the power to deal with such questions. On his part the interview would have come to an end forthwith had not Kirsty, who had evidently bethought herself that if one purpose had failed they must not fail to press another, broken in with an involved story about their 'bran'it coo gyaun aff 'er milk,' and the best calf 'takin' the blin' staggers;' and all shortly after a certain neighbour had taken the huff at some slight offence they had given him; the moral being that my Uncle the Baillie might also offer his judicial aid in what was evidently a case of the evil eye; a hint which my Uncle, unhappily, was not prepared to take more than the other. At this point indeed his magisterial gravity got slightly upset; and he was tempted to make the averment that in questions of 'trailin' the rape,' and the exercise of an 'ill ee,' the practical skill of young Skairey, as a reputed Professor of the black airt, was sure to be more effective than the services of a half-dozen of baillies. In uttering that sentiment I am afraid my Uncle did much to lower the public conception of a toon's Baillie's power and authority in Strathtocher, as expounded by the Souter.

When Francie and Kirsty Tamson had got over their day's exertions up to my Uncle Sandy's tea hour – (they had returned upon Mrs Geils to an early dinner, carrying a load of tin and wooden table furniture, as caups, ladles, timmer spoons, and platters) – they seemed disposed to settle down for a time; and it was then that Francie, in a tone of more than half chagrin, for the first time told my Uncle Sandy of his real errand, viz., the matter of the Tes'ment, and in so telling conveyed more that was fresh information than he had anticipated.

'Ye ken the muckle feck that Meggie hed wud 'a gane to Tam my nevvy, an't hed been sae; but he's awa'—

'Awa?' said my Uncle Sandy, – 'Oot o'the pairt ye mean? What's the maitter o' that?'

'Gweeshtie, Sandy! Ye seerly ken that Tam's deid sax ouks syne.'

'The tailor deid!' exclaimed my Uncle with a start. 'I never heard o' his bein' ill even.'

'Weel, ye see, he hed been freuchle noo an' than for a file; an' fernyear he was clean aff 'o wark in a decline,' interposed Kirsty. 'He tyouk a vaege hame, but made naething o't; an' he's worn awa.'

'An' left a young faimily?' asked my Uncle.

'Twa; a bit stump o' a laddikie, an' a tsil,' said Kirsty. 'But they canna be ill upon't. Tam, though but a fen'less cheelie, was aye a gweed tradesman; an' their mither's a stoot young 'oman; ye'll min' upon 'er – Elsie Robertson.'

'At ony rate they sudna be enteetl't till fat's belang't to my sister Meggie,' added Francie. 'Cudna *ye* help's to get oor richts, Sandy?'

'Your richts!' said my Uncle, whose thoughts were evidently moving strongly within him. 'Your richt to rob the fatherless an' the widow?'

'Weel but we're sibber nor them,' insisted Francie, 'noo, fan Tammie's awa'; an' were nae seekin' but the siller that belangs till's.'

'To bury i' the yird wi' ye in half a score years' time at far'est! The curse o' God be in the "siller that belangs to ye" if ye mak' ony sic claim,' said my Uncle Sandy, with an energy that made both man and wife stare. 'Lat me, at least, never hear anither word on that subject.'

What were the reflections in my Uncle Sandy's breast that evening, as he thought of Tammy Tamson dead, and his wife a widow under such circumstances as those dimly known to him, I cannot say. For the rest of it, Francie Tamson and his wife Kirsty, kept both him and Mrs Geils pretty well at it, not only for the remainder of the day, but far into the night. They had sought and found lodging with Mrs Geils – rather they had been courteously invited to stay. Ostensibly they had gone to bed about ten o'clock, but certainly by midnight Francie was to be heard up and bickerin' loudly about the door, in the endeavour to look out upon the state of the weather. By two o'clock next morning they were out of bed for good; and so was Mrs Geils, for breakfast had to be made for them. They had determined to be at the Stabler's by three o'clock to resume their homeward journey half-an-hour later; and I think everybody was truly thankful; at least I was very glad when I had heard the last creak of the wicker creel, as they marched out of the house, followed by the 'good mornings' of Mrs Geils and my Uncle Sandy, and the door closed behind them.

CHAPTER TWENTY-ONE

The Last of Tammie Tamson

TAMMIE Tamson, the tailor, was dead; and the circumstances of his death, typically viewed, were of a sort probably far from uncommon. From his last vain search for health in the air of his native region the poor tailor had again turned his steps southward to the populous town where his home had latterly been, with only the faintest flush of renewed freshness in his hollow cheek, and that soon to fade away once again, and for ever, in the murkier atmosphere in which he must thenceforth remain. As he lay sore and wearied with the very weariness of exhaustion, the thought that most burdened his mind was the future of his wife and children, left with the scanty means they would be able to call their own. And as he thought of their future, in his helpless feebleness of body and mind, so would he ever and anon link it on with the past in words of regret concerning all the might-have-been had matters been differently ordered. Had he never left Strathtocher he might have been a wealthier man, and a healthier man; and so able to make everyone in whose welfare he was concerned happier than he had done, or could now ever do; and, to be sure, it was all quite true. But had he never left Strathtocher, he had, in all human likelihood, never met Elsie Robertson under circumstances in which she would have consented to be his wife. And, at the time he so met her, though his business prospects were no better than they had been after, had it not seemed to him that Elsie's consent to join her fate with his carried him utterly outside the range of dull economic laws, and above the pressure of mere material conditions? And who shall say that Tammie's conceptions in this respect were either singular or remarkable; or that they contravened the canonical idea of the 'happy marriage' of two

116

loving hearts, guileless of experience in the world's rude ways, and all unheedful of certain inexorable laws of this mundane life? It was not that Elsie had not been to him a faithful and devoted wife; yet, as the dying tailor mused brokenly over it all in the tightening grip of the last fell foe, he tried to gather the thread of his dim and wandering thoughts into one never finished sentence of regret:—

'Elsie, there's been a great mistak' – but I leave you to the care – o' your—'

And they carried the tailor to his burial in an obscure corner of the town's cemetery. Kindly enough were the hands that helped to lay out his corse; and kindly enough the hearts of those that followed the hearse and stood by till the closed grave had fully got him for its own. Only they were the hands and hearts not of kindred but of strangers; all except the newly-made widow and her now orphan son, whose duty it was to do the part of chief mourner. The boy, with that air of calm care and matured gravity, which once seen on a juvenile face may not be readily forgotten, and which bespoke a deep realisation of all that was signified by his sombre surroundings, had walked in front of the procession as the one solitary being there who felt that his part was other than perfunctory; and he had stood by the grave with a feeling of bewildered desertion as the company one by one shook hands, and bade him good-bye. They had all left but the gravedigger and one or two others, when a dilapidated-looking elderly tailor, also a north country man, who had known Tammie as his shopmate, taking pity on the lad, offered comfort as he could in the words—

'Come awa, noo, Jamie; that's the last we'll see o' him till we graip doon the same dark lane oorsel's, an' get licht o' the tither side. The warl' 'll be a gey teem place to you eenoo, laddie; an' deith a grim spectre that'll never leave your side nae mair. But we maun aiven warsle on, an' jist mak' the warl' as habitable for oorsel's as we may; an' it's mair nor likely that the langer ye live the less ye'll be disturbit aboot deith's doin's amo' your fellows; though it's as certain as the nicht follows sindoon that his tussle wi' yoursel's a' the distance nearer at han'.' And the elderly dilapidated tailor walked with the boy to the door of his now desolated home, where he too bade him good night.

CHAPTER TWENTY-TWO

Genealogical Pursuits

FROM the date on which my Uncle Sandy had accompanied Richie Darrell on a certain Sabbath day's journey he had been fully aware that the genealogical connections of his family were a matter of prime importance with the bookseller. It curiously happened that though Richie Darrell had violently quarrelled with the greater part of his living relatives, and had for many years been in a state of entire estrangement from those most nearly connected with him by blood, he had used much paper and ink, and not a little personal effort, in clearing up questions as to the affinity between himself and various others of his distant kindred. Among these was a certain brewer in the south of England, whom he had never in his life seen, but who, from the inscription on an old tombstone in the Kirkyard of Bieldside, he had been able to identify as a third cousin of his own. To determine the particular branch of the tree to which the brewer's ancestor belonged, and the particular position on that branch which the brewer himself ought to occupy, had been the subject of the bookseller's latest research.

'Tell the Deacon to luik in as he gaes up the street this aifterneen,' said Richie to me one day about this time, with an air of business-like directness. 'Dinna forget, noo.'

My Uncle looked in accordingly, and as I happened to be about at the time I took the liberty of following uninvited.

'I taul ye I had written Mr Augustine Darrell, the great brewer at Croydon,' said Richie.

'I believe ye did,' answered my Uncle. 'That's the man ye claim as a relative?'

'Read that!' and Richie pulled a letter, which had been

folded in the old-fashioned way and sealed with red wax, from his desk and handed it over the counter.

'Lood oot!' he added, as my Uncle proceeded with a silent perusal of the missive.

The letter was couched in rather formal terms, but thanked the writer's correspondent for the information conveyed by him concerning the 'branch of the Darrells' that had found their way to the north of Scotland, and which no doubt was quite correct. Indeed Mr Augustine Darrell had heard that branch spoken of as being in the line mentioned, and he added 'you are no doubt aware that the family is believed to be of French origin, and I incline to have some searches made in the view of determining the point more exactly.' In his P.S. he asked Richie's acceptance of a small keg of double XX porter in acknowledgment of his pains in the matter of the family tree.

Without uttering a single word further, the bookseller opened a small cupboard beyond the fireplace, took out a tumbler which he carefully wiped with the corner of his apron; and then unlocking the door of his back closet, exhibited the keg of double XX with an air of much satisfaction.

'The dominie tells me its o' the vera best London mak'; an' far afore onything manufactur't here-aboot.'

My Uncle Sandy had to prove the quality of the porter, which was pronounced good, but, of couse, too potent a liquor for one of my years. It was only when all this had been done that the bookseller approached the real object for which he had desired to see my Uncle Sandy.

'It's the maternal side o' the faimily that I'm concern't wi' noo,' he continued. 'They're i' the north countra, maistly in good positions, an' by your leave, Deacon, I mean to pay a visit to their place vera soon for a special purpose. It'll cost me twa days at least; an' the dominie's promis't, wi' your help, to keep an open door for me. Fat say ye?'

'Wi' a' my hert,' said my Uncle, 'only my help amo' books an' stationery cud be but sma'. Though I were at the back o' the counter already, I wud ken neither books nor prices. Ye'll hae to trust Mr Greig for that.'

'Ye can tak' aff the shutters; an' turn the key i' door fan

its necessary. The dominie 'll tak' twa three hours here i' the forenoon; an' fan he tires he'll jist need to gae hame – it winna be like him if he mak muckle speed at sellin'. An' ye wud maybe tak' a turn in for a minute whan ye gae to your four hours, jist to lat the community ken that the place is nae forhoo't a' thegither.'

It was on this footing then that Richie Darrell set off on the excursion that was to keep him absent for the unwonted period of two whole days. The purport of his journey had been more freely confided to Dominie Greig, with whom as an old friend he had professed to take counsel, though in the estimation of the dominie with a foregone conclusion in his own mind all the while.

'A queer compound truly this human nature o' oors,' said the dominie. 'O' a' men aboot the least liable to be suspeckit o' indulgin' in the romantic, wud be oor frien'. Yet here he is on the ae han' interrogatin' the monumental records o' the place in behalf o' those he never in his life-time saw, an' neist makin' lengthen't expeditions if perchance he may be able to vindicate the memory o' ithers lang deid an' gone.'

'Some o' his mither's relatives is't that he's concern't aboot?' asked my Uncle Sandy.

'Yes; at least ane o' the objects o' inquiry 's aboot some o' his "maternal ancestors;" but as I gaither't fae broken hints, the main drift has connection wi' his duty to the memory o' ane that comes into the parallel line – a cousin – a veritable cousin – whose memory – she's been deid a full thirty years – he deems it incumbent upon 'im to vindicate.'

'To vindicate! Hoo to vindicate?'

'That,' said the dominie, 'is a stage beyond me. I only un'erstan' there was something unpleasant conneckit wi' 'er death; that's a'. Oor excellent frien', followin' scriptural example, had appeal't to a nearer kinsman first, an' findin' that to be in vain has ta'en up the cause 'imsel', a cause, on his ain statement, affectin' nae human bein' noo alive. But what o' that, ye might jist as weel think to argue that copy o' Baxter oot o'ts sheepskin brods as convince 'im that he's gaen on a Quixotic erran'. In fact he got uncommon kittle upo' me whan I hintit at sic a thing.'

'Weel I daesay oor frien' wudna be likely to get credit for errin' on the side o' the romantic wi' maist folk. But that's merely because they dinna ken human natur i' the abstract; nor him as a comprehensively compoundit concrete specimen thereof,' observed my Uncle, half seriously half jocularly.

'Learnedly an' truly utter't,' responded the Dominie. 'In my experience the true spirit o' romance an' pathos is to be socht nae amo' your men gi'en to mouthin' sentimentalism an' full o' self-conscious ideas o' their ain high motives; but raither amo' the unconsider't an' inconsiderable section that, hae'in' faced some o' the sterner facts o' life an' being, wi' little disguise on either side, are mainly content to seem what they are an' to be what they seem.'

'Weel, but apairt fae the instance in han', hoo dee you account for this particular pedigree craze generally, if it may be so describit', in a man that professes to despise distinction o' birth; an' seldom loses an opportunity o' snubbin' the person who presumes on ony advantage o' the sort?' said my Uncle Sandy.

'I dinna attempt to mak' oot ony complete theory on the subject, answered the dominie. 'But ye maun observe that though Richie's very carefu' to set doon fat he deems impertinence or needless assumption, he is equally carefu' to gie a' the honours to fat he's pleas't' o' his ain free will to recognise as birth an' position; an' though he can be brusque an' peremptory to rudeness even wi' folk that misfit him, his politeness whan he cares to show't carries wi't an air that's actually un-Scottish in its finish, so, to speak – witness his reception o' yer austere frien', Miss Spinnet, for example.'

'Weel, there's nae doot his gracious courtliness wi' favour-ites o' the safter sex is in raither strikin' contrast to the snell inceesiveness that marks nae inconsiderable pairt o' his intercoorse wi' the male pairt o' humanity.'

'Especially the consciously important an' well-to-do sections o't,' said the dominie. 'but in this maitter o' genealogy, in fact, I've had a notion for lang that Richie 'imsel's nae originally o' Scottish descent ava. On that point his newly-recognis't kinsman the brewer's probably no sae far agley. The name 'Darrell' has a soun' little aneuch suggestive o' sentiment or euphony, such as our mair southern neighbours cultivate, to be sure. But alter the spellin' a wee bit an' mak' it 'D'Aurelle,' an' ye hae the suggestion o' some refugee faimily, say in the times o' the Huguenot persecution, lichtin' doon in this northern region, an' makin't their hame. Then the pure Protestantism o' the Huguenot, dash't wi' a little covenantin' Presbyterianism; an' the blood o' the Latin mixed with that o' the Norseman wud be likely aneuch to result, theologically as weel as mentally an' physically, in a character like that o' oor worthy freen. What think ye?' asked the Dominie.

My Uncle Sandy laughed; but in laughing declared himself mightily struck with the ingenuity of Dominie Greig's theory; and, if not absolutely convinced of its truth, not in the meanwhile prepared to question its validity.

'Weel; weel,' said the Dominie, 'it's the mere fancy o' an idle man, it may be; only ye winna hin'er idle men indulgin' in siclike mair than men that profess to be the reverse o' idle.'

CHAPTER TWENTY-THREE

The Tailor's Son

THE season of the year when Richie Darrell set off on what his friend Dominie Greig styled his Quixotic expedition to the north, was a little after midsummer – Tammie Tamson's death had occurred in the previous spring. The Dominie, as Richie's substitute, was anything but an expert shopkeeper and salesman, being in point of fact hopelessly confused concerning prices and the location of even the most commonly used requisites in the shop. Therefore it was that my Uncle Sandy felt bound in passing to look in as frequently as might be with the view of rendering what assistance he could during the bookseller's absence. While in the shop on one of these visits a boy stepped in and asked for

'A ha'penny pencil an six sheets o' ruled paper.'

'Eenoo, my man,' answered the Dominie, who felt that the order was one within the compass of his limited shopkeeping capacity.

Whether it was the voice that awakened his recollections or what, my Uncle turned sharply round as the boy spoke, and scrutinised him closely.

'Are ye the laddie that wantit to buy a Latin book here last autumn?' asked my Uncle.

'Yes, sir,' said the boy.

'What! what! – a Caesar said ye,' asked the Dominie, 'An' can ye construe Latin?'

'Yes; if it's only simple prose.'

'An' read Caesar?'

'I've read most o't.'

'Well done; well done.'

'An' do you live i' the toon?' resumed my Uncle.

'Yes, sir, noo.'

My Uncle Sandy paused and looked at the boy for a minute or two reflectively, as he asked with a half-hesitating air—

'Do you live wi' your parents?'

'Wi' my mother. Father's dead.'

'An' what's your name?' said my Uncle.

'Jamie Thomson,' said the boy.

My Uncle paused again. He did not ask more; he simply looked at the boy with a curiously intense sort of look; and when Dominie Greig appealed to him concerning the proper sizes of the ruled paper, and the right price to charge, he replied in a way indicative of a certain measure of abstractedness. The thought of asking the boy in which street of the town he lived, and at what number, with sundry other points tending to identification, had come up in my Uncle's mind, and made a little bit of tumult there. But he had no feeling of difficulty or hesitation in refraining from farther interrogation. And what need for such? Did not the boy's face, as he perused it once and again, speak to him with a stronger certainty, and a more suggestive significance than words could. 'Yes,' thought my Uncle Sandy, 'as sure as the heavens are o'er us, an' the earth beneath, Elsie Robertson's his mother! What richt hae I to speer anither syllable?'

'Noo, man, that's maybe nae jist so ticht fauldet as micht be; but ye see the maister o' the estaiblishment's nae upo' the premises the day – Three bawbees; ay, thank ye, thank ye. Gie ye 'im a call again at your convainience. He'll be glaid to see you I'm sure.'

So said Dominie Greig, as he dismissed almost the only customer with whom he had that day managed to transact business as interim bookseller and stationer.

'He's a thochtfu' birkie that, nae doot,' continued the Dominie. 'An's mither's a widow, ye say? Weel, weel. I houp the laddie 'll go on an' be a comfort till her.'

That evening my Uncle Sandy's thoughts carried him irresistibly abroad; now backward to the scenes of his youth, now forward again to the totally different realities into which the dreams and aspirations of his early days had grown. He had not the faintest doubt about the boy he had that day for the second time encountered – curiously enough in the very same place – being the child of her who had once been so dear to him. But how it had come to pass that the boy should have turned up in Greyness now, as he had turned up nearly twelve months earlier, was something he could not well make out. He was sufficiently familiar with the early part of the story of Tammie Tamson, the tailor of Trotterburn; he recollected well the time that Tammie had got tired of supplying moleskins and corduroys to the clodhoppers of Strathtocher – (the needs of the few broadcloth persons in the capital of that region were far from sufficient to keep a furnishing tailor establishment going) – and in the 'wudden dream' that had been begotten of disappointed love had gone off to achieve fortune by accepting a partnership in a more fashionable but doubtfully stable town business, which had turned out but poorly. And he knew the after history of Tammie in its bare outlines; only he did not know that when he had made his last hapless 'vaege' home in search of health, he had brought his boy with him; and that the two were returning southward together at the time when the latter came first under his notice. The circumstance of the bookseller having never again got sight of the lad was accounted for by the fact of his stay in Greyness being so brief. His reappearance now admitted of an equally simple explanation. Had my Uncle Sandy felt it was his part to put one or two simple questions further he would have found out all that was to be told. Briefly related, it amounted to this, that Elsie Robertson, the tailor's widow, as a stranger in a strange place, that had few happy memories for her, in her utter down-heartedness at the prospect of commencing the struggle for life so heavily weighted on the scene where adversity had already caught her, had felt that a change to almost anywhere would bring a certain sense of relief. And thus, though not it might be without a sense of misgiving and pain, she made up her mind to return to Greyness. There was not much feeling of home in the world for her then; but in so far as the feeling had place at all, it clung faintly and tremulously to the old town that was the capital of her native shire.

CHAPTER TWENTY-FOUR

John Cockerill

FROM the very day on which my Uncle the Baillie first took his seat on the judicial bench, my office companion, John Cockerill, had, as has been already said, felt his own personal importance, as an adjunct of a high civic functionary, to be sensibly enhanced. He was one of those good-natured empty fellows whose vanity and immense fund of self-satisfaction enable them – when they are kept in the right groove – to get on in a way that is surprising to think of, though when they happen to get a little too much rope they are apt to make a considerable mess of it. To be able to speak sounding nonsense with an air of confident assurance, and perfect unconsciousness may be a gift denied to the man with brains, yet, where possessed, it is a gift far from valueless in its effects upon the mass of mankind. Mr Cockerill's particular weakness was to be recognised as the magistrate's clerk, or private secretary. My Uncle the Baillie had at first exhibited some stiffness toward John when he made advances in that direction; but John understood not a rebuff, unless it happened to be made unusually emphatic; and gradually his attentions gained on my Uncle, who could not shut his eyes to the fact that, after all, it did look magisterially well to have the service of a private clerk occasionally.

John Cockerill had contrived to become the owner of a showy-looking ring, the brilliants in which were probably not of the purest water, which he liked to wear on the little finger of his left hand, with evidently no desire to hide it, except when my Uncle Sandy was by. At such times, warned by experience of Sandy's habit of uttering uncomplimentary and sarcastic remarks on what he deemed undue personal display, John would contrive to keep his left hand covered to the needed extent by a page or two of the ledger; and I have even seen him in an extremity furtively slip the ring off and quietly put it into his pocket for the time. Toward my Uncle the Baillie John acted quite differently. When my Uncle, preparing for a heavy day's judicial or other public work on the morrow, would call out to him of an evening, 'Cockerill! Put up your ledger an' come here; I want you,' John would march into my Uncle's sanctum, not only wearing his ring, but carrying the ring finger with a sort of ostentatious official air. And he would talk about the technicalities of affidavits, warrants, summonses, and the like, in a manner suggestive of profound legal knowledge. He was jealous of my Uncle's reputation as a magistrate and member of the municipality, and concerned himself about his public appearances. He had come to do the part of amanuensis in preparing the manuscript of certain of the Baillie's chief efforts as a speaker; and there were not wanting indications that on special occasions he had even endeavoured to go the length of culling flowers of rhetoric from the classics known to him, with a view to weaving them into the needed peroration.

It is not to be wondered at if John Cockerill's zealous services gained for him a goodly measure of regard in the family of my Uncle the Baillie. John had figured at the last election dinner, among older men, including the leading members of my Uncle's committee. But that was not all; he had been once and again asked to private parties with such young people of good standing as Mrs Macnicol thought it meet for her daughters to associate with. It was amazing how quickly John Cockerill learned to do his part gracefully and with *empressement* in all this. He plumed himself on being able to sing somewhat, though his voice was none of the most melodious, as I was wont to think when doomed to listen to his practisings at hours when we two had the warehouse to ourselves; and he would turn the leaves of the music book, as Miss Macnicol warbled at the piano, with an assiduity and grace that could not be surpassed. Next time he would engage in a grave conversation with Miss Macnicol's mamma regarding public affairs in the burgh of Greyness.

'He's grown an uncommon sensible, discreet lad, Johnny Cockerill,' said Mrs Macnicol, addressing my Uncle Sandy on the occasion of one of those parties. To do her justice, she seldom omitted him from the list of her invitations, whether he accepted or not, and Sandy was always in request, amongst the junior portion of her family at least.

'Div ye think so, Mrs Macnicol?' said my Uncle.

'Deed, I do; there's few young men hae sic a knowledge o' public maitters or tak' sic an interest i' them.'

'I daursay't John's quite able an' ready to talk at lairge aboot ony mortal thing; except it may be the vera things that he ocht to ken aboot.'

'Noo, Sandy; it's raelly nae becomin' to speak that way o' the lad. Look hoo usefu' he's been to the Baillie mony a time sin' he was pitten in'o the first cheir – 't my father – fill't – for mony a day – an' hed to tak so mony public duties upon 'im.'

'Oh ay. I've nae doot John has an eye to the chyne 'imsel' some day; an'll think it a' weel spent time, seein' it'll fit 'im for the high duties o' the office. But waes me for the gap atween the office stool an' the Bench.'

'Ye're owre censorious noo, Sandy; the lad's a smairt weel-meanin' lad, an' hoo sudna he hae a joost ambition? If he's grantit grace he may even mak' a position for 'imsel' yet. We a' ken the story o' Dick Whittington an' his cat.'

'Of coorse. In the meantime look at the elegant figure o' 'im! I'm satisfiet John thinks 'imsel' quite an irresistible object o' attraction amo' the young ladies.'

'Oh fie, Sandy; hoo sud ye speak sic nonsense?'

'Nae nonsense, I assure you. If John cud be gravely serious in ony point it's there.'

'But indeed the lad's mainners are won'erfu' for ane that's nae conneckit wi' people in an upper station.'

'Hoot, hoot, fearna ye, but John 'll think 'imsel' quite a fit match for the dauchter o' ony Baillie, or aiven a Provost, for that maitter; tak' my word for't,' said the incorrigible Sandy.

At this point the conversation was for the time broken up by Annie Macnicol and some of her companions getting temporary possession of Sandy's ear on a subject interesting to them. By and by my Uncle the Baillie desired to exchange ideas with his brother, who had that day returned from an absence of a week on business, which was a matter of periodical

occurrence with him. As the Baillie approached, a small group
of seniors had formed. My Uncle the Baillie's wife always
arranged for the presence of a few of these at her junior parties
as consonant with the gravity of the magisterial character.
Amongst them was Mrs Baillie Gudgeon – that respected
ex-Magistrate had himself been unable to put in appearance.
And in her presence, duly invoked, Mrs Macnicoll at once
revived the subject and appealed to her husband concerning
the merits of his chief clerk, and the promise he gave as a
member of general society.

'Ye see the Baillie's put the lad forrit in a mainner that few
cud 'a deen; takin' 'im under his own eye in so much public
business. He micht set up for a lawyer maist; an' he had had
some Laitin.'

'Oh yes' said my Uncle the Baillie, who with Sandy standing
by was perhaps less diffuse than he might otherwise have been,
'The lad's naitral pairts are middlin' – vera middlin' – but he's
smairten't up a great deal ae wye an' anither. Of coorse he's had
good expairience for some years – expairience that may be vera
usefu' till 'im a's life.'

'I'm weel sure o' that,' said Mrs Gudgeon. 'Hoo cud it be
ither, Baillie? It's a mervel to me, as I ees't to say to my nain
man, that your heid's nae clean turn't wi' sic a wecht o' toon's
affairs upo' you.'

'H – m,' said my Uncle, whose thoughts were not altogether
abstracted from Sandy, who at that very moment was again
luckily caught and carried off, *pro tem.*, by some of the juven-
iles.

'But it's rael true, Baillie,' pursued the lady with emphasis.
'Ye sid raelly gie't up, an' nae mak' yersel' an aul' man afore
yer time.'

'Public duty first an' oor ain feelin's syne, Mrs Gudgeon.
Only I'm a magistrate's dauchter!' said my Uncle's wife, with
a significant giggle.

'Well,' said my Uncle the Baillie, now quite at his ease,
'well, Mrs Gudgeon, I'm not the person to blaw my ain horn;
but the duties o' office are gettin' heavier an' heavier, wi' the
increase o' population – Greyness is a lairge city noo – an'
the multiplication o' statutes. An' Mrs Macnicol here can tell

you the sacrifeece that a man must mak' noo-a-days whan he serves the public i' the wye o' takin' office. It costs time, it costs labour; as Baillie Gudgeon kens weel it did aiven in his time; it costs serious thocht, an aiven interferes wi' the preevacy o' domestic life. An' fat for? Nae aiven thanks for recompense. It's only a strong sense o' public duty, an' the satisfaction o' oor ain conscience that induces a man to tak' up sic responsibilities at first, an' that susteens 'im in the dischairge o' them.'

The speech was perhaps not very necessary, but it was at least satisfactory to Mrs Macnicol to hear it delivered. To be sure, John Cockerill had been a little pushed to one side by it; but as the two ladies directly thereafter took to a quiet confidential gossip on matters interesting to themselves, my Uncle the Baillie once more sought out Sandy for a bit of chat, in which John, as it happened, was by no means remotely interested. It amounted to nothing more or less than this, that as John Cockerill had already been retained in the warehouse a couple of years longer than it was usual to retain old apprentices, my Uncle the Baillie had at last made up his mind that, notwithstanding his valuable services, John could be kept no longer; but must push his fortune in the usual way further south, with a recommendation under my Uncle's hand to various firms with whom he did business. The situation as it affected him was now to be formally communicated to Mr Cockerill, who had already got a sort of general intimation on the subject, and had, indeed, as he had hinted to me, a sort of half impression that the present meeting was in the nature of a farewell entertainment to him; and meanwhile my Uncle, as the most business like way and to save himself bother, had, through Mr Sneevle the solicitor, made certain inquiries relative to a suitable apprentice to occupy my stool when I should be advanced to that about to be vacated by John Cockerill. And as the final selection must rest with my Uncle Sandy, my Uncle the Baillie had arranged that he should see the lawyer at his office on the morning of the succeeding day, and decide the matter.

CHAPTER TWENTY-FIVE

Engaging the New Apprentice

AS my Uncle Sandy walked down to the office of Mr Peter Sneevle, solicitor, to perform the duty devolving upon him of selecting an apprentice, the absurdity of the lawyer being employed in what seemed so simple an affair came up in his mind once and again, as a fresh illustration of certain weaknesses to which the Bailliehood was liable. He was not however aware, till informed, of the elaborate fashion in which Mr Sneevle had gone about the matter intrusted to him. That gentleman's business was of an omnivorous sort. He liked to style himself an agent; and his agency comprehended much from the compilation of an ordinary roup bill to the drafting of a feu charter, from the sale of a wooden shed to the purchase and bonding of some of the best heritable subjects in Greyness. And he did everything according to the most ponderous legal form, a peculiarity of Mr Sneevle's method, moreover, being that in place of the formality diminishing in proportion as the business was trifling, it seemed rather to increase.

'Of coorse we advertis't,' said Mr Sneevle.

'Indeed!' said my Uncle Sandy.

'There were just thirty-four candidates – the replies are here. Wud ye like to hear them read?' asked Mr Sneevle, lifting a bundle of variously sized sheets of paper, folded and duly tied together and marked.

'Oh, no, no!'

'Well, they're all classified here, I can give you a *précis* of the whole as we go along.'

'I understan' ye've reduc't them to a leet o' three. I'm quite willin' to trust your judgement so far, Mr Sneevle.'

'Ay; vera good; but it'll be mair in form if I report generally.

There's a synopsis here; let me see. Good penmanship, you know, is an essential requisite. Well, o' the total number o' thirty-four, twenty-one were below par in the formation o' the letters, wi' mair or less bad spellin'; six passable writers also spelt badly. That reduc't the list to seven. Then a closer scrutiny became necessary. O' the seven, twa that wrote weel had nae feelin' for capitals, an' even spelt the first personal pronoun wi' a single i; a habit nae radically incurable, perhaps, but indicative o' a tendency to looseness in form. The neist twa – perhaps ye wud like to see them;' and the lawyer lifted the bundle and began to pull at it with the intention of drawing out certain of the papers.

'No, no,' said my Uncle, 'go on.'

'Weel, in a sentence; ane was blotch't wi' ink, an' the ither tussl't an' torn at ae corner. Here they ae. Noo I think that's the substance o' my report almost – No – let me see—'

'Can ye lat me see the three laddies?' said my Uncle a little impatiently.

'Stay, stay, Mr Macnicol, we haena come to that yet. Allooin' that ye pass fae the ithers; we come to a leet o' three a' eligible; but nae equally eligible it may be. Afore we come to questions o' personal appearance, mainner, an' the like, we can mak' a comparative analysis o' the han' writin''—

'Weel, really, Mr Sneevle, my pooers o' discrimination are nae equal to that. If the boys write decently it's a' that ye can expect, an' I wudna care a button for ane bein' a little better an' the ither a little waur – jist lat me see the laddies.'

'Weel, Mr Macnicol, if ye're satisfiet, though it doesna exhaust my remit in a formal mainner, I'll do as ye wish, only there's a risk o' miscairriage – Will ye tak' them ane an' ane for scrutiny or a' in a bunch?' and Mr Sneevle dabbed down the button of his table bell as a call to his attendant clerk.

'Oh, bring them a' in, an' we'll judge the han' writin' as far as needs be aifter seein' the writers.'

'Simon, sen' in the boys in the waitin' room,' said Mr Sneevle to his oldish and impoverished-looking clerk, when that functionary had pushed the door half open and looked in for his order. '*In cumulo* Simon,' he added, as the clerk seemed to hesitate with an inquiring look; '*in cumulo* – not *separatim*

– but *seriatim*, and in alphabetical order – Anderson, Baxter, Thomson – you have the check list.'

As the boys were ushered in in single file, Mr Sneevle, with an air of grave importance handed over to my Uncle Sandy the specimens of their handwriting furnished in the written applications, each of which, in addition to being subscribed by the name of the writer, was docquetted with that name written in large letters outside.

'Much o' a muchness, Mr Macnicol,' said Mr Sneevle, after a minute's pause, during which the three boys had ranged themselves inside the door. 'I forgot to mention that the parentage in each case seems fairly respectable – I can gie you the particulars here as to birthplace, whether one or both parents alive, employment of father, &c., an' put ony ither questions.'

'It's nae in the least necessary,' said my Uncle, who had been about to ask the boys how they had been employed hitherto, when his eye having rested on the boy ranged third in Mr Sneevle's order, he found a look of recognition returned which carried him back to Richie Darrell's shop. 'Thomson' – Jamie Thomson, of course, with his grey blue eyes and intelligent expression. My Uncle nodded, with a kindly 'Ah, I've seen you afore,' but put his question all the same, with one or two others following, and then dismissed the aspirant warehouse clerks, each a sixpence richer for their interview with him.

'I'll lat you know in course o' the day which boy to engage,' said my Uncle.

'Will you tak' the papers wi' you, or shall I file them?' said Mr Sneevle.

'Or burn them,' had almost escaped my Uncle's lips, but he only said 'Gie me the three letters; an' mak' what use ye like o' the rest.'

The duty of selecting an apprentice had turned out a more delicate and difficult one than my Uncle had anticipated. Had he been a man of coarser fibre than he was perhaps the difficulty would not have been much felt, if felt at all; perhaps it might have assumed the form of an opportunity for doing what would have ministered to the doer's sense of self-satisfaction either in choosing or rejecting the boy toward whom it was impossible his feeling could be that of pure indifference. As my Uncle Sandy mused over it he felt his position to be one of real perplexity.

'Is that boy o' a' boys on earth to follow me henceforth like my ain shadow?' was my Uncle's hastily formed mental interrogation. And then he by and bye bethought him of what was most probably signified by the fact of the boy's figuring there at all as a candidate for the lowest stool in our warehouse; he who but recently had seemed so earnestly bent on giving his early years to the pursuit of learning. Cramped means on the part of her on whom he depended – the *res angusta domi* so pressing as to compel him to quit school and the books he loved, and take what employment he could get if he might thereby earn some addition to the pittance.

My Uncle Sandy did not by any means relish the task before him the more he looked at it; but he felt that he must endeavour to get through it conscientiously, trusting to see his way more clearly as he went on. His first thought, namely, that the specimens of handwriting, or the synopsis of ascertained particulars, with which Mr Sneevle had been at the trouble to furnish him might, after all, supply tangible elements for a decision, he found illusory. The candidates were thus far at least 'much of a muchness,' as Mr Sneevle had expressed it. And, at any rate, he could see no plausible reason why, on an impartial examination of their merits, Jamie Thomson should be set aside and another preferred. Quite possibly it was a piece of sentimental weakness in my Uncle to balance the matter on such fine lines; or, indeed, to give such a trifling affair much balancing at all; yet could he not escape the feeling that the simple act of his accepting or rejecting this boy as an applicant for a humble apprenticeship yielding less then five shillings a week, touched issues of no mean significance in his own life. Reject him, and he was in all probability doing what was equivalent to frustrating the best hope of obtaining a much needed aid in procuring the means of daily subsistence to one from whom he might now be forever and irrevocably separated, but toward whom he could not entertain a harsh thought, much less do an unkind act. Accept him, and almost of necessity a new set of relations sprung up. The idea of putting himself openly and gratuitously in the position of a patron to, or benefactor of, Elsie Robertson's boy, was altogether repugnant to my Uncle. And, apart from that feeling, would not the bare fact of the boy being so intimately in connection with him day by day tend to the revival in a way that he would much rather avoid of thoughts that even yet had the power to depress and wring the heart, concerning what was and might have been, but had passed and now could never be? Nay, might not the whole facts tend even to the revival, or origination rather, of gossip of an objectionable or sinister kind? 'I'll let my brother decide,' said my Uncle Sandy to himself; but his second thought at once checked him. 'If he reject the laddie an' prefer anither, what better am I? In that case it is I aifter a' that have wronged her, an' done it in a cowardly way too, an' a' to forestall something that'll never happen.'

Having made up his mind honestly that all things considered Jamie Thomson had the best claim to fill the office of our new apprentice, my Uncle Sandy deliberately resolved to sink his own personal feeling and let the future bring what it had in store for him. And he accordingly instructed Mr Sneevle to complete the engagement in due form.

CHAPTER TWENTY-SIX

New Points of Departure

JOHN COCKERILL had left our office, and he had left Greyness to achieve fortune in one or other of the great cities of the south. It was not to be supposed that a person of John's importance could be allowed to quit the city that had hitherto had the benefit of his labours without some tangible recognition of the estimation in which he was held. John was the 'corresponding secretary' of a certain Debating Club, which had assumed to itself the imposing title of the Greyness Dialectical Association and Social Institute, and it was this society that was understood to move in the matter of the Cockerill Testimonial. I only know that it was John himself who half-badgered half-bullied me into giving a subscription of sixpence; and who suggested that it would be a fitting thing of me to canvass my two uncles to contribute, although they were not members of the society.

'Ye ken unco little aboot it gin ye dinna ken that that's the wye that the feck o' testimonials 's gotten up,' said John, in answer to my weak remonstrance about the bad taste of canvassing in that fashion in one's own behalf.

'The siller wud never be rais't mony a time an' fowk themsel's didna think it worth their pains to luik aifter't,' was John's rejoinder on the point.

'A massive gold Albert chain' was presented and John Cockerill declared himself utterly taken by surprise by a gift so unexpected, adding the usual statement to the effect that, great as the intrinsic value of the testimonial was, it was as nothing to the value he would ever attach to it as the symbol of friendship so spontaneously expressed. And all this had been duly recorded in the Greyness organ of public opinion as happening, on the eve of Mr Cockerill's departure to 'enter upon a more important engagement in the south,' prior to which, and following on the presentation, the members of the association and a number of other gentlemen from the wide circle of private friends, contributors to the testimonial, had 'thereafter sat down to a sumptuous repast' in the Crown Hotel, 'the president in the chair, and Mr Benjamin ———— (meaning myself), who succeeds Mr Cockerill in his present appointment, efficiently discharging the duties of croupier.'

John Cockerill had been gone for several months, and, despite the startling eminence to which I had so unexpectedly attained, I had been feeling myself fully at home with humble Jamie Thomson as my companion and successor on the lower stool. Shy and reserved for a little, he had not scrupled latterly to confide to me fully his deep disappointment at being obliged to become a warehouse apprentice. It is not, however, easy at fourteen to believe that a cherished ideal is impossible, and he accordingly entertained still the full hope of being somehow a learned man yet. Meanwhile he was in a high degree diligent and attentive to his duties, approving himself to the heads of the establishment as in every way a satisfactory apprentice.

Probably the best evidence as to the relations between the new apprentice and myself was, that we had begun to exchange visits systematically at our respective homes. My own opportunities of entertaining visitors were strictly subject to the arrangements of Mrs Geils and my Uncle Sandy; and the measure of liberty allowed was apt to increase or diminish according to their ideas of the company I happened to introduce, not always, it must be allowed, to my entire satisfaction. It so fell out, however, that Jamie Thomson speedily found favour with both, and accordingly I had never the slightest tremor concerning his visits. My first visit to his mother's house marked a sort of era in my history, if only by reason of the sheer paucity of fresh events at that time. The house was placed in a quiet street in the north-eastern suburbs of Greyness, where rather well-to-do people had at one time resided, though the street was now reckoned old-fashioned. The houses had accordingly come to be inhabited by people a shade lower in the social scale than the former occupants, either on their own account or for the purpose of keeping lodgers. The house was not of large dimensions. The single parlour and bedroom which it contained had, at a cost of a little effort and contrivance, been furnished with a view to accommodating one, or it might be two, lodgers; and the widow and her small family made shift to find accommodation as they best could in the narrow and ill-lighted kitchen and small bed-closet that adjoined it. A couple of well-dressed young men of what may be termed the brutal class of lodgers, occupied the parlour and bedroom. They paid at the lowest rate they could, rang their bell violently and frequently, destroyed the best pieces of furniture in a way that only low-bred curs could have allowed themselves to do, always spoke to their landlady with an assumption of vulgar authority, and never by any chance took the slightest notice of their landlady's children, or the slightest interest in her comfort or convenience. The contrast to the *status quo*, under Mrs Geils's hospitable roof, was too marked to escape the notice of even a thoughtless youth like myself.

I had not then the faintest idea of the relations in which the widow Thomson had stood to my Uncle Sandy, and on the general subject of widows – basing the induction on my knowledge of the class, as personally acquired at the time (my own mother naturally was not taken into the count, one way or the other) – I had implicitly arrived at the conclusion that the entity known as a widow was in all cases rather elderly and wrinkled. Great, then, was my surprise when, on proceeding to carry out my first visit, my new friend's mother turned out to be a woman, as it seemed to me, yet in the very prime of her life, and goodly alike in form and feature. Her open forehead and regular features, shaded still by masses of wavy fair hair, impressed me so much that I could not forbear to descant on the same to my Uncle Sandy on my return.

'Jamie's mither's a richt bonnie 'oman'—

I had got thus far, when my Uncle rose abruptly to fetch a book, with the remark that

'That point's in nae need o' enforcement by you, Benjie, man. – Is the little girlie like 'er?'

'I think she is,' said I, in a vague sort of way, as driven suddenly off the line. 'She has curly hair.'

'A white heidit lassikie, wi' bonnie blue een? Aboot fat age?'

'Weel, maybe sax or aucht year aul',' said I.

My Uncle Sandy had buried himself in his book, and the talk went no farther with him. Naturally Mrs Geils had a few judicious queries to put, albeit her curiosity was certainly not of the maliciously gossiping sort; and neither recognising nor ignoring my utter ignorance of my Uncle Sandy's old affair of the heart, she, after a little, delivered herself to me in a sort of half soliloquy in this wise—

'Weel, weel, it was little I kent aboot 'er weel a wat. Only fan we ken the gate that young fowk's traivel't till they've come to faur they are at mid-life or so; an' better ken the road that they refees't to tak', we begin at my time to be able to set ae thing forenent anither in gey near their true licht. Gin the tailor's widow hedna become the tailor's wife – but fat for sud I haiver aboot that. It's only the lesson that comes o' the wardle's hard an' unfeelin' grip driven fairly hame in her ain experience that enables mony an 'oman either to ken 'er ain min' or the worth o' a true man's affections. An' the mair seemin'ly fawvourable her chances the mair likely is she to dree that lesson in a' its bitterness. – Far be't fae me to say ae single word to fau't 'er. I've nae richt aiven to say that she ca'd 'er hogs till a peer market aifter bidin' bode in a better; but o' ae thing we can weel say oor say an' be debtor to nae ane – Fan the wife's been made widow an' the wardle to face anew on 'er ain can, the worth o' true friendship in man or woman is little likely to gae at oonder value; or if it dee, the case maun gae fairly oot o my ken. – An' aifter a' that's come an' gane, if the grip o' rael distress cam upon 'er I can hae nae doot faur help wud come fae, open or secret, an' withoot bein' socht. But fat need I speak; she is as she is, an' maun aiven mak the attempt to winnow on 'er ain cannas. The mair she's deservin' o' help the less she'll like to seek it; an' noo that she's open't hoose, I've nae doot her frien's in Strathtocher'll need nae adverteesement to lat them fin' oot that she's in a braw wye o' deein', an' "fell handy atween han's", as Francie wud say, fan they're takin' a bit scour throu the toon.'

So thought and so said the practical Mrs Geils.

CHAPTER TWENTY-SEVEN

Another Sabbath Day's Journey

'THANKS to ye, Deacon; thanks to ye for helpin' the Dominie to keep an open door for me,' said Richie Darrell, on first meeting my Uncle Sandy after returning from his journey to the north.

'I hardly ken fat for,' replied my Uncle. 'To speak honestly the twa o's did unco little to promote your business, or your reputation as a bibliopole; an' mine bein' by a lang way the least pairt, I'm mair than dootfu' aboot my title to thanks.'

'Ou, weel; jist as ye tak it. Fowk can dee but accordin' to their capacity, ye ken. I was obleeg't to ye for liftin' the shutters at onyrate,' said the bookseller.

Concerning the nature and results of his northern journey Richie Darrell was, on the whole, somewhat reticent. I have reason to believe that on certain points of it he had taken an early opportunity of unbosoming himself to no other than his greatly respected friend, Miss Spinnet, in the full belief that that high souled and severely virtuous woman would be the first to appreciate and commend his action in reference to the main object of his journey, which, as he had proceeded to explain, was to vindicate the memory of a deceased relative. But Miss Spinnet did not even want to hear the whole story.

'Richard! I think you have given way to a vain sentiment. "Let the dead bury their dead," ' said Miss Spinnet. 'Our duty is to care for the souls of the living – those corporeally quick, whose day of grace may not be run; and who may be made spiritually alive. To be concerned firstly, as you seem to be, about the name and reputation of those who are dead must surely seem to a person of your discernment a waste of precious means and opportunities.'

No wonder that the dead effect of such a speech from such

a quarter should be rather staggering. As a direct consequence of it, Richie Darrell – whose own heart, or the part of his mental constitution so called, told him he was right in what he had done, while by his formal reason he was equally convinced that the paragon of womankind as known to him could not be wrong – in his communications with my Uncle Sandy, made but brief and cursory references to the subject which of late had occupied the main part of his thoughts; and which still very evidently engaged a considerable share of his attention. To Dominie Greig, so soon as he had a little recovered the shock his feelings had sustained, his confidence was more largely given; the Dominie being a very old friend, and a man from whom counsel might be asked in a case where the promptings of the finer instincts and the voice of high external authority seemed to be in collision.

'Ou, weel,' said the Dominie, 'I hae nae doot Miss Spinnet's a perfect embodiment o' the soondest doctrinal conceptions, but did it never strike you that there's an absolute calamity involv't in gettin' so much high theology, an' sae mony abstract virtues embodiet in a bein' that, on the ae' han' is devoid o' a' the ordinary passions o' frail human nature – ostensibly so at least – an', on the titherhan', is carefu' to the last degree in ha'ein' the necessities o' the flesh minister't to, in so far as concerns personal comfort an' convenience, aiven if it be at the cost o' discomfort an' inconvenience to ithers? It seems to me that fowk o' that kin' – an' we come on specimens noo an' than, female as weel as male – wud need a place o' habitation by themsel's, different fae this peer earth below; an', in my sma' judgment, still mair widely different fae that heaven above, which belangs to the poor in spirit.'

To this homily Richie Darrell merely replied, that the Dominie should be taken before the Kirk-session and censured for entertaining and uttering loose opinions.

In the meanwhile he was more than usually engrossed in carrying on a correspondence, and attending to other matters external to his business, and more or less connected with the affairs about which he had recently been taken up. And, on a certain day, near the close of the autumn, he bespoke my Uncle Sandy's companionship on another Sabbath day's journey. On the Sunday then next ensuing, the two, who had started betimes, as was their wont on these occasions, pursued the same road, pretty much after the same manner as they had done fifteen years previously; and when they had again in their devious way reached the old Kirkyard of Bieldside, the bookseller once more went straight to the family gravestone.

'Ye wud maybe min' upo' the blank on the lairstane?' said Richie, addressing my Uncle, and pointing to some newly-cut letters near the bottom of the stone – 'ALSO, MARY, ONLY DAUGHTER OF THE AFORESAID JOSEPH DARRELL, WHO DIED AT PORTCASSIE, 18 – AND WAS BURIED THERE.'

'I min' upon't weel,' said my Uncle, 'an' ye've fill't it in at last.'

'A simple act o' justice to the deid; an' to the faimily name. It micht be little my pairt; the claim o' full cousinship by blood – I'm a Darrell on baith sides – is nae the strongest, an' it wasna made stronger by time and chance; deed no, Deacon. But if nane else wud tak' the pains to clear an unjust reproach fae the deid that had suffer't mair than aneuch as the livin', it cud hardly be unfittin' that I sud try't.'

'Certainly not,' said my Uncle, rather puzzled with Richie's enigmatical speech, though desirous of avoiding any appearance of seeking to pry into what he had not chosen voluntarily to reveal. 'Certainly not. But she's not buried here – your cousin, I mean; ye simply put the name on the faimily stone?'

'Ye saw the stane as it was, an' ye see't as it is. It was to mak' gweed her claim to Christian burial that, at the cost o' a het feud wi' them that sud 'a kent better, yon blank space had been keepit unlettered for full five an' twenty year. It micht be wrang-heidit to mainteen a body's richt to control i' the maitter at first; an' it may be aside o' the foremost duty to tak' the needfu' pains about fillin' in the record noo. But hooever that may be, I'm content that fat's deen's deen; an' me still here to see't wi' my ain een.'

The two Sabbath-walkers worshipped with the rustic congregation as before. It was several years since Richie Darrell, formerly a more frequent visitor, had last been there, and his re-appearance was the occasion of a general and prolonged scrutiny by the occupants of the various pews within view of that in which he had taken his place. Several parishioners twisted themselves round as they sat, till their spinal adjustments must have ached, to get a proper view of him; and one old fellow, as he went up the pass, stood absolutely still, took off his hat, and deliberately adjusted the specs on his nose to enable him to obtain a satisfactory look of the stranger. If any other feature in the service was notable, it was the impatience of the bookseller as he listened to an extremely formal and commonplace discourse. This feeling he signified by frequent resort to his snuff-box, and violent inhalation of its contents. And yet, when the big bullet-headed rustic who occupied a corner seat a couple of pews in front of him fell fast asleep, and lay backward open-mouthed, and happily oblivious to all that was going on, he excited the attention not only of the bulk of the congregation, but of even the parson himself, as he read and thumbed along his MS. by the vigorous style in which he punched the man's ribs with the top of his old-fashioned stick, and then when his object of arousing him had been accomplished, ministered to his startled consciousness by openly handing across his buffalo horn snuffbox, to give him an opportunity of taking a pinch.

'An' its fifteen year ye say sin' ye war here last, Deacon,' said Richie to my Uncle, as they pursued their way home together.

'By my reckonin' it is so,' replied my Uncle. 'I've been wi' you elsewhere, repeatedly; here only ance.'

'Ay; ay, time slips past; an' we af'en lat opportunity gae wi't. Fifteen years is a gey bit slap in a man's lifetime, be he young or aul'; an' fan ance we've come to be o' the side o' the hill faur the shaidows lengthen, though we're apt to be aiven less impress't wi' the lapse o' time than in earlier life, it signifies a space that we've sma' chance to see twice taul' owre our heid ere we maun quit this mortal scene. Ye may begin to tak' the lesson yoursel' Deacon; ye're nae a laddie noo.'

'Vera true,' said my Uncle; 'but hoo sud a man seek to forecast the day o' his death? He's surely happiest that fills up his time to the last quietly an' steadily, be't lang or short.'

'Spoken like a philosopher Deacon; only oor philosophy doesna aye stan' proof against the vera sma' trials an' vexations o' oor material daily life, ony mair than it sairs to set at rest the inner questionin's o' the human spirit. Hooever, lat it dee its pairt as far as it may – Gie me your airm a bit up the hill, I'm gettin' "fat an' scant o' breath".'

'I'm maybe walkin' owre fest?' said my Uncle, easing his pace, as he offered his arm to the bookseller; 'we'll tak' it cannier.'

'The autumn o' human life, sir, like the autumn o' nature, nae only lacks the lusty life-pulse o' the spring an' simmer tide, but the vera stirrin' o' the air that suggests upspringin' growth i' the tane only marks the rustle o' the deid leaves across your path i' the ither – see hoo they go quiverin' doon fae the bare brainches an' seekin' a quiet haven for decay an' death at the boddom o' the ditch;' and the bookseller stopped as he spoke, to take breath and look upon something like the reality of what he had been describing, as presented by an open clump of wood alongside of which they were passing. Perhaps it was the unexpectedness of the symptoms of exhaustion manifested by the bookseller; perhaps it was the fixedness of his look and the prolongation of the silence which ensued that made my Uncle offer to lighten the subject by remarking—

'Oh, weel, we're here at the tap o' the knowe. It's an easy step hame noo; an' spring'll be here again, ere we think o' anither Sabbath day's journey at least.'

'True; true, oh, Deacon—

> The spring returns, but not to me return
> The vernal joys my better years have known.

Hooever, it's but the autumn that we're speakin' o', an' it's the autumn wi' its russet mantle, gettin' black an' bare at elbows, that's wi's; an' the winter comes neist. – We'll be steppin' again, by your leave.'

And they quietly walked onward to Greyness, my Uncle to his homely home-like lodgings, where, as on all such occasions, he found his landlady nursing certain pots and platters about her kitchen range, with a religious miscellany occupying her spare thoughts; and mightily exercised all the while about his dinner being 'oot o' sizzon,' and what he personally was sure to suffer by such reckless treatment of himself.

In Richie Darrell's domicile, which may not be here described at length, the domestic aspect was essentially different. When the bookseller had turned the key in the lock, and pulled up the little blind on his front window, the narrow grate, with its rusty bars, and its uncheery freight of spent cinders and grey ashes, was there silently staring him in the face. The little table, which still carried the breakfast dishes on the tray that occupied the main part of its surface, stood in the middle of the floor in a straggling and uncomfortable sort of way, and the empty tea kettle hulked upon the hob with its back to the door and its spout into the chimney. In this state of matters it behoved the bookseller to set about setting his fire alight, and doing what else was necessary for refreshment and solace of the man as he stood, body, soul, and spirit.

CHAPTER TWENTY-EIGHT

The Romance of the Bookseller's Life

'AN' Richie has never taul' you the origin an' outcome o' his visit to Portcassie at the time that we twa keepit shop for 'im?' said Dominie Greig, addressing my Uncle Sandy on one of his not infrequent visits soon after the date of the second Sabbath day's journey.

'He seems mair bent on gi'en me 't in a kin' o' pantomime fashion,' said my Uncle.

'Weel, I can believe there micht be some points he wud raither avoid excep' wi' the like o' mysel' that's kent 'im so lang that the familiarity existin' atween's has grown to be a rootit' habit that can be disturbit only by a positive effort; an' I've sufficiently the advantage o' 'im in point o' years to enable 'im to luik upo' me as a kin' o' father confessor.'

'He has hintet a sort o' outline bit by bit o' pairt o' the family history,' replied my Uncle. 'But I've raither steer't clear o' the subject; his reticence leadin' me to suppose that something unpleasant, mair or less, had possibly been conneckit wi't.'

'Your surmise was richt in pairt at least. An' as I'm aware that Richie wudna be displeas't to ken that ye war inform't on the chief points, I'll put the story thegither in a rough fashion, as I've gaither't it up fae time to time owre a lang series o' years – but indeed it leads me back in a way upon the essential points in our frien's ain history to get at the heart o' the nit; an' may rin the risk o' bein' a little tedious.'

'If it doesna weary you in tellin', it certainly winna weary me in hearin',' said my Uncle.

'Weel, in relation to this craze aboot the faimily tree, an' to begin at the beginnin', it was Richie Darrell's hap as a young man to fall violently in love with his own cousin, a Darrell tee – Mary Darrell – Marie D'Aurelle say – by name. Hoo

far the fair Marie reciprocatit his passion is to me unknown.
In poor Richie's estimation it was only necessary that sinister
influences sud be kept oot o' the way, an' in due course Marie
without question wud be his ain; ither folk averr't that she
hedna the vera slichtest regaird for 'im as a lover. Onyhoo
the sinister influence, as Richie view't it, cam' in the shape o'
anither wooer, a relative likewise, an' as it wud seem an aul'
companion o' his ain, though noo a resident at Portcassie, to
whom Mary Darrell in due course gave her han' if no her hert.
They were join't in wedlock, an' Mary left the hame o' her
parents at the Glack o' Bieldside for that o' her husband at
Portcassie. By some accounts the husband – a man in a good
enough position – was nae better in morals than he sud be; by
ither accoonts the wife's temper was nane o' the least irritable
or sweetest. But we may pass that point under the lee o' the
gweed aul' maxim *de mortuis nil nisi bonum*. It seem't their
marriet life hedna been a' thegither o' the happiest at ony rate;
an' our frien's grudge against the man that had, as he thocht,
deen him deidly injury, by and by assum't the form o' bitter
an' unrelentin' hatred. "The unprincipl't villain that was a
traitor first, an' a heartless oppressor neist," was the emphatic
sentence pronounc't on the livin' man, an' I'm nae aware that
it was relax't or qualifiet in the least fan he raither suddenly
descendit to the grave. This latter event happen't at a time
whan oor frien, who then follow't his original occupation o'
a damask weaver, was a considerable way remov't from the
scenes o' his early life. There had, it seems, been a sombre
shade for maist pairt owre the widow's latter years, pairtly
throu' faimily dissensions o' an acrid kin'; an' it didna lift, but
fell closer doon at the close. An' Mary Darrell, wha had lived
a troubl't life, died a suicide's death. So it was bruited abroad
in Portcassie, an' the statements o' the nearest relatives, that
cud speak to the circumstances only too minutely, confirm't
the current report. Mary, who amid a' her troubles had grown
stout and apoplectic lookin', had been found dead in her lone
dwallin', half restin' in an easy chair, with a hempen cord
drawn tightly aboot her neck.'

'Ah!' said my Uncle, 'that explains what oor frien' suggestit
raither than said; an' why he didna say mair.'

'To the primitive community o' Portcassie the idea o' suicide was not merely revoltin'; it inspir't a kin' o' sanctifiet horror; an' it was deem't mair than their Christianity was worth to alloo the body o' the self murderer to be buriet within the hallow't God's acre, whaur the crumblin' remains o' those wha had left this mortal scene by fair strae death war interr't. Burial at a cross road atween the gloamin' an' the licht was the fit sepulture for such; an', in Mary Darrell's case, the compromise made was to bury her body ignominiously in a waste piece o' ground, far ootside the little toon, thus showin' that she had, by her last act, made hersel' an ootcast fae the society o' the livin' an' the hope o' the deid. Some years had pass't ere Richie Darrell kent o' the story, even thus far. Whan it cam' to his knowledge, he relentlessly pronounc't an aggravatit doom on the man who had robb'd him o' his cousin, Mary; an' unhesitatingly chairg't him wi' the responsibility o' her dark endin'. An' so the maitter stood for nearly a quarter o' a century; Richie Darrell, whan under the necessity o' reluctantly referrin' to Mary's history, contentin' himsel' by declarin' vehemently that she *cudna* a' ta'en 'er ain life. At lang an' last, ha'ein made up his min' to revisit Portcassie aboot the beginnin' o' his pedigree campaign, he was pleas't beyond expression to licht upon some traces o' fat he thocht positive evidence that Mary Darrell *didna* tak' 'er ain life. These he treasur't secretly in his ain possession till, bit by bit, at the cost o' a voluminous correspondence, followin' up his personal inquiries, he had fully satisfiet 'imsel' that the maligned woman had really died o' apoplexy, an' that, as persons yet livin' cud testify, the false report concernin' the mainner o' her death had been set on foot by neighbours wi' whom she had liv't on bad terms, an' ane o' whom – a relative, it was averr't – with a fiendish malignity, had sought to blast her reputation beyond the grave even, by actually puttin' the cord by which she seem't to hae strangl't hersel' in the place whaur it was got. Weel, ha'ein' got things so far, it only remain't, as our worthy frien' believ't, to write a triumphant letter to the great man who is the heid o' the Portcassie brainch o' the faimily, who is a near relative o' the deceas't husband o' Mary, an' wi' whom he had been in vera frienl'y correspondence aboot genealogical maitters, proposin' that the time had noo come to vindicate the memory o' their common relative, by gettin' 'er remains exhum't fae the barren-blastit heath an' convey't to their legitimate restin' place in the pairish graveyard. To his intense mortification, and even disgust, the reply was a stiff an' formal declinature to tak' pairt in or coontenance ony sic "romantic an' imprudent undertakin'." It micht be a' true that he said aboot the actual mainner an' circumstances o' Mary Darrell's death, but there was no use in openin' up old sores; the circumstances were fast dyin' oot o' recollection, an' respec' must be had to the position an' feelin's o' the livin' as weel as the memory o' the deid. Ye can imagine the explosion that follow't, I daresay, better than I can describe it?' And the Dominie paused in his narrative.

'I can imagine it in some reasonable degree, I daursay,' said my Uncle. 'But dear me, Mr Greig, wha cud 'a believ't there was so much romance in the history o' oor frien'?'

'A common-place remark that raither. Ye surely dinna need to be taul' that the truly romantic in human life is not seldom to be found in quarters the least like it,' answered the Dominie. 'Hooever, to proceed wi' my tale. When maitters had come to the point jist spoken o', the coorse o' duty was clear, lat the big kinsman think or say what he micht. It wud seem that the pairis' parson's a man o' sense an' feelin'; an' the grave digger nane less so. Baith the ane an' the ither lent him willin' assistance at the ootset in the way o' fortifyin' his information aboot the hapless Mary Darrell. The parson pronounced the principle o' vindicatin' her memory laudable. He scrutinised the session minutes done under the eye o' his predecessor about the time o' Mary's death; he made extracts, and even concerned himsel' in obtainin' the evidence o' the maist valid witnesses. Aboot an' actual exhumation he was not so clear; nay he had his doots aboot the propriety o' the step. Not so the sexton; the vera aesthetics o's craft compell't him to gie an' emphatic endorsement to Richie's open proposal to have her bones forthwith exhumed an' in the face o' day, wi' the kirk door open an' the bell twice toll't, duly re-interr't in the grave o' the faimily to which by marriage she belong't.

"Seerly," said the Sexton, "I wud apen the graiff for naething man, raither nor hae a Christian 'oman keepit oot o' the yard aifter ony sic haethenish mainner." An' in point o' fac' he firmly refees't to tak' a copper mair nor the ordinar' chairge for fat cost him at least dooble duty. An' so the lang maligned cousin had proper burial at last. "It was fae nae love o' them that lay there already nor o' them 't may follow; but it was wi' her choice in life she gaed there, an' it was her richt in deith to lie faur she's laid," said Richie, in windin' up the last chapter o' his cousin Mary's story.'

'An' do ye mean to say the re-interment o' this unfortunate woman a quarter o' a century aifter her death 's been carrie't oot at oor frien's sole chairge an' oversicht?'

'That was his business on his last visit to Portcassie. By the aid o' his stedfast frien', the Bellman, he had asked the favour o' the company o' maist o' the adult male inhabitants o' the place to atten' the funeral. Some cam' o' pure goodwill; ithers fae various causes. It had been speedily discover't that the influential kinsman disapprov't o' the proceedin', an' naitrally those that fear't his frown staid awa', while those that despis't it or bore him a grudge made it a special duty to atten'. Hoo the bookseller himsel' gravely headed the slow an' sombre precession, through groups an' groups o' speculatin' villagers o' a' ages an' baith sexes, an' under the vera windows o' the recalcitrant kinsman wha sud by richt hae occupiet his place that day, on to the open grave, which, wi' uncover't heid, he saw feenally clos't, cud be taul' only in his ain brief an' pithy words. But the thing is done an' his min' at rest. The last act was to remit, per draft, the amount o' the undertaker's and sexton's chairges; an' though the sum total – a maitter o' near by twenty poun's – representit, as I happen to be aware, little less than the half o' a' that stan's on the credit side o' Richie Darrell's bank account, never, I verily believe, was money paid wi' less o' a grudge, or a mair assur't conviction that it was money weel spent.'

'An' wha sall say it wasna money weel spent?' said my Uncle in an earnest and half-absorbed tone.

'Weel it michtna be either you or me, Sandy,' said Dominie Greig. 'But I'm no sae sure that oor frien' 'll be held free o' censure by folk that wud tak' in han' to teach baith you an' me.'

'Of coorse his lady frien' wi' the blue goggles had better ken naething aboot it,' said my Uncle.

'Too late, sir. Your discernment in this instance is just. But Miss Spinnet has heard the cause an' deliver't her adverse judgment; but for the staggerin' effect o' which judgment, comin' fae such high authority, on the pairty at the bar, ye wud surely hae got the whole story at first han' ere noo.'

'Is't possible,' exclaimed my Uncle. 'By a' that's best in heaven an' earth, an' the dearest hopes o' here an' hereaifter, save me fae that fashion o' formal religion – Christianity it is not, nor even a healthy Paganism – that seeks nae only to frown doon the finer, mair pathetic sentiments an' promptin's o' the human spirit, but reckons their active operation in the nature o' an actual sin. An', abeen a', save me fae't in the shape o' a woman.'

'Nae doot; nae doot;' said the Dominie, rising to his feet, and pacing the floor with his hands behind his back. 'But ye ken the siller mitha deen creditable service in the wye o' aidin' the temporal or spiritual weel-bein' o' the livin'. An' nae doot, too, Richie's conscience maun bear the responsibility o' disregairdin' an' traversin' the sound instruction which Miss Spinnet has taul' him weel baith he an' she were privileg't to hear fae the pulpit o' Dr Cleavahair, an' to which his ecclesiastical successor has faithfully adher't to this day. Still an' on; still an' on; sic sins as carin' to excess for the moral reputation o' the deid, are not, I verily believe, o' so deep a dye but that the like o' you an' me, that hae nae claim to risin' abeen the feelin's an' sympathies o' frail humanity, may aiven venture to forgie 'im, if we canna dee mair for the poor graceless bodie.'

CHAPTER TWENTY-NINE

An Unexpected Reappearance

'FRANCIE Tamson i' the toon again! Fat i' the face o' Fortune can the creatur' be seekin' back already – Has your Uncle seen 'im?'

The words were uttered by Mrs Geils, in reply to a certain piece of intelligence I had communicated to her on returning from the warehouse to my dinner.

'No,' said I; 'nae Sandy. He was in o' my Uncle the Baillie's officie; but Sandy was oot.'

'An' didna he wyte for 'im?'

'No; he didna speak to me ava; but jist gaed straucht throu to the Baillie's ain room.'

'An' said naething comin' or gaein?'

'Forbye that, fan the Baillie call't me in to dictate twa letters for the post, an' him sittin' there, he never said a word nor luikit as gin he kent me. The only thing that I heard 'im sayin' was speerin' fat 'onwal' the 'toonship' was gi'en eenoo; an' fan they took in siller. He hed been consultin' my Uncle Dawvid aboot takin' chairge o' some o's siller, I think.

'Siller say ye. Fat i' the wardle wye cud the creatur' hae siller to hoord eenoo an' it rent time? But fat need aw say that. He wud scrape siller aff o' the vera links o' the crook.'

'He hed a gweed puckle notes in's aul' pocket buikie ony wye,' said I, rather pluming myself in having scrutinised Francie's action thus far.

'Weel, weel,' said Mrs Geils, 'I may jist mak up the attic bed at onyrate; we'll hae anither nicht o' im.'

In this case Mrs Geils was mistaken, however.

This fresh visit of Francie Tamson had struck even myself as rather odd; in so far as that, when he come into the warehouse, in place of asking for my Uncle Sandy, who for aught he could have known might have been in some part of the front premises, he had made directly for the rearward corner, shut off for the exclusive use of my Uncle the Baillie. And, in point of fact, the cool and secretive kind of way in which he had advanced to the inner apartment – which of course was known to him from his former visit – while apparently out of keeping with the rusticity of his general manner, rather suggested the notion that he did not desire to attract general attention in the warehouse at all. At any rate Francie put in no further appearance; and my Uncle Sandy, when he came home, was not able to give the slightest information concerning him. Still, Mrs Geils would prophesy – 'Bide ye still; he's nae here for naething; an' gin he dinna turn up some gate, I'se eat a peat.'

I think Mrs Geils was not off the expectation that Francie Tamson would somehow turn up at her door, even on the next day. It was late in the afternoon of that day, and I was about to close the warehouse, the two principals having left, when my companion, Jamie Thomson, upon whose mind something seemed to have been weighing during the day, confided to me that his grand-uncle, Francie, had been at his mother's house for such part of the night as he could be kept indoors – his mother and little sister having to give up their bed to him, and sleep on a shake down in the floor – and that he had said or done something that was causing his mother much trouble and vexation.

All this I should, no doubt, have communicated for information on reaching my lodgings; but, on getting there, I found I had been, in an unlooked-for way, anticipated.

CHAPTER THIRTY

Francie Tamson's Errand, and What Followed

IT was somewhere approaching six o'clock in the afternoon, when Mrs Geils's door bell rang.

'Wud that be him noo?' thought Mrs Geils with herself. She had not anticipated any caller at that hour, and in going to answer the bell herself, her mind was in rather a defensive attitude than otherwise. When she opened the door, there stood before it, not Francie Tamson, but a youngish-looking woman, with somewhat careworn but comely face, and dressed in widow's weeds.

'Weel?' said Mrs Geils interrogatively past the edge of the door, as soon as she caught sight of the figure before her.

'Is Mr Macnicol in?' asked the lady caller, in a very quiet and subdued tone.

'Mr Alexander Macnicol is't?' asked Mrs Geils. 'It's only him that's lodg't here. There's nae ither ane but's nevvy.'

'It's Mr Macnicol 'imsel',' said the lady. 'If I could see 'im for a vera few minutes,' and she glanced at Mrs Geils with a look that plainly said I know who you are, and you might at least guess who I am.

'I'll see; ye better come in,' said Mrs Geils, who up to that point had held the door, only three-fourths open, in her hand. It was plainly manifest that she objected on principle to subjecting her lodger to any such ordeal as that of a good-looking young widow calling on him; and consequently there was extremely little cordiality in her tone or manner.

'Ye'll be Mrs Tamson?' said Mrs Geils, arresting herself for a moment, as she showed the visitor into the best parlour.

'Yes; an' I think this is Mrs Geils?'

'It's the muckle feck o' fat's for me,' said Mrs Geils. 'Mr Macnicol'll jist be gaein oot eenoo; but I'll see fat he says – gin he can speak to ye – sit doon for an instant.'

How it was I do not know. I am certain that my Uncle Sandy was not an eavesdropper, and from the small library parlour where he ordinarily sat it was equally certain that one could scarcely hear any person talking at the door or entrance lobby unless they happened to speak in an unusually loud tone, and the colloquy between Mrs Geils and the visitor now in the parlour had been a very quiet one; yet before Mrs Geils had opened my Uncle's door, and looking in with a very inquiring face, had said, 'A lady i' the parlour wud like to see you for a minute; will I tell 'er 't yer busy?' he had somehow – whether by sound of footfall, reflection of voice, or what else, he probably could not have told – become fully conscious of who the visitor was.

'Yes,' said my Uncle, 'I'll see her in a single minute.'

Mrs Geils had only to repeat his message, and then, leaving the lady alone where she sat, return to her operations in the kitchen.

The idea of again meeting the woman face to face, who at an earlier period of his life had stood to him in the position that one tacitly-accepted lover stands to another, and in view of all the intervening history, had once and again pressed itself upon my Uncle; and he had been totally unable to make up his mind either as to what was the fitting action or attitude for him in the matter; or the state of feeling into which either side might be thrown. He had casually learnt enough to make him certain that the widowed Elsie Robertson's circumstances were straitened and difficult; and had the way seemed open to offer his service in aid of her friendless condition he would readily have done it. But except in so far as his hand and act could be effectually concealed, my Uncle believed it would be alike presumptuous, and lacking in delicacy of feeling, were he to put himself forward in the light of a benefactor. To seem to thrust himself in any wise indeed upon the widow was utterly repugnant to him. And so it was that she had been for more than six months in Greyness and they had never once met, or been in any way brought into personal contact.

As my Uncle stept into the parlour, which he did immediately after Mrs Geils had disappeared, it was beyond question
that a certain feeling of nervousness had possession of him for
a moment; but it was only for a moment.

'How are you?' said my Uncle, stepping rapidly across the
floor and taking his visitor's hand, which he grasped firmly
and closely as his wont was. 'Be seatit,' he added, putting
forward the chair off which the lady, whose agitation was too
visible to admit of concealment, had risen; 'be seatit an' tell
me hoo you are.'

Thus cordially greeted the visitor resumed her seat with
an evident feeling of satisfaction and relief, though still
exhibiting tokens of unmistakable embarrassment.

In my Uncle's case all feeling of nervous emotion had now
gone. As Elsie Robertson, the sedate widow of to-day, sat
there before him, and their eyes met, a vivid image of Elsie
Robertson, the bright-eyed, light-hearted, girl of fifteen years
ago, instantly rose in his mind; and my Uncle thought with
perfect calmness of the face once so familiar, now so much
older, not with the oldness of years it might be, but with the
oldness of an experience which, on its external side at least,
had not been free of such vicissitude as was fitted to imprint
some lines of care prematurely on the brow. If he had thought
too that – perhaps – in the inner life of the heart's affections a
certain rankling void had existed, my Uncle might have been
excused. But he was after all a kindly soul, my Uncle Sandy;
and as he looked again straight in Elsie Robertson's eyes, and
she with tremulous emotion looked in his, he simply felt this
– that she had known sorrow, that trouble was her portion,
more or less, still, and that despite it all she would trust in
him more fully, more readily, than she could in any other
human being; that, in fact, she could not help so doing if
she would. There was a memory of keen and bitter anguish
which he could even yet recall – the price he had paid for
having loved only too well – but all that had passed, or could
only be seen in mellowed light on the backward horizon of
his life; and he knew at that moment that it was elsewhere
than in his breast if aught remained to wring the heart or
make reflection bitter. And even had it not been so, it was

hardly in my Uncle Sandy's nature to do otherwise than feel that in whatever his visitor had now to ask he must be at her command.

My Uncle had no great command of commonplace talk to serve him in an emergency; and consequently when Elsie Robertson had fully answered his renewed interrogation, and in turn asked after his own welfare, he had just begun to feel the inconvenience of so large a region of common interest being utterly tabooed to him, when the conversation took a direction by the lady saying,

'Ye'll excuse my callin' in this way, Mr Macnicol; but if it had only been to thank you for your great kindness to my boy, it was my duty'—

'I'll perfectly excuse you callin' Mrs Thomson, but hardly if ye speak o' thanks whaur nae thanks are due. I hope ye can still believe that I wudna willin'ly see a laddie suffer injustice or inflict it mysel' knowingly; an' that's aboot the extent o't.'

'If I hadna believ't a' that an' mair, I couldna 'a ventur't to come here the nicht,' said the widow with strong feeling. 'An' the best proof that I can trust your frien'ship, is my bein' here to ask your advice in a maitter that's brocht me to my wit's en'.'

'Ou, weel, like enough my advice mayna be able to cairry you far; but ye needna want it at what it's worth, nor ony ither sma' help that I can render, or ye can accept.'

'You're vera kind indeed'—

'Noo, pray, nae mair idle sentiment ye ken,' said my Uncle, interrupting, with a half-comical look. 'I'm a strictly maitter-o'-fact man, you know; an' eager for business at a' times. An' forbye, forehan'it paymen' mak's slicht-han'it wark.'

Thus admonished, the lady proceeded to say how, in accordance with the last will and testament of her late husband's aunt, a certain small amount of moveable property, hardly exceeding a hundred pounds in amount, had been bequeathed to her family; that from the date of her husband's death, which occurred directly before their receiving the bequest, his Uncle Francie had not ceased informally to urge his claim as nearest of kin; that on the preceding day the aforesaid Francie had paid her a visit, and incontinently taken up his quarters in her house for the night; that, after his arrival, he had very broadly hinted at the invalid nature of his sister Meggie's Tes'ment; that, before leaving, he had plainly intimated that as restitution had not been offered, he would 'tak' advice upon't'; and that, as evidence of his having done so, a portentously worded letter, drawn up by Gabbin' Gibbie, as 'instructed by Mr Francis Thomson,' threatening a process of count and reckoning, or alternately demanding an immediate offer of compromise, had been received by the widow that afternoon.

'The mean, contemptible aul' villain,' exclaimed my Uncle Sandy, forcibly, the moment he had heard the story.

'But do ye think they've a legal claim?' asked the widow. 'It's nae use incurrin' expenses if ye think that. I maun jist tak' a less hoose an' try an' sattl't some way.'

'Nonsense, Elsie – Mrs Thomson,' said my Uncle correcting himself – 'I dinna believe he has the shadow o' a claim; an' whether or no, he's pay for't ere he finger a shillin' o' the money, if ye'll trust it to me. If I micht ask, ha'e ye got the whole that Meggie left?'

'Except what was got for the sale o' her furniture an' things.'

'But the sale's past; an' Francie wud hae in's han' there? Ah, weel – if ye'll trust me wi' that precious document, we'll see whaur the count an' reckonin' has to be. In the meanwhile gie yoursel' nae trouble whatever aboot the maitter – the detestable aul' scrub – ye'll excuse my plainness o' speech – it'll be an act o' charity to expose his cunnin' an' greed.'

I have reason to believe that the widow Thomson went to her home that night, not only with a less troubled heart than she had on leaving it, in so far as the immediate object of her visit was concerned; but also with a certain feeling of being in all that concerned her less unprotected in the world than before. And all this, combined with an ever recurring sense of absolute and insuperable distance from the man to whom at one time she had a feeling of such intimate confiding nearness; and whose right worthily to own her perfect trust and confidence was, she keenly and vividly felt, not less than it had been of old – more she knew in her innermost consciousness it could not be.

'She hasna hurrie't awa', weel awat,' said Mrs Geils to herself, as she heard the parlour door open. But she stopped short in her outward advance as she heard my Uncle Sandy's voice in the lobby. 'He's lattin' 'er oot 'imsel', is he! Na, sirs! Is that the door? Wud he be awa to see 'er hame, no? The road's nae sae lang nor the nicht sae dark, seerly, as a' that – Weel, weel. They've left the gas bleezin' at a bonny rate; I may pit it doon ony wye.'

CHAPTER THIRTY-ONE

The Last of Meggie's Tes'ment

I T is a trite observation, that when a man of a naturally placid and peace-loving disposition has got provoked to the extent of fairly rousing him, his anger is not easily withstood. In this way it had happened that my Uncle Sandy had occasionally, under exceptional circumstances, left the impression upon people who did not know him better that he was, after all, a man with a rather violent temper. The attitude he had assumed toward Francie Tamson, in respect of Francie's movements relative to his sister Meggie's Tes'ment, was well enough fitted to support this conception of his character. To Francie himself his opinion had been delivered with sufficient emphasis to induce him to avoid the chance of hearing it repeated; and we know that Francie's subsequent procedure had been of a sort that was well adapted further to rouse – as indeed it had further roused – my Uncle's indignation. When he called on a personal friend of his own who was a member of the Greyness bar to ask him to take up the case, defensive or offensive, against the old Strathtocher crofter, my Uncle indulged in what was to him very strong language.

'It's nae use to ca' 'im a villain or a swin'ler because words o' that kin' dinna express the idea,' said my Uncle. 'But the wretch is ane o' that kin' o' creaturs – I'm sorry to think that they sud be nae vera seldom o' countra growth – that are so encased in, an' owrelaid wi', sordid greed that ye actually need to get doon through the coarsest stratum o' their character afore ye can beat into them a distinct apprehension o' fat constitutes particular crimes, as swin'lin, theft, an' siclike.'

'I see,' said the lawyer laughing. 'An' ye wud like to gie this interestin' old gentleman a lesson in that direction?'

'Weel, I certainly wud; if merely for his ain sake. Only

whan a man gets into the state that pure greed o' wardle's gear fairly obscures a' sense o' moral right an' wrong, it's nae easy. There's only ae sensitive point at which ye can touch 'im.'

'An' ye've nae scruples o' conscience aboot touchin' 'im there, if it can be done?'

'Nane; I'm persuadit in fact that it's the only method o' salvation for 'im, to teach 'im through personal experience that hoardit' siller can burn like fire the vera han' that hoards it.'

'Strong meat doctrinally, nae doot,' said the lawyer. 'However, the first thing is to see the terms o' this will.'

'I expeckit as much,' replied my Uncle; 'an' so procur't Meggie's Tes'ment fae the aul' minister who drew it, as he has drawn mony a similar deed in his day. The phraseology may be a sma' thing antiquatit, but I'm greatly mista'en if ye dinna fin't a' perfectly formal an' valid in its scope an' purport.'

It was even as my Uncle had said. The lawyer on examination, declared Meggie's Tes'ment to be a very distinct and definitely drawn will, under which her nephew Thomas and his wife and bairns were expressly named as sole testators, her brother Francis being equally explicitly set aside with a small special legacy for the trouble he might have in disposing of her effects.

'He hasna a leg to stan' on. An' Gibbie, in his eager desire for business, must hae written in entire ignorance o' the contents o' the will,' said the lawyer. 'Surely his client himsel' must have been under some delusion.'

'Siclike delusion as is bred o' unconscionable selfishness an' love o' pelf. An' I can weel un'erstan' hoo Gibbie sud ken little forbye the story he micht be taul'. They're nae owre observant o' business forms in my native region o' Strathtocher. An' abeen a' they're never owre hurriet in windin' up a piece o' business. So when I call't upo' the minister the last time I was that road, "Hoot Sandy, man," says he, "the Tes'mentie's never been oot o' my dask sin the day it was pitten there. But ye'se get it i' yer pouch." An' so I did; an' as ye may suppose, Gibbie wud'a gotten little knowledge o't fae me though he had socht it.

Kennin what ye dee noo, ye'll aiven turn the tables on 'im at ance.'

'Well, well,' said the lawyer, looking at Gabbin' Gibbie's letter, 'in due course. But ye say ye wudna be sorry to see a little wholesome punishment inflicted on Francie Tamson. Noo Gibbie doesna write the like o' that document free gratis an' for nothing, an' whan he has a client by the lug that he thinks can pay, he doesna spare his missives. So I think, wi' a' due consideration for your desire to be at 'im, we may e'en dee waur than lat him hae the opportunity o' rinnin up his account against Mr Tamson a little farther – he'll get every farthing o't to pay, I'll be bound – an' syne we can serve him wi' a summons, if need be, for payment o' the proceeds o' Meggie's sale, wi' the needfu' amount o' threatenin' legal verbiage; an' as he'll get a' the costs to pay, I warrant you we'll hae deen a fair stroke towards his possible salvation by that time.'

And on this understanding my Uncle left the case in the hands of his lawyer friend; who forthwith intimated to Gibbie that any further communications in behalf of his client should be addressed to him as agent for Mrs Thomson; an intimation which had evidently rather staggered the little pettifogger, who by-and-bye indicated a desire for a personal conference with a view to compromise or adjustment of particulars. This being promptly and flatly refused, Gibbie addressed an urgent letter to his client asking him to come speedily to town, and bring copy of the will so as he might be fully 'instructed' in his case.

'Weel man, aw doot he winna be gryte lawvyer that; or he wud 'a made oot wuntin' sae muckle by vreet, an' word o' mou fae you,' said Kirsty Tamson, when Francie had spelt out the purport of his agent's letter.

'I canna gae near 'im onywye till the crap be in'o the grun,' answered Francie, who, sooth to say, did not relish the idea of having to search after the will, believing, as he did, that the fact of his being in pursuit of his 'richts' was still (as he desired it to be) a secret in Strathtocher. He not only did not go to Greyness as wished, but being 'nae dab at the pen' he sent not the slightest acknowledgment of Gabbin' Gibbie's letter to him; a piece of neglect that speedily brought down on his head a second and greatly more ferocious missive, which conveyed a threat, to the effect that if he did not show himself in his agent's office within three days he would for once in his life have experience of something as near as possible to a process of horning. Resistance or evasion was then felt to be out of the question. Under the portentously savage terminology of the second letter, painfully deciphered line by line, even Kirsty could not longer afford to doubt that Gibbie was sufficiently formidable legally to be dreaded; and another and reluctant journey to Greyness was the result.

'Tell me ye've come here again wantin' that will!' said Gabbin' Gibbie. 'Faur i' the wordle is't min?'

'The minister gya't to Mister Macnicol,' answered Francie.

'Gya't to Mister Macnicol! An' dee ye think that I can get throu' wi' yer case, an' be keepit i' the dark this wye – lat alane yer ain deceit an' duplicity – go and get that will, sir; or I'll throw up yer case, an' ye'll see faur ye'll be – go to Macnicol at once.'

That Francie Tamson should go to my Uncle Sandy concerning his sister Meggie's Tes'ment, if not absolutely a startling idea, was a proposition that certainly was very far from commending itself to him. If he had had the faintest belief that Sandy would be disposed to be in any way helpful to him, he would not have hesitated at the mere cost of a good deal of personal humiliation. But after what had passed he knew the case was hopeless. The notion of appealing to my Uncle the Baillie was faintly entertained but speedily abandoned. Francie was conscious of having told him a story in which was omitted a good deal that would now have to be revealed in order to define the position coherently, and the revelation of which would not be exactly comfortable. Even to call upon Mrs Geils or the widow of his nephew for his dinner and bed, seemed a perilous sort of proceeding, though he was getting both hungry and tired. And so he landed at the stabler's much bewildered concerning the next step; which, after a few uncomfortable hours, towards the close of which he and the ostler got mutually confidential, and Francie, much bewildered over a half mutchkin of bad whisky, proved to be his sudden return to Strathtocher without further communication with his agent.

'Preserve me, man,' said Kirsty, when Francie had reached home at an unexpectedly early hour next day; 'you here a'ready luikin' like a vera wraith; but fat i' the wardle's things comin' till? Mair papers – Peter Thain the Shirra's offisher's been here sin ye gaed awa, wi' a summons for ye to pay owre the ootcome o' Meggie's roup; or be poin'et for't.'

The action in this case was, of course, at the instance of the lawyer employed in the interest of the widowed Elsie Robertson. Poor Francie; his troubles were thickening on all hands! Kirsty declared him to be like a man 'fit for the lunatic;' and donning her straw bonnet and tartan shawl she set off to the manse to lay her case before the minister, and implore his intervention for the purpose of unravelling the tangled skein of his troubles. And the shape in which the parson intervened was by compelling Francie to accompany him to Greyness, where he had first of all to face my Uncle Sandy and the lawyer he had employed.

'So ye daur't, an' ye've dreet my ill prayers, Francie man.' said my Uncle.

'Oh, Sandy, I wuss I had ta'en yer advice a-time.'

'Tak it noo an' disgorge the gear that's nae your ain; an' jist pay the smairt for your dishonesty.'

'But will 'a be sair soosh't wi' expenses, Sandy; the like o' me kens little aboot fat it is to gae into the witters o' the law; an' I'm jist naar-han' herriet a'ready wi' a' this rinnin' oot an' in to the toon, an' negleckin' the wark at hame.'

'I daursay it's a' true, Francie; but ye've naething to thank but your ain unchristian greed.'

'Eh, but he's a terrible creatur' yon lawyer mannie – wudnin ye sattle wi' him for me, Sandy?'

'Deed, Francie, he may tak's will o' ye; an' ten thousan' pities if he dinna fleece you weel.'

'Eh, gweed keeps Sandy, man; fat's to come o' me, fan you't's kent me a' yer days wud say the like o' that,' whined Francie, by way of a last appeal.

It was like taking the life-blood from Francie Tamson to compel him to part with money once in his possession; but he now paid over, with a certain air of relief, the sum he should have paid before, a matter of twenty five pounds, as the result of the sale of his sister's effects. His lawyer's bill for bad advice had been run up to £12. Concerning this he complained very grieviously; at first flatly refusing to pay, and latterly living in a sort of sleepless distraction under fear of a threatened process to compel payment. Ultimately my Uncle Sandy, who had been again specially appealed to, probably deeming Francie's punishment fairly adequate at that rate, got an offer of half the charge made to Gabbin' Gibbie, by whom it was, with little real difficulty, though with a good deal of strong language, accepted.

CHAPTER THIRTY-TWO

John Cockerill's Progress

JOHN COCKERILL was getting on. He did not omit the duty of writing to his old friends by any means. I was favoured with occasional epistles; so was my Uncle Sandy; and so, sooth to say, was my uncle the Baillie. Who else I might surmise, but was not so certain. My Uncle Sandy, I incline to think, had proved to be not a very regular correspondent; for myself, being rather under John Cockerill's mark, I was kept in hand mainly for utilitarian purposes rather than treated on the footing of equality implied in a properly established friendship. If John had an inquiry to make which no one else would attend to, or desired to be remembered by or have a message conveyed to some one, to whom, for reasons of his own, he did not desire to write, I have no doubt he felt it convenient to have somebody at command; and why not myself. Only as time went on and John, forming new connections and companionships, began to have a vaguer feeling for the old, my communications from him became gradually fewer and more formal in character. In the case of the head of our establishment it was otherwise. I don't think my Uncle the Baillie did much in the way of directly encouraging John Cockerill to correspond with him. Indeed I know as matter of fact that his replies to John were rather stiff and curt in their scope and bearing, and far from prompt and regular in transmission. But John heeded not this. He persisted in favouring my Uncle the Baillie with the results of his observation of the doings of the great unpaid magistracy of the city in which he now dwelt, criticising, comparing, and offering suggestions on points on which he thought his widened knowledge might be useful.

By-and-bye my old fellow apprentice came out more strongly in a business capacity. He had become traveller to a wholesale firm; some said one of no great account, but John represented differently, and he delighted to send forward cards to customers, actual or possible, intimating with a considerable flourish that 'our Mr Cockerill will have the pleasure of waiting on you' at such and such a date. It was only eighteen months after he had left Greyness that, heralded by a liberal distribution per post of such cards, John Cockerill revisited it. Men of his stamp sometimes contrived to carry their samples in their hand; but that did not suit John's ideas of the dignity of his calling. He had a porter attendant conveying his strapped boxes in a hurley from street to street, as he went through 'the quiet old place,' as he styled it; and the impression made by 'our ex-townsman' was far from inconsiderable.

John wore a shaggy longish-tailed kind of coat, the exact likeness of which had not been seen in Greyness up to that date. On his head he had an imposing white hat, and he now wore not one but a couple of showy rings on the fingers of his right hand; and spoke with an appreciable southern accent of the kind that may be described as imitation Cockney. Though somewhat lofty and patronising in his manner toward such inconsiderable characters as myself, John was not too haughty to recognise and greet any of his old acquaintances; nor indeed to go out of his way a little to see them. And in this way he had among other places called at Richie Darrell's shop, stepping in with a loud

'Holloa, old man; still in the land of the living, an' inside your ancient counter.'

'Ye've the advantage o' me sir,' said Richie in a steady tone, and with a fixed look at his visitor.

'What, Richard Darrell, not know his former friends?'

'Ah!' exclaimed Richie, with an air of sudden recollecton. 'Loons commonly grow oot o' shape mair or less aboot the pulpy, beardless stage, fan they're i' the likeness o' neither man nor laddie; but I wud not 'a kent ye Jock, man. Maybe it's your uncouth claes; but seerly ye've clippit a nyeuk aff o' yer tongue ere ye cud 'a gotten sic a lingo. Hoo far south hae ye been – Newcastle?'

To my Uncle Sandy, Richie avouched his opinion of my old companion by the statement that 'that chiel Cockerill's grown a greater ass than ever,' and Sandy answered that John was developing in perfect consistency with the promise he had given. With my Uncle the Baillie, John Cockerill contrived with some difficulty to have one or two semi-confidential interviews, ostensibly on business, when he put on an air of more than his usual matured wisdom; and what was more, he contrived to get invited to my Uncle's house. His reception by my Uncle's wife was very much of the sort John desired, inasmuch as he was drawn on, or at least allowed, to expatiate on the enlarged experiences of life he had acquired since leaving the humdrum of Greyness, and the prospect that lay before him. And, of course, John did not fail to manifest his wonted gallantry in all becoming attentions toward the elder Misses Macnicol. The impression he had made thus far, there was reason indeed to believe, had been reasonably favourable. Mrs Macnicol had had her previous good opinion of him rather confirmed, and Miss Macnicol reproved her sister, Annie, for styling him 'a goose.'

Subsequent visits to Greyness in the like capacity, showed John Cockerill in the light of a man, always satisfied with himself, and always in the van of an advancing world. And when only some three years had expired, John was able once more to astonish his slow-paced friends of Greyness by the receipt of circulars, intimating that he had commenced business in company with another 'experienced in the trade,' under the firm of Cockerill & Sharp, importers of Spanish and Portuguese wines.

CHAPTER THIRTY-THREE

The General Situation

THE story of how Francie Tamson had been compelled to
disgorge the small amount of funds realised from the sale of
his sister Meggie's effects has been already told at sufficient
length. It was the acquisition of this money that had tempted
him to negotiate with my Uncle the Baillie concerning a loan
to the 'toonship' of Greyness, inasmuch as he felt that, by
clubbing it with the hoardings he had previously in hand, he
could make up a sum that, at the corporation rate of interest,
would earn as much as would make him sensibly richer. Now
that idol was smashed, and an actual loss had followed his
travail in the matter, equal to more than a year's 'onwal,'
on the sum total of his investments. How far the moral and
spiritual effect was beneficial, we are not prepared to say. At
any rate, if Francie did not repent of the part he had acted,
he at least lamented what had befallen him with sufficient
sincerity. By my Uncle Sandy's instructions, though not
through his hands, the money was at once paid over, in full
tale, to the proper recipient.

'The expenses? Oh; there's no charge for expenses; an' ye
may be perfectly sure ye'll have no further annoyance from
that quarter,' said the lawyer, as he counted out the cash on
his desk.

'But ye must have had trouble about it, an' should be paid,'
said Mrs Thomson.

'Oh, if that's a' – there are different modes o' gettin'
payment. An' we lawyers prefer takin't aff the defaultin'
side, d'ye see.'

Elsie Robertson warmly thanked the lawyer; and I have
not the least doubt she felt truly grateful to him. But as
she revolved in her mind the whole circumstances connected

with what, though a small matter in itself, was to her a matter of very considerable importance, she could not help the conviction that the deeper gratitude was due to another. On learning the issue her thoughts had at once flashed to my Uncle Sandy; and now, as she thought over it, she saw his hand in it all more and more. To express articulately her heartfelt thanks to him would have been an inexpressible privilege. But how best to do it without the appearance of unwarranted intrusion was a question that admitted of no very ready solution, especially as my Uncle did not afford the slightest opportunity for anything of the kind. To call upon him again formally for such purpose would have seemed like taking a doubtful liberty; and the thought of writing revived the long past even more keenly. And so, in the hope that the thanks so strongly felt might thereafter still be directly spoken with propriety, the widow simply sent a verbal message by her son Jamie.

And thus the days passed on. My Uncle the Baillie was still a leading figure in the public business of Greyness; and he had in addition somehow got on to the directorate of nearly every one of the larger joint stock concerns in the place. He was chairman in one or two cases, and in every case he attended his directoral meetings with wonderful regularity. In the chair at an annual meeting he had in large measure the notable and very useful faculty of being able, when the report was unsatisfactory, to cheer the shareholders by dwelling on the fact that, if the revenue had been bad there were a number of occult circumstances discovered by the directors tending to establish the belief that it might have been much worse. And he would group their own past figures and the figures of other similar concerns in various attitudes, either to show that these latter were in a worse plight than they; or that there was yet a deal of latent elasticity in their business. It is not needful to say that a chairman of this sort is invaluable to the undertaking that can command his services. It was indeed averred by some that my Uncle loved and cultivated his numerous directoral meetings as an easy and safe mode of earning the guinea and half-guinea fees allowed, and that for that end he would without fail put in appearance even when he was well aware that there was no business to transact. But I suppose my Uncle would just have said 'If others do the same, why not I? and it is not every man that has as good faculty for exigent occasions as myself.' At anyrate, it had come to pass that, in consequence of all these extraneous engagements, the business done in the warehouse of Castock & Macnicol was now controlled, as well as superintended, mainly by my Uncle Sandy.

Toward this another circumstance contributed. Whether my Uncle David ettled at some day exchanging the function of senior Baillie of Greyness for that of Provost of the burgh I know not. But, at anyrate, the question of social position bulked largely with those who would aspire to that highest position; and Mrs Baillie Macnicol never ceased to regret that, though one favourable chance occurred of her late lamented father aspiring to the Provostship, the fact that Baillie Castock persisted in dwelling in the old-fashioned family house up a narrow court, and actually eating his porridge sometimes before he was shaved in the morning, stood fatally in his way. The man who would be Provost did wisely to fortify himself in all matters of social dignity; and it so happened that my Uncle the Baillie was suddenly tempted to become the purchaser of a suburban residence, with forty acres of land attached. The proprietor of 'the Grove,' who could invite people out to see his 'place,' was in a position to patronise Greyness if need were, rather than be patronised by it in respect of municipal dignities, and my Uncle David was not likely to put his foot in it by offering his services too cheaply.

In the business of Castock & Macnicol the time had now come when, my apprenticeship being expired, I, in the natural course of events, should have been pushed out into the world; and a new apprentice being taken in the work would go on as before, the senior apprentice taking the position of first clerk. Several things conspired to change this order somewhat. The numerous outside engagements and frequent absences of my Uncle the Baillie, first and chiefly by throwing the business more exclusively upon my Uncle Sandy, made it needful that he should be relieved from the function of occasional traveller and so forth, which at once fixed my position so far. Then there was the case of the other apprentice, Jamie Thomson, for whom an exceptional arrangement was made.

Toward Jamie Thomson, during the two years he had been in the warehouse, my Uncle Sandy, while acting with all reasonable kindliness, had seemed to maintain a greater reserve than was his natural wont. On Jamie's side there was a feeling of something like unbounded respect for, and belief in my Uncle Sandy. As it concerned my Uncle David I am bound to admit that we had been accustomed occasionally to speak of even him with a certain levity as 'the governor;' and latterly he had been mentioned at times as 'the laird' – in playful allusion of course to his newly acquired landed property. In speaking of my Uncle Sandy, the idea of styling him governor could not conceivably have occurred to me, inasmuch as all my life long he had seemed so intimately bound up with my own individuality; and far less to Jamie Thomson, to whom he was on all occasions either 'Mr Macnicol' or 'the maister.' Now it so happened that, while diligent and attentive to his duties in the warehouse, Jamie Thomson had never foregone his desire to obtain such an education as should fit him for some of the learned professions; and in the pursuit of his studies, as he could contrive to go on with them in his leisure time, he too had become a stated customer at the shop of Richie Darrell, where his earlier literary furnishings had been acquired. In so visiting the bookseller, however, he was careful to avoid calling at the hours when my Uncle Sandy was likely to be there; and, indeed, seemed generally shy of his getting to know of his bookish tendencies; though all his aspirations in that way were freely enough confided to myself.

My Uncle Sandy knew all about it perfectly well, however; and as Richie Darrell had with some emphasis delivered his opinion concerning the 'bit knap o' a laddie' that came about his hand in search of this and the other book at attainable prices.

'He has the makin's in 'im o' something better nor a mere quill driver,' said Richie. 'Fat are ye gaen to mak' o' the birkie, Deacon?'

'Me mak' o' 'im!' said my Uncle. 'It's wi' 'imsel, I tak' it, that the decision o' that question lies. I cudna mak's future though I were to try't, nor if the richt material's in 'im cud I mar't.'

'Nae sae freely cynical noo, Deacon. Ye ken brawly the boy has pairts; an' if ye dinna, lat me gi'e ye the Dominie's word for't. He 's seerly a sufficient judge; an' he declares 'im to hae made remarkable progress. – It's a pleasure to hunt up a cheap copy for 'im fan it's to be had i' the toon.'

'Weel,' said my Uncle, 'I think the dominie an' you have judg't richt. I believe nane in pushin' loons beyond their capacity; or hoistin' them into this or the neist position without regaird to their fitness or merit, an' merely because ye may hae 'influence' to be able to dee't. But I do believe in affordin' opportunities to a lad that has gi'en some earnest o' bein' able an' inclin't to tak' advantage o' them; an' it may be offerin' a word o' counsel or advice if ye think ye hae such worth gi'en'—

'Dinna gae so far aboot it, man. He sud be a perfect idiot that had liv't to forty or fifty, an' learn't naething fae the lessons o' experience or itherwise that would enable him to be counsellor to youth o' fifteen.'

'Weel, weel; I defer to *your* wisdom at ony rate. An' aboot this laddie, what I've jist deen, aifter some cross-examination, an' a spate o' sic counsel as I had to gi'e, has been to arrange his hours an' duties, so that he can tak' the necessary classes at the burgh school; an' we'll see what comes o't – will that satisfy you that I'm amenable to some o' the promptin's o' humanity, even yet?'

'Verily, Deacon, ye're a man an' a Christian – though far fae a prudent person,' said Richie Darrell. 'The laddie'll dee credit to your discernment yet.'

The course adopted by my Uncle Sandy was one that exactly suited the circumstances, as it exceeded the most sanguine expectations of his beneficiary. Jamie Thomson's gratitude was unbounded, and his diligence continued unabated. And all this while the intercourse between my Uncle Sandy and Jamie Thomson's mother was of the slenderest and most incidental sort. As it happened that they both went to the same kirk, while their paths otherwise occasionally crossed, it could not but be that my Uncle should now and again come in contact with the Elsie Robertson of his more youthful days. Such occasions of meeting he neither shunned nor sought; and when they incidentally met the interview, in so far as my Uncle was concerned, was marked by perfect cordiality and perfect self-possession; that the latter feeling always prevailed on the other side I am not prepared to say. It did not seem that the intimacy here would increase. In another direction it was totally different.

One of my Uncle Sandy's most frequent visitors continued to be my cousin Annie Macnicol; and Annie's most recently acquired and cherished pet companion happened to be no other than Jamie Thomson's sister Jeanie; a bright-eyed merry-hearted girl of now ten or eleven years of age. Possibly led by Annie's example, possibly not, Jeanie Thomson got to claim my Uncle Sandy as a sort of universal referee on all subjects of interest to her. And that without the slightest reserve or the slightest doubt concerning his superior wisdom, or his willingness to hear and be interested in what was told him or asked of him. And evidently her instinct did not lead her far astray in this. Perhaps it was that the bonnie blue een and soft luxuriant ringlets of Jeanie Thomson reminded him of a time long ago; perhaps not. I don't know; only it was most clearly evident that in wee Jeanie Thomson my Uncle Sandy's interest was strong; and his liking for her unmistakable. He would sit watching her with an intent and occasionally abstracted look, as she prattled away confidentially, stroking her hair, it might be, at times, or even setting her on his knee in defiance of cousin Annie, who had now overgrown that privilege; and all in a way that was suggestive of my Uncle being a man who had a certain inner history to which his thoughts were at times wont to revert.

CHAPTER THIRTY-FOUR

Richie Darrell in the Great Shadow

'FAT an' scant o' breath' was the phrase used by Richie Darrell to indicate his early sense of failing strength and physical infirmity. From the date on which he had first uttered it in returning from a certain Sabbath day's journey with my Uncle Sandy, the bookseller had aged quite visibly. His walk was less nimble; and his long country excursions had been finally given up. Visitation of the churches had indeed ended on the occasion when he had gone to the graveyard of Bieldside, and satisfied himself that the name of the posthumously slandered Mary Darrell had at last been inscribed in its proper place. And not only so; for even the walk from his shop home to the Braehead had by and by become fatiguing, and latterly it had at times been more than enough for him. He would pause now and again by the way for a breathing space, and willingly enough lean on the arm of a friend, such as the placid Dominie Greig, when occasion offered. And when the air was moist and thick, or the raw eastern haar came up from the lower end of Greyness, days would pass on which the shutters of the shop would not be taken off at all.

That the bookseller was failing with a rapidity which his years did by no means account for, was manifest. But keen as his temper was he bore his infirmities uncomplainingly, and awaited the outcome with a steady and resolute onward look.

'Your complaint I fear is beyond the physician's skill, Richard; I hope you are not allowing your thoughts to rest on the frail perishing body, and neglecting the health of the immortal spirit,' said Miss Spinnet. She had come to the Braehead on finding the shop door shut, partly it might be from real interest in the bookseller, chiefly because she did not know how else to come at some book she wanted cheaply second-hand.

'The frail perishin' body's jist a little apt to assert it's maisterfu' control owre the feck o' your thochts an' sensations tee at times,' replied Richie Darrell. 'It's hardly a question whether ye'll alloo your thochts to rest upon 't.'

'Ah, my dear friend, you must not give way to such rational and materialistic ideas. A living spiritual faith will lift us above all that concerns the flesh.'

'I'm weel aware, Miss Spinnet; I'm weel aware o' the principle, only it's been strikin' me mair an' mair that siclike words spoken wi' the greatest unction, under the play o' full bodily health and ease, an' the enjoyment o' a' needfu' comfort an' even luxury, hae aifter a' but a vera shadowy an' uncertain spiritual value; and may even turn oot to be pure unreality an' sham fan the actual pressure comes that rends an' o'erwhelms the spirit through the body that's so closely and mysteriously linked wi't.'

Miss Spinnet did not pursue the argument further.

'It's a great inconvenience to me, Richard; but you don't think you could made an effort and get what I want?' said the lady.

'I mith as weel think to put my shouders to the twa door cheeks an' lift the hoose body bulk, as think to traivel to the middle o' the toon eenoo; lat alane searchin' fae place to place for hours it micht be,' was the bookseller's answer.

Miss Spinnet was very sorry; very sorry indeed; and having said so, she left with a fresh exhortation bearing on the sinfulness of ministering to the flesh.

To an ordinary eye this would have seemed about the least likely cause of lapsing on the part of the bookseller. For now that he was confined at home a good part of his time, with no stated female superintendence of his domestic arrangements, the general lack of comfort that distinguished his unpretentious abode had become very distinctly apparent. The fireplace manifestly had never once been properly redd up of late, neither had the dishes been quite cleared away or fully washed out. The floor had been only partially swept, and by a glance into the little back closet it was seen that

purpose-like bedmaking was a neglected art. The infelicity of
the existing state of matters in this respect had not apparently
struck Miss Spinnet further than that it led her to keep the
skirt of her spotless silk dress closely about her to avoid soiling
it on the dusty bits of furniture. To my Uncle Sandy, who
was not as a rule specially observant of domestic details, this
lack of comfort about the house had come to present itself as
a rather painful feature; and as things had been on the whole
getting worse, while the increased debility of the bookseller
made him less able to bear discomfort and privation, my
Uncle had a certain feeling of perplexity on the subject,
knowing, on the one hand, how readily active interference
even with the best intentions might be misconstrued and
resented, while, on the other hand, he felt strongly that the
friendship could not be reckoned very warm or sincere that
would not attempt something, be the risk what it might, in
order to effect some obviously needed ameliorations in the
domestic surroundings of the bookseller. Under the normal
state of things Annie Macnicol had been wont to do her
best occasionally at setting Richie Darrell's house in order;
but meanwhile Annie was elsewhere; and in any case my
Uncle felt that the occasional aid of some one with a more
experienced hand was wanted; but how to secure that, unless
the Dominie, who might venture where he could not dare,
could suggest a mode, he knew not.

After an interval of nearly a week, my Uncle Sandy had
gone to visit the bookseller with some such ideas as these
in his head, when his cogitations were pleasantly broken
up by finding Richie with his white nightcap on, seated in
his old-fashioned easy chair, the chintz cover of which was
evidently newly washed, while the grate was clean, the fireside
free of surplus cinders and ashes, and the place generally in
a wonderfully comfortable and tidy condition. Even Richie
himself was brighter and in better spirits than he had been
for weeks. He talked for a little freely on his favourite topics as
his 'bellows-power' would allow him; and by-and-bye, when
more personal matters were touched upon, he spoke with a
certain vivacity, and a good measure of his old chivalric air,
of 'a lady' who had called to see him, once and again, and

had not scorned to use her own hands to put his house to rights. Whether the bookseller knew who the lady was or not he gave no indication; nor did my Uncle in the least care to ask, being quite satisfied to witness the result of what he felt to be her labour of true Christian charity. In referring to the subject, however, Richie Darrell could not withhold a slight corruscation of appropriate jocularity.

'Ay, Deacon man,' said he, 'I doot my chance is but sma', life bein' unco near the back o' a day noo, but she's worth luikin' aifter to ony man o' sense like yoursel'. The feelin's an' faculty o' a true Christian woman, an' the gentleness an' pityin' sympathy o' a lady by nature, if no by birth, an' ane that has kent some sorrow 'ersel.'

The bookseller, whose tone had become serious and reflective, paused for breath, and then continued. '"Ministerin' spirits sent forth to minister;" it wud seem that as lang's we're i' the flesh, the ministry maun be manifestit through the flesh; yet hoo near hame to the invisible spirit it may come! But for a' the kin'ness an' comfort her presence has brocht to me, I can but say, God bless her, an' a that wish her weel.'

'A fervent Amen to that,' said my Uncle, 'an' I dootna the least that the blessin' 'll come.'

And shortly thereafter, bidding the bookseller good night, he left with the promise to return at an early date.

CHAPTER THIRTY-FIVE

An Old Compact Revived

WHEN my Uncle Sandy had left the bookseller's to pursue his homeward way his mind naturally reverted with a feeling of satisfaction to the improved state of comfort in which he had found him; and which seemed to put him in about as good a position domestically as his temper and habits of life would allow. Whoever the woman might be whose gentle and beneficent hand had been so opportunely stretched out to aid him, he did not doubt of her good offices being continued while needed; and upon Richie Darrell himself the effect thus far had evidently been both physically and mentally beneficial. My Uncle, in place of going straight to his lodgings, had turned in the direction of the north-western suburb of Greyness, with the purpose of enjoying the air of a fine spring gloamin', and cogitating meanwhile on the likelihood of the returning season bringing a partial restoration of health to the bookseller. He had walked on for a few minutes when his eye caught a female figure advancing by an intersecting street in the direction in which his own steps were bent. A single glance told him that the figure was none other than that of Elsie Robertson, and he at once crossed the causeway to meet her. My Uncle's greeting, as usual, was cordial, and his manner, as had been the case on every occasion on which they had incidentally met during the past two years, was free and unconstrained. They walked on together leisurely for a space, discussing the commonplaces of the hour; and when a turning had been reached at which the widow, whose purpose evidently was to go on to her home, would naturally diverge, my Uncle, with a slight appearance of hesitation but no actual pause, turned aside in part from the route he had meant to pursue, and accompanied her some distance further.

Another turning had been reached, considerably nearer Elsie Robertson's home, when my Uncle stopped short, as about to say good night. For a few minutes before but little had been spoken on either side; and it was evident that the lady had some struggle to find words in which she might express the feelings that for the time seemed to sway her mind.

'I'm asham't o' mysel',' she began, 'but I ken ye winna misun'erstand how I've never been able to thank you as I ought for a' your kindness.'

'It's hardly likely I'll misun'erstand if ye'll just lat me hae my way, an' say naething farther on the subject.'

'But, believe me, I'm deeply grateful Mr Mac—

'Elsie!' exclaimed my Uncle hastily and half impatiently. He looked up, and something like an angry cloud passed over his face, but as he looked again he saw her lip tremble and the tear start to her eye – 'Weel, weel,' said my Uncle quietly and seriously, 'ye see I'm nae wiser than ever I was.'

My Uncle paused for a single moment; he once more looked straight in the eyes of the woman by his side; and then silently drawing her arm closely within his own moved onward, not in the way she would naturally have taken in going homeward, but in the way he had meant to go himself.

'I only wished to say that I canna an' winna be styl't Mr Macnicol by you,' said my Uncle after a pause, and in half jocular tones. 'An' we must hear nae mair o' thanks, as ye value your ain peace o' min'. The idea's really oppressive to me; an' ye ken I cud never brook bein' cross't, hooever absurd my notions.'

'I can only say it's my pairt to be content wi' what ye think richt,' was the reply, uttered in a tone of eager earnestness, that was almost pathetic.

My Uncle had not asked Elsie Robertson whether she would be pleased to step out of her direct path, and accompany him on such route as he might choose to lead her. He had simply put her unresisting arm in his own, and walked on, as he might have done at a time eighteen years earlier, when she had the full control of his youthful affections, and he, as he fancied, of hers. And by-and-bye, he had thrown himself back upon old recollections of Strathtocher common to them both.

For a time his talk ran freely and discursively on. He spoke, though but briefly, of some whose faces and forms were gone for ever, but touched chiefly on scenes and incidents of a more general cast, and such as were fitted to illustrate Strathtocher life, as a whole, in its more characteristic aspects. And, as he went from point to point in his treatment of his subject, there were not wanting touches of the grotesque, and even ludicrous, that compelled something beyond a mere smile. In this fashion my Uncle had prolonged his very leisurely walk for a full half mile, when it seemed suddenly to strike him that another will than his own might desire to be consulted as to the proper direction in which their steps should be bent. He pulled up with the exclamation—

'But really this is too bad to take you out o' your way. We'll turn, an' I'll go along a wee bit wi' you.'

And so they walked on, and yet more slowly, my Uncle with Elsie Robertson's arm still closely linked in his, and Elsie herself with downcast eyes, and rapidly beating heart, walking by his side. Once or twice, when about to meet respectable denizens of Greyness, out for their evening stroll, and to whom she thought it probable, or certain, that my Uncle Sandy, as a moderately prominent citizen, would be known, the widow had indicated the intention of timeously withdrawing her arm from its place, and on each such occasion my Uncle, with a perversity all his own, had silently but effectually resisted such intention; once or twice with a comical glance into his companion's face, as who should ask, 'They have said; what say they? Lat them say.'

They walked and walked slowly; and now for a space but few words were said. But round-about as the way had been, the door of the widow's home was reached at last; and she turned to bid her companion a peaceful goodnight.

'May I come in?' said my Uncle Sandy, in a tone which one who had heard his previous speech would have called extremely deferential.

'Certainly; an' most welcome,' exclaimed Elsie Robertson, in pleased surprise at his making a request where she would not have dared to proffer an invitation.

In a couple of minutes thereafter, my Uncle was seated

in the neat but sparely furnished parlour, into which the descending sun still cast a flood of mellowed light. Elsie Robertson had taken her place at some distance. Her emotions were evidently not altogether to be kept under restraint, despite her best efforts to appear calm and at ease, and, for the first time since they had met, there seemed now to come the appearance of an awkward pause. It was only for an instant, however; when my Uncle, with the greatest deliberation and composure, rose from his place, and, taking her by the hand, led her across the floor and gently seated her beside himself. He uttered no other word, but, folding her closely in his arms, with the exclamation – 'My ain Elsie yet!' impressed a long and impassioned kiss on her lips.

And as they sat side by side, her hand fast locked in his, my Uncle stroked her cheek, and smoothed over the tresses on her brow, as had been his wont in the time byegone.

'My ain – my ain heart's love can it be? I'm unworthy surely, surely o' this;' and the tears came plenteously, as Elsie Robertson clung passionately to the man on whose breast her head had often fondly rested so many long years ago.

'Time has taught each o' us lessons,' said my Uncle, 'but it has made neither less to the ither. So let it be. If life is less in duration noo, it needna be less in aught else that mak's it worth havin'.'

CHAPTER THIRTY-SIX

Is it the Unexpected that Happens?

IT is the unexpected that happens we have been told, and the saying is doubtless true, literally, with a qualification. The qualification is found in the fact that, after all, an appreciable proportion of actual events in every man's experience do happen in accordance with previous expectation; and the simple reason why a greater proportion have not been looked for, and thus come as the unexpected, is that, through force of habit and otherwise, we each and all contrive systematically to shut our eyes to many of the considerations and circumstances that are expressly fitted to lead to the expectation of what is about to fall out in our experience.

Such philosophisings as these are not meant to apply particularly to the personal affairs of my Uncle Sandy in their latest recorded phase. The idea of the unexpected having in any wise overtaken or dominated him was not to be at all entertained; and I don't believe it had just then occurred to him in the least. True it was that his meeting with a certain woman had been unexpected when it happened, but the incident was substantially a repetition of what had happened repeatedly before, and might happen any day under very similar circumstances, and pass without the least noticeable influence on the life or history of the parties concerned. What followed was, I venture to believe, done with a very settled purpose and a very certain expectation. Seventeen years earlier, when she was less than twenty-two, and he but twenty-four, a courtship, dating on either side respectively, from boyhood and early girlhood, had been broken up disastrously for both. The fault was hers first, but my Uncle had years and years ago come to doubt whether it might not be his in part, secondly; and as the lapse of time and the lessons that life brings to all wise men and women taught him to judge more dispassionately of himself and others, he only felt the more that if at twenty-one a woman fails to know her own mind and at once to take up the guiding of her truer instincts under testing circumstances, it was not to be held a mistake such as ought never to be condoned. And, indeed, could the experience of seventeen years in advance have been compressed into two in his own case, he felt that his behaviour toward the repentant Elsie Robertson sixteen years ago would probably have been wiser than it had been; and possibly their relationship to each other might thenceforth have been very different. But all this was in the nature of conjecture and hypothesis. It was a matter of certainty that while my Uncle Sandy had learnt so to discipline his tastes and feelings as to be in large measure independent of others, and able on his own resources to find what gave life a rational interest, the place once occupied in his affections by the sweetheart of his youth had never been filled by another; nor had he cared to ask himself too closely whether the question of its ever being or not being filled was still an open one.

The practical point now reached by my Uncle, and I think quite deliberately, was just this – that he would begin his courtship again exactly where he had left it off seventeen years before. A deplorably unromantic business, considering the age and circumstances of the lovers, it will be said! I don't know, good reader, why it should; or why the loves of a man who has honestly breasted the blows of circumstance, and along with his gathered life-experience still retains the buoyant heart and genuine sympathies of youth; and a woman just come to full womanly maturity, who has known something of trial and sorrow and faced difficulty enough to show her womanly qualities, and put light and shade in her past experiences, should be held of so much less human interest than the loves of some boy and girl pressing ecstatically toward the goal of matrimony, with notions so totally self-centred and crude concerning all that lies before them in life; with so little actual knowledge of the demands that must inevitably overtake them, and so indifferent to all relative claims and duties outside of their two sweet selves, that the dispassionate onlooker is almost driven to the reflection that after all, 'youthful love' in its practical aspect is not seldom about the sublimest illustration of blind reckless selfishness that human nature affords!

But all this in passing.

It was Friday evening when my Uncle Sandy had called to ask after Richie Darrell. He had meant to call again on the Sunday, but did not get his purpose carried out; and ere Monday came, no further visit but one was needed.

'It's a' owre at the Braehead. The en's come an' come suddenly, as was to be expeckit' exclaimed Dominie Greig, stepping into the warehouse soon after ten o'clock on the Monday morning, and making directly up to my Uncle Sandy.

'The bookseller dead?' asked my Uncle, in a tone of surprise, 'When?'

'That question I can hardly answer vera precisely. Indeed, though I'm straucht fae that this minute, I haena ta'en time to look into particulars till I sud tell you the main fact.'

'Dear me; an' Richie's dead! Did he die alone?'

'Alone – quite alone. The death seems to ha'e been in a sort o' curious harmony wi' the life.'

'An' the particular time an' circumstances of course naebody'll ken exactly?'

'Nae exactly. He was seen by mysel' an' at least anither yesterday late i' the aifternoon; an' was at that time much as he had been for days, an' certainly nae appearin' to be worse. This mornin' aboot an' hour ago, I had a hurriet call fae the neebours wha had notic't the window blind undrawn, an' perfect stillness about the place; an' hae'in chappit at the door wi'nae result, an' syne try't to peep in at the window, only to obtain sic suggestions as the silence an' dim lichts o' the room cud gie, they cam' for me.'

'An' ye wud speedily ken what was to be kent?'

'It took a few minutes – indeed it seem't langer than patience could weel brook – till the door cud be forc't. Nae that I had the least doot o' fat had happen't within. But though I had my min' made up as to hoo it was wi' him, I cudna in the least 'a pictur't the circumstances o' the last scene as it evidently had been.'

'He was quite dead – had it been for some time?'

'Manifestly; but, truth to say, the time may be approximately fix't nearer the exact hour than I've yet try't to dee.

Upon his last Sabbath day even it had been substantially as on mony a previous ane. He had fastened his door for the nicht, steppit back to his easy chair, and, takin' aff his nichtcap, read his chapter in the big Ha' Bible, an' then half shut it, enclosin' a limb o' his favourite spectacles atween the leaves of the Book; an' aifter a meditation maist likely had ta'en his aul' silver watch aff the pin to wind it up. The outer cases were open't, the watch held in ae han' an' the short metal chain across his knee, as the fingers o' the ither han' had been layin' haud o' the key. But there an' then the arrest had come. An' there is a' that noo remains o' Richie Darrell: simply reclinin' a wee bit to ae side in the aul' easy chair; but, except that he has ceas't to breathe for some hours, wi' features as compos't an' peacefu' as if sleepin' the sleep o' perfect health, an' a' the pain an' weariness o' his later days gi'en place to an expression amaist o' quiet joyousness. – Ye'll aiven come an' see 'im as he is ere a han' is alloo't to touch the body or lay it oot as it maun be laid.'

My Uncle did not hesitate a single moment, but at once acceded to the suggestion of his friend the Dominie; and the two set out for the Braehead together. 'Tis enough to say that they found the state of matters there literally as described by Dominie Greig. The figure of the departed bookseller lay in a more than half-upright position, simply reclining backward a little in the left hand corner of the easy chair, with the face upturned, the eyes shut as if in peaceful sleep, and an expression that seemed to have wiped out the past ten years of his life, and carried him back to his physical prime; only the look was more radiant, and, so to say, spiritual, than either the Dominie or my Uncle could quite realise as familiar to the well-known features on which they now gazed. The limbs were cold and stiff, and the left hand still held in its rigid grip the bulky, old-fashioned silver watch, the outer cases of which had been taken off, and hung over the thumb in preparation for winding-up. The hour hand pointed to midnight; and not many minutes thereafter had been numbered when it too had ceased its beat, and lay still and silent in the stiffening palm. It was the bookseller's wont to go to bed at ten. To wind up his watch was the closing act of the day; and at that stage, on his last Sabbath evening, unseen by human eye, and without the faintest struggle, he had passed away from this scene.

'Truly, ye said, weel, the death had been in harmony wi' the life,' said my Uncle, after a brief pause, during which they had both gazed silently on the dead form before them. 'An' it strikes me that, if he had had his choice he would hae preferr't so to depairt, giein trouble to naebody.'

'It were a wise man's choice at least, I can fully believe, to desire to be cut off so,' replied the Dominie, 'as if death were the sudden lapse into a deep sleep – an' a' that we can judge by here seems to testify to that – for, ah me! to few, aiven o' the weakest and weariest, does the great change come withoot a hard and sair struggle, when the faintin' spirit must face a warfare in which there is nae dischairge all alone; an' whaur human aid an' sympathy can only stan' helpless in the dim an' recedin' background.'

They had next consulted about the steps necessary to be taken, and sundry dwellers in the neighbourhood, male and female, had gathered about in groups to retail what they knew, and what they conjectured, concerning the startling event that had occurred; to express their *ex post facto* vaticinations concerning the man that now lay dead, and about whom they had formed remarkably sage conclusions while he was yet alive; and to manifest their interest in, and intentions relative to, what ought now to be done. In this way, a certain number had found their way inside the house when the Dominie interposed with a quiet but decided request, that they would forthwith cease, and for the present retire to the scene of their own affairs, as he was master there meanwhile, and other authority had to interpone and make due inquiry.

''Twere aneuch to call back his spirit to the frail clay tenement, to think o' sic uncouth hysterical claiks puttin' han's on his remains,' said the Dominie. 'But I'm thankfu' beyond expression that ye sent sic suitable an' welcome help to soothe his last days. She'll nae doot be willin' to return an' see decently deen fat's still adee.'

'Me send help?' exclaimed my Uncle, in bewildered surprise. 'I'm asham't to say that at this moment I ken naething o' fa it was that gae the help ye speak o'. My niece, little Annie, your frien', gaed oot and in wi' the best intentions nae doot for a time. But the help needit cam' to be far mair than a lassie but half through her teens cud gie. Forbye, Annie's been fae hame; an last day I saw 'im he spak in his ain wye wi' the greatest satisfaction an' gratitude o' some 'lady' that had been statedly visitin' 'im.'

'I understan' it a' perfectly. Only it's little Annie I sud credit then, an' nae you. Weel, weel, she contriv't to get a service deen for which we sud baith be gratefu'. An' ye dinna aiven ken fa the lady was? Ye mauna be surpris't if I say that I thocht ye had been on sic terms o' intimacy wi' her as warrantit my supposin' that ye baith kent, an' had been instrumental in obtainin' her services; nor maun ye be disappointed when I tell you that it was the young widow, Mrs Thomson.'

'Excuse me, Mr Greig,' said my Uncle hastily, 'The time is hardly fittin' for explanation. That I may gie to you at another time so far as needit. But though my intimacy wi' the woman you name is at this moment as great as it properly can be, it is literally true that I kent naething o' this. Yet, if I am a little ta'en by surprise, believe me that, so far fae being disappointit, nae news to me cud 'a been mair welcome or gratifyin'. An' in proof o' my sincerity I hae nae hesitation in sayin' on her behalf that she'll be prepar't an' willin' to dee fat may yet be requir't, as soon as ye've tauld hoo maitters are.'

And so it was arranged. As it happens to all men similarly circumstanced, and not on the paupers roll, relatives male and female started up in abundance from various unascertained corners of the earth to prospect for the amount of property and the terms of settlement, but Elsie Robertson had full sway in laying out the corpse and otherwise caring for the ordering of the house until it was taken thence, and the door finally locked, to be reopened ere long to make clear way for some other; and Dominie Greig himself filled the office of chief mourner, till all that was mortal of Richie Darrell was also laid under the broad family gravestone in the quiet churchyard of Bieldside. And I even think, had the bookseller had the ordering of his funeral obsequies himself, he would have wished to have it precisely as it was.

CHAPTER THIRTY-SEVEN

My Uncle the Baillie has an Aristocratic Illness

WHEN the door of a once familiar howff has been conclusively shut upon you, and shut because the face that gave you welcome there has disappeared for ever, and the voice that was so well known to you in unceremonious greeting, familiar banter, or stiff debate has ceased to be heard in your ears, pensive thoughts concerning the instability of all things on this earth, and the ultimate significance of human life itself, are apt to take possession of the mind. It so happens, however, that, in the great majority of cases, the pressure of external circumstances in the never-staying current of time leaves the man who would keep in his rank and have steady footing amid the onward course of events little superfluous leisure to indulge in such reflections.

It was very much thus with my Uncle Sandy. His intimacy with Richie Darrell, the bookseller, had begun at a point in his own personal history that marked impressions of life he could not well forget, and which, under a gradually mellowing light, had so far shaped and shaded all his future. At precisely the most sanguine period of life, he had found himself a man triply broken – in health, in such worldly prospect as seemed before him, and, hardest of all, in his heart's dearest affections. The caustic, half-misanthropic, and occasionally wayward utterances of the solitary bookseller had at once caught his attention in a half-inquiring, half-combative kind of way; and they more or less continuously possessed a certain fascination for him. And, while that was so, he had found occasion to note and steer clear of the impenetrable angles of Richie Darrell's character, which prevented his fitting in to some circle of social or family life as he otherwise might, and as his sterling worth would have enabled him to do to the advantage of others as well as himself. Thus had he been helped, as he believed, to a somewhat juster view of his own past and its experiences, and of himself as related thereto. And though there remained a certain feeling of regret that his path had been perforce turned aside from the kind of pursuits he had naturally chosen and loved, to such as he had adopted merely to earn a piece of bread, my Uncle had long ago come to see that there was a purpose served by what had befallen him—

'Doubt the doctrine o' a special Providence!' he was wont to say. 'The man's history maun hae been o' a radically different cast fae mine that wud find it possible to dee onything o' the sort. I can luik back wi' humiliation upo' follies, an' waur than follies, o' my boyhood, that hae had issues so far reachin' that I canna to this day estimate their full ootcome. But if I had been alloo't my full swing, if I hadna kent what it was to be batter't doon, fairly defeatit, even to the upsettin' an' erasement o' a' my cherish't purposes in life, an' compell't to go where I had nae wish, I feel morally certain, that o' little value as my life may hae been, it wud nae only hae been o' less value, but, in a' probability, wud hae been fettered an' marred in ways from which, nae thanks to me, I've been keepit free; an' marked by collapse an' failure whaur the crudities o' a sanguine temperament led me to look forward to certain an' unqualified success.'

But as suggested, my Uncle Sandy did not find the affairs of life so arranged that he could well sit down and indulge pensive musings concerning the decease of his friend the bookseller. As has been already indicated, the recent course of my Uncle the Baillie had been that of so far withdrawing from the active management of his rather quiet-going old-fashioned business. He liked to cultivate his directoral engagements, and though he still had the largest share in the business of Castock & Macnicol, it had come to be more in the sleeping-partner fashion. He knew that his interests were perfectly safe in the hands of my Uncle Sandy, whose first thought always was conscientious performance of his full share of work; his reward for such performance being only an after consideration. A combination of qualities, which, if admirable on general grounds, was not perhaps the one best fitted to achieve 'success' in the usual acceptation; and I think that as between the two partners the order given was pretty much reversed in the case of the senior, not altogether to his disadvantage. Anyhow, my Uncle the Baillie did not grudge to allow my Uncle Sandy the privilege of looking after the warehouse as assiduously as he chose; and for himself he was equally careful that his own full pecuniary claims should not be overlooked.

In the normal condition of things, my Uncle Sandy's hands were in this way pretty full, but a special cause of engrossment in business had arisen from the fact that my Uncle the Baillie had fallen sick. What the exact nature of his illness was, was never precisely stated, only it was suggested to be of the select corporation character that attacks only baillies and people of such-like status; and the vulgar and elderly man who acted as our warehouse porter, had nearly put his foot in it, by declaring aloud to several inquirers that the Baillie had 'jist gotten a snifterin' kin' o' caul' in's heid, an' a touch o' the rheumatics aboot the sma' o's back to keep it company.'

With much assiduous doctoring and nursing, my Uncle the Baillie, who up to that time had been a remarkably healthy man all his life, had been got to the stage of convalescence, when a new and irresistible idea struck his wife. Hitherto, when society in Greyness felt the need of physical recruitment on approved lines, it had been 'the thing' to undertake a journey to the famed mineral Spa of Pitcaithly. Strathpeffer had indeed received some attention, but Pitcaithly was the proper resort; as for Pananich it was by far too common to be thought of. Latterly, however, such places as Harrogate and Buxton had come into notice in select circles; and as it was known that certain red-nosed choleric old gentlemen, with tender toes, connected with the county, had been visitors at either of these places, the report was speedily abroad that Baillie Macnicol, whose 'constitution' generally was understood to have got more or less impaired, had been suffering from gout ('gut' Mrs Macnicol inadvertently pronounced it), and was going to Buxton for the benefit of the waters.

Now as it was universally known that no Provost of Greyness, even, had up to that date taken the waters at Buxton, it will be believed that the stroke accomplished by Mrs Macnicol in this matter made rather a sensation. Whether the Macnicols meant to rate themselves as gentry or what, was the great point. Strathpeffer or Pitcaithly were emphatically declared to be good enough for them; while some were uncharitable enough to declare that 'fient a flee ails 'im; jist anither attempt. Was there ever sic a woman! She made Dawvid a Baillie at the first shot; an' neist a bit bonnet laird; an' noo she wud fain hae fowk to believe that the generation o' 'im's been eatin' venison an' drinkin' wine sae lang 't the canker o't's bizzin' oot at's nose an' the point o's muckle tae!'

While my Uncle the Baillie and his wife were absent at Buxton, the charge of the household was entrusted to their elder daughter, Miss Amelia Matilda, in whose prudence and circumspection her mother had the fullest confidence. How far these qualities were generally exercised I may not here say, though certainly Miss Macnicol contrived to bring me pretty promptly into hot water; the cause being her sister Annie. Annie had never foregone her habit of visiting my Uncle Sandy and myself at Mrs Geils's lodgings; and as she happened to be a special favourite with that worthy person, one of the features in whose character was the rare and invaluable one of being able at seventy to enter with the keenest interest and zest into the thoughts and feelings of mere unsophisticated girlhood, it was not likely she would soon do so. And why should I not like my cousin Annie to be about me, with all her homely honest inquisitive ways? What her elder sister, as temporary head of the house now did, was to write to her parents expressing her strong sense of the extreme impropriety of 'a young man of eighteen,' and 'a grown girl of sixteen,' persisting, against all sense of shame, and the express warnings of those who were older than themselves, in being so much together 'under such unbecoming circumstances;' in addition to being frequently 'out in the streets in company late at night.' The latter charge, of course, referred to my seeing Annie safely home as occasion required.

The consequence of this interference of Miss Amelia Matilda was, that I received a letter from my Uncle the Baillie (mature reflection led to the conclusion that it had been written at the sight of his wife), in which my conduct was commented upon with a severity that took me utterly aback; and almost staggered me into the belief that somehow, unconsciously to myself, I must be an abandoned young villain after all. A remedy in the shape of dismissal from the service of Castock and Macnicol was hinted at, and warning given that my future behaviour alone would determine my fate.

It was the first angry missive I had ever had from my Uncle the Baillie; and being emphasized with some formidable references to the writer's ample judicial opportunities of testifying to the truth of the maxim, *facilis descensus,* &c., it so discomposed me that I could not make up my mind to show it even to my Uncle Sandy, my invariable counsellor in matters that seriously perplexed me.

CHAPTER THIRTY-EIGHT

A Passage in the Family History

FROM the time that the youngest of my Uncle David's numerous family of daughters had got beyond the stage of mere childhood, and the two elder ones were fairly entitled to be recognised as marriageable young ladies, the cares that devolved upon my Uncle's wife had naturally changed in character; but it could not by any means be said that they had lessened in amount. To each of the young ladies opportunity had been afforded of acquiring what in Greyness society was understood to be a finished education. And with the single exception of the erratically disposed Annie they all gave good promise of turning out accomplished young ladies, according to the standard and requirements of Greyness society. It was the ruling desire of their mother that they should do so; and if they were granted grace to respect their position and themselves as its occupants, she felt that she could be happy and hopeful of the future. The natural probability being that a black sheep will occur in every family, Annie had almost necessarily come to be viewed as giving strong ground of suspicion. And hence her elder sister's commendable vigilance already mentioned.

But my Uncle David's wife had begun to think much about the prospects that lay before the two eldest of her daughters in particular; Annie she had frequently pronounced hopeless, declaring that if she ever got married at all it would be to some man of low position, if not questionable principles. And the subject had come to be introduced by her as a matter of connubial conference quite as frequently as my Uncle found to be agreeable.

'Bless me, 'oman,' said my Uncle David. 'Are young women, fan they get past bairnhood, to think o' naething but hoo they're to get marriet?'

'Noo, Dawvid Macnicol, dinna gie way to feelin's unbecomin' your position; an' min' ye've ye're duty as a pawrent,' said Mrs Macnicol.

'Weel hae I been tell't that; but fat has my duty as a pawrent to dee wi' stuffin' the lassies' heids fu' o' notions as gin only gentry were fit company for them?' replied my Uncle, rather impatiently.

'Gweed forgie you, man, to say the like. Hoo sud I stuff their heids wi' ony thing o' the kin'. Its talents an' mainners that mak' the man, an' wi' that he may belong to ony rank in life. Ill wud it become *me* to say itherwise. Only it's necessary, ere a woman condeschen' to mairry below 'er position, that she sud ken that she's mairryin' principle an' capacity, an' nae takin' peertith an' shiftlessness baith.'

I don't know exactly how far my Uncle felt flattered or otherwise by this speech; or whether it recalled visions of the time when he had been a suitor for the hand and heart of the fair Miss Castock – vulgar report had it that, as matter of fact, the lady, not being unduly troubled by rival suitors, had come pretty rapidly 'ben' the string' on her father's 'strappin' weel-faur't chiel' of an assistant. Still less can I say whether my Uncle's wife spoke at all in the knowledge of forthcoming events. But certain it was that by-and-by, and some time after the return of my Uncle and his wife from Buxton, Greyness society was set agog by the intelligence that Miss Amelia Matilda Macnicol, eldest daughter of David Macnicol, Esq., of the Grove, senior magistrate of Greyness, was about to be married to a rising Glasgow merchant. Who the merchant was had been modestly kept in reserve for the time.

My Uncle David and his wife had acted prudently, no doubt, in all the circumstances. When it had first come to light that John Cockerill was keeping up an inflammatory correspondence with Amelia, Mrs Macnicol had endeavoured to temporise by getting Amelia's attention engrossed in the subject of new and fashionable dresses, and family excursions hither and thither. This for the time seemed to have the desired effect, and Mrs Macnicol went to Buxton reposing the fullest confidence in her dear child. It somehow happened, however, that during her absence John Cockerill found it necessary to pay one or two lengthened business visits to Greyness; and it was certain that a good deal of his leisure time, which seemed ample, was spent in the company of Miss Macnicol either at the Grove or squiring her here and there.

It was at the very date of this visit, as I afterwards maliciously noted, that the tell-tale letter was written by Amelia, which caused me so much trouble.

Be that as it may – as Mrs Macnicol speedily found, her darling Amelia Matilda's passion had burst out afresh, and at least as fiercely as ever. When the fact had come to her knowledge, and she had endeavoured to make the maternal voice heard in a severer key, Amelia had hysterically declared that to die would be a simple and easy matter, but to live without John Cockerill was the sheerest example of the impossible. Mrs Macnicol was still disposed to exhaust all likely measures with a view to ward off at least for a time an alliance about the propriety of which she was not by any means assured. She argued that John was a mere youth and had got no definite position, had hardly even given proof of possessing the qualities that would enable him to attain such. But Amelia promptly retorted by quoting her mother's own laudatory estimate of John as the Baillie's confidential clerk and amateur adviser, in proof of his capability. The extreme sordidness of the views urged upon her that he had not yet got time to become wealthy shocked Amelia, who, if her fate could only be linked with her dearest John could joyfully face poverty, hardship, or trial in any form. But, so far from poverty, it was only needful that he should have the comforting presence of one who loved him to enable him to hold on assuredly in the path to certain opulence and civic distinction. My Uncle's wife came irresistibly to the conclusion that John Cockerill's powers as a wooer had been exercised to effectual purpose while she was partaking the amenities of life at Buxton. The case being as it was, she had no help but reveal it in all its seriousness to my Uncle the Baillie.

My Uncle had not fully heard what his wife had desired to tell him when he incontinently exhibited tokens of getting choleric, and forthwith denounced the whole affair as outrageous, and John Cockerill as an empty impertinent cub and pretentious adventurer.

'I'll seen pit my fit upo' that,' said my Uncle.

Perhaps my Uncle thought he could; and I have not the least doubt that he very willingly would have put his foot upon it. But I suspect when a daughter is sufficiently resolute in such circumstances, and when she has got her mother round to the point of being apprehensive of what may happen if her dear child's wishes are thwarted, the authority of the father and all the sanctions he can bring to bear in the opposite direction do not count for a great deal. And accordingly, though my Uncle the Baillie stormed in a way that produced tears in some abundance, and peremptorily prohibited all further correspondence, the question of Amelia's marriage was fully settled by the time his wife had taken to concealing the advent of John Cockerill's letters by allowing the outer envelope to be addressed to herself, while she expressed her fear that the result of postponing the marriage for even a twelvemonth would be that in the interim Amelia would 'die in a decline.' And that at least was prevented by 'the happy event' being celebrated at the Grove within six months.

I am not particularly concerned with the marriage settlement of my Uncle David's daughter and son-in-law farther than to say that it was understood to have caused some disappointment to, and even to have upset certain business calculations of, the firm of which the latter was senior partner. With the caution native to him, my Uncle had seen fit to tie up his daughter's dowry so that her husband had next to no control over it. To the young and enterprising firm of Cockerill & Sharp a certain amount of cash, even if it were got off a marriage portion, would have been very acceptable; indeed, had become indispensable if the business of the firm was to go on at all. And as it was not forthcoming the usual result ensued. When John Cockerill had exhausted his resources in the sort of operation vulgarly known as 'raising the wind,' he once more addressed himself to the composition of a private circular, in which it was set forth with regret, that owing to 'failure of the vintage, and consequent heavy losses through our foreign correspondents,' the firm of Cockerill & Sharp, importers of Spanish and Portuguese wines, &c, were under the necessity of temporarily suspending payment, and with a view to an ultimate favourable solution, the concurrence of creditors in an interim payment of 2s 6d in the £ was hoped for.

Unhappily, the creditors took a different view, and stringent measures being threatened, the junior member of the firm, Mr Sharp, who, unbeknown to the leading partner, had adhibited the firm's signature to certain bills of a questionable sort, quietly took permanent leave of the business on a certain morning, leaving John Cockerill to wind up or go on as he might find convenient.

CHAPTER THIRTY-NINE

Changes in the Warehouse of Castock & Macnicol

THE burden of the letter of reproof I had received from my Uncle the Baillie had lain heavily on my mind for some days when I resolved that I would take my office companion, Jamie Thomson, into my confidence and obtain his assistance as a casuist in establishing a clear mental vindication of myself. I would not have dared to make a formal reply to my Uncle; and indeed he had proceeded on a series of assumptions and reasonings that excluded my right to do so. Jamie heard my statement with a sort of fixed half-abstracted look, not altogether usual on his face, and when it was ended, very much to my surprise, said in an abrupt tone, not by any means familiar to him,

'Weel, I think yer Uncle sud ken better than ye dee fat's richt.'

'But he's been taul' clypes 't's nae true!' exclaimed I, under some feeling.

'Ye ken brawly it's true aneuch, the principal pairt.'

'That Annie comes to oor hoose?' asked I.

Jamie Thomson looked an affirmative with something like a gleam of anger in his eyes, but without speaking.

'An' dee ye think 't my Uncle Sandy wud alloo onything that's nae richt?' said I indignantly. 'Or that he disna care as muckle for Annie as her ain father can dee?'

Jamie Thomson, as has been already said, had unbounded faith in my Uncle Sandy; and the quotation of his name in the way of sanction or authority was never without its effect upon him. Still he was clearly not satisfied concerning the integrity of my position in the matter; and we parted under a certain degree of misunderstanding, if not also of mutual distrust. I had on the whole an increased feeling of perplexity where I had counted on the opposite; and the more I reflected on my companion's peculiar view and short, sharp utterances, the less could I understand the position he seemed to have assumed. Nor did I get to understand it for a long while after.

It was soon after this that, Jamie Thomson's apprenticeship being out and something more, my Uncle Sandy took him into his own room one day and expressed to him his belief that the time had now come when the proper following out of his studies rendered it desirable that his time should be more fully at his own disposal than was compatible with certain fixed office hours daily. Jamie acquiesced, but went on to say that he did not see his way quite to that yet, when my Uncle said—

'Oh, weel; but I'll arrange a' that; an' ye had better go on at ance wi' your classes regularly.'

So Jamie Thomson entered on his work as a medical student. Thereafter I saw him only now and again for several years. A new apprentice – a dull, matter-of-fact lad – came in his place; and while my responsibilities were increased, the nature of my companionships was so much altered, that I, for almost the first time in my life, began to think this earth a mutable and disappointing scene.

CHAPTER FORTY

My Uncle Sandy Wedded

THE unlooked for resumption between two persons of a correspondence that had suffered absolute and complete interruption for the space of seventeen years is fitted, under any circumstances, to stir feelings that go somewhat deeper down than the mere surface. Of course, where the correspondence has been out-and-out commonplace, and the individuals between whom it has existed partake of the same character, even such an event may pass over without the thought occurring that the circumstance affords any particular material for reflection. But in the majority of cases we should imagine the mere lapse of time, and the change that such lapse inevitably makes upon the individual himself, as a reasonable being, must bring the reflective faculties into play to more or less useful purpose. And at any rate, where the correspondence that had been broken off and has been renewed is a correspondence of the kind that brings the individuals concerned into the closest relations that can exist between two human beings on this earth, an event such as that cannot happen without both the one and the other being moved by feelings pretty nearly as profound as their natures are capable of entertaining. I don't mean in the least to trouble the reader by analyses of the feelings of either my Uncle Sandy or his old sweetheart, Elsie Robertson, on, and subsequent to, the night on which he had met her by accident and accompanied her home, with results which the reader already knows. Neither shall I attempt to settle such questions as whether it would have been better for one or both that their loves had been consummated in marriage seventeen years earlier; whether, as Elsie had undeniably been unable ever fully to undo the grasp with which her affections clung to my Uncle, she could have gone through all the experience of being married to, and suffering with and for another, and yet remained worthy the man of her first love; and whether, consequently, my Uncle Sandy, who, in the course of all these bygone years had, without his seeking it, acquired among his confreres the reputation of a prudent and rather wise man, was not now about to commit himself to the one egregiously and irretrievably foolish act of his life.

Human nature is a decidedly composite affair; and if our judgements of it would be other than mistaken, superficial, or unjust, they must not only be discriminating, but the result of a considerably more patient and sympathetic study and interrogation of all the facts and circumstances under which we find it acting than we are occasionally prepared to bestow.

It simply came to this, that with his eyes perfectly open to it all, my Uncle Sandy, when he once again looked in Elsie Robertson's face and took her hand in his in Mrs Geils's parlour, felt that he stood precisely as much nearer to her than any other human being, as he had done before their parting; and in so far at least as that which on her part caused their separation was concerned, something in the nature of instinct or intuition told him that there was less between them than there had ever been. On her side, as has been already in part indicated, the irresistible feeling was that, with an insuperable barrier placed between them, all the former power to command her affections remained with my Uncle; while within her bosom there was a willingly yielded sense of trusting respect which perhaps had never so fully existed before as now, when the opportunity for its exercise must be restrained within narrow and formal limits.

Of my Uncle's renewed courtship, what need to speak? No tremulous impassioned pleadings, no formal words of asking even, were used in settlement of the great question toward which it all tended. To either or both that done in articulate form would have seemed too purely mechanical and unreal to be from the heart. By the one single act of deliberately seating her at his side, and calling her his 'ain Elsie,' my Uncle had wiped out all that had ever come between them as lovers. And thus far they stood to each other as they had done seventeen years before – with this difference, that Elsie Robertson seemed now more eagerly anxious to rest with submissive confidence in my Uncle's judgment than it was even possible for her to have been when they had last stood on a similar footing.

Naturally enough my Uncle neither sought to conceal nor to publish abroad the position in which matters stood with him. If people took note of the fact that he omitted no legitimate oportunity of being in the company, abroad or at home, of the woman of his earlier and later choice, he saw no reason why they should not; and if they failed to take note of it and draw the fitting conclusion, he was not disappointed. As every man ought in such circumstances, he felt honoured and not ashamed if his name were coupled with that of the woman he meant to make his wife; and on fit occasion in fit company would not shrink from letting it be known that he was proud to own the relationship.

'Ah! an' aifter a' I was richt in a blin' kin' o' way in my guess aboot the lady,' said Dominie Greig, when my Uncle had made a certain communication to him, first of all men, concerning his intentions.

'Richt certainly in the essence o' the maitter, though the detail was owre complicated to be seen through accurately by you, or maybe ony ootsider,' said my Uncle.

'Weel, weel, never min'; the details concern you an' her; the main fact has certainly its interest for me. An' I hae seen enough to be able to say she's a person o' sense an' true feeling, wi' the womanly faculty an' gentle tact that are least heard an' quickest felt whaur the need is greatest.'

'It wud be sheer affectation in the cast o' ane that I've deliberately re-chosen as my ain aifter the testin' o' time, an' sic chance an' change as micht weel hae made oor separation perpetual, if I didna confess that I hold every word ye've uttered to be the literal truth,' said my Uncle gaily, yet with a sincerity that was unmistakeable.

'I sud think little o' your hert or judgement if ye didna,' replied the Dominie. 'An' forbye it's the only sure an' lastin' foundation o' every true mairriage that a man respect the woman o's choice on clear grounds, as well as love her for what his instinctive promptings hae led him to see as loveable in her.'

'An' if there's ae thing I'm surer o' noo than ever afore it is that I can yield that respect in full measure.'

'Ah, weel, weel,' said Dominie Greig, 'The event has come wi' some feelin' o' surprise, it wud seem, in the case o' ane that had been suppos't resolv't on the gweed aul' maxim *festina lente*; an' I congratulate you wi' a' my heart.'

What will Mrs Geils think of it all? had been a keenly-revolved problem in the mind of my Uncle Sandy. Not that he dreaded any directly expressed disapproval of his purpose; but it would be a considerable something deducted from his sum of happiness if she merely maintained a negatively hostile attitude. To my Uncle's great satisfaction Mrs Geils asked to be introduced to his prospective wife, when she forthwith declared her belief that it was full time he should be married, and that the woman he had chosen had all the manner of a prudent and, capable as she was, 'an engagin' person.'

When the news had reached the family of my Uncle the Baillie, Mrs Macnicol desired her husband to say how far he had of late been keeping himself personally cognisant of the business affairs of the firm of Castock & Macnicol.

'What d'ye mean, my dear?' asked my Uncle the Baillie, in a tone of some severity. 'Lat that alane, 'oman. My brither's deein' what 'll be a wise thing for 'imsel', an' for the business he'll see his ain interest suffer seener than mine.'

'Dawvid Macnicol, dinna pit *your* meanin' upo' *my* words. Forbid't I sud cast doot upo' Sandy's integrity or his diligence; but – if it hed to be at his time of life – he mith 'a min'et 't's position's different fae fat it was at the time't he cam' here, a raw countra lad.'

'We've nae call to say a single word i' the maitter. There's every reason to believe that she's the woman that'll mak' 'im happy; an' that's aneuch.'

'An' aifter fat's come an' gaen atween them! I'm sure if he had wantit to tak' up hoose, as I've af'en urg't 'im to dee, ony o' the girls wud 'a cheerfully devotit themsel's to makin' 'im comfortable. But I'se – haud my – tongue!'

It was in the very recent past that the firm of Cockerill &

Sharp had collapsed, one incident of which had been, that to prevent certain ugly proceedings being taken against John Cockerill in connection with one or two firm bills, signed by his absent partner (but of which John to do him justice had known nothing), my Uncle had had to pay down a considerable sum. And the whole matter still weighed on the family. Otherwise I am not sure that Mrs Macnicol would have been disposed to hold her tongue quite so readily.

And so the wedding of my Uncle Sandy came off in due form. Of the leading assistants thereat Dominie Greig occupied a chief place, inasmuch as he performed the duty of giving away the bride; and my cousin Annie, to her own extreme satisfaction, had devolved upon her the onerous function of bridesmaid.

CHAPTER FORTY-ONE

The Status Quo

WHETHER my Uncle David should or should not ever become Provost of Greyness was a problem that for a while seemed to hang in doubtful suspense. Certainly that high honour had been fully within his grasp had his ambition goaded him into action. But my Uncle David was naturally a cautious man. A space of five or six years had passed since the date of the events last recorded, and he remained my Uncle the Baillie still. All risk of his budding into Provost might now be regarded as nearly over.

And I think my Uncle David was right. The gentle persuasions to which he had been subject may have been difficult to withstand; and to forego the honour of having one's name inscribed in the roll of municipal dignities of the highest rank certainly implied a large sacrifice. Still when a man has got to the highest pinnacle, the 'white light' in which he stands is apt to expose whatever of feebleness, inanity, or vacillation there may be about him in a rather merciless way; thus revealing, it may be, a personality of dimensions considerably smaller than had been anticipated; whereas he who might have stood on that pinnacle, but prefers to continue on the second-rank level of the sage and trusted senior baillie, with all the unexhausted possibilities of his character about him, may go on to the end of his life with an unquestioned reputation for fathomless profundity and a capacity of the highest order.

The circumstances just stated make it fitting that our story should now take end; as it shall take end with the briefest possible indication of how matters have gone with certain others with whom the reader has been made acquainted.

My Uncle Sandy has lived through those years in his own undemonstrative fashion. Utterly eschewing municipal ambitions, his spare time is amply taxed by a variety of extraneous matters in which his help and advice are sought; yet does he ever contrive, come what may, to spend an ample portion of his leisure in his own quiet and comfortable home, in the company of the woman who is more to him than all the earth besides, and to whom it is the intensest satisfaction to find fit and helpful association in interpreting his purposes, and aiding their accomplishment; in acting the part of sympathetic listener, and by quick and appreciative suggestion resolving the doubts that otherwise would have been cumbersome on many matters of detail; and generally in doubling to him the value of life by the most intimate participation alike in its joys and its sorrows, its pleasures and its trials.

The home of my Uncle is graced too by the presence of one who is a true daughter to him in all loving attachment and confiding regard – Jeanie Thomson, now a blooming, womanly girl of eighteen.

My old companion, Jamie Thomson, has followed his medical studies to excellent purpose. Graduating with honours, he next, after a period of hospital practice, and further study in the great metropolis, competed with marked success for an appointment in the public service. And during his time of waiting till he should go abroad, Jamie returned to spend a couple of months in Greyness. I too, in my small way, had been a short distance abroad in the world, and had returned shortly before on the footing of undertaking duties of a more responsible kind in the business of Castock & Macnicol. When I now met Jamie Thomson it was under my Uncle Sandy's roof, and in the company of my cousin Annie and his own sister Jeanie. Annie, who had certainly grown to be the handsomest, as she was the best informed and most pleasantly unconventional, of my Uncle David's daughters, had, as was no doubt right and proper, replaced her unsophisticated romping girl habits by a somewhat more coy and maiden-like demeanour. Yet was the evening we spent together a very enjoyable one to all concerned; and, at its close, when not I but Jamie Thomson was asked to see Annie to her home, the manifest alacrity with which he undertook this duty brought forcibly to my mind the unaccountable severity with which he had at a previous time regarded similar intercourse between my cousin and myself.

'Oh, ay; ye think it a' richt to gae hame wi' Annie yoursel'! What gar't you think it so reprehensible in me?' asked I on the succeeding day.

'Me! Did I?' said Jamie with a laugh, 'I suppose I must hae been under some grim hallucination!'

'Surely I had as gweed a richt to tak' care o' my ain cousin as ony body cud?'

'Ah, Benjie, ye was but a mere laddie than. It was proper to gie you a caution!'

'An' ye think caution's nae needit noo?'

'Far fae that. I'm nae sure but ye stan' as much in need o't as ever in some quarters.'

'Oh, aye; only ye think Annie may be alloo't what freedom she thinks proper noo?'

'Nae quite that; jist siclike freedom as ye wud think fittin' for my sister, Jeanie!' said Jamie, somewhat slily, as it seemed to me.

And so, as long ago as the date of my Uncle David's angry letter, jealousy of myself as a rival in Annie's affections had found a lodgment in the breast of poor Jamie! And it was only now that I became fully aware of the fact, when – I must freely admit – all risk of such contingency had passed away.

Before Jamie Thomson left Greyness to go to India he and my cousin Annie had become formally engaged lovers, and as Jamie's reputation as a distinguished student and young man of high promise had ere then made his name notable even among the notables of Greyness society, Annie's position and credit in the family of my Uncle the Baillie had become not a little enhanced. Indeed without thought of such a thing on her part she found herself now in some danger of being held up by her mamma as the model daughter of her family; a circumstance accounted for in part it may be by the fact that none of the others had as yet given definite hope of passing from her charge into that of some proper guardian of the opposite sex.

As for Amelia Matilda, John Cockerill, fairly beat out of his sphere as an importer of Spanish and Portuguese wines, had once more returned to Greyness, where he has a thriving family of four small children. His profession is that of commission agent; he is still powerful in the preparation of circulars; and the promulgation of ideas concerning various newly patented articles of high value engrosses much of his attention. But as the purchasing community and he do not seem to be usually of one mind on the merits, he has always a considerable amount of spare time on hand for philanthropic and municipal purposes. Indeed his latest attitude is that of offering his services, in accordance with a 'numerously signed requisition,' as a member of the Town Council of Greyness; and the grounds of his claim are avouched to be 'public spirit and business capacity.'

GLOSSARY

Words cited below are glossed as far as possible to preserve the nuance and implication they bear in their specific context in the novel; uncertainty is indicated by a question mark.

'*a*, I
a', all
abeen, above
aboot, about
accoonts, accounts
adee, to do
ae, one
aff, off
agley, crooked
aifter, after
aifterhin', after
aifterneen, afternoon
ain, own
airm, arm
airt, art
aitseed, oatseed
aiven, even
alane, alone
alloo, allow
amaist, almost
amo'/amon', among
an', if
ance, once
ane, one
aneth, beneath
aneuch, enough
anither, another
apairt, apart
apen, open
a'thegither, all together
atween, between
atweesh, between
au', ?awl [?misprint aul'?]
aucht, eight
aul'/auld, old

ava, at all
avizandum, take under further
    consideration
aw, I
awgent, solicitor
ay/aye, yes

baillie, senior magistrate
baith, both
banes, bones
bannin', cursing
barfit, barefoot
bawbee, halfpence
belang, belong
bickerin', rattling
bode, bid, offer
birkie, youth
bittie, little
bizzin', buzzing
blaw, blow; boast
blebberin', blubbering
bleck, beat
bleezin', blazing
blether, chatter
blin', blind
—*blin' staggers*, ?disease of cattle
boddom, bottom
bodie, person
body bulk, entirely
bonnet laird, small landed
    proprietor
bookit,
—*little bookit*, modest in
    achievement
boordin', boarding

braid, broad
brainch, branch
bran'it, brindled
branks, bridle, restraint
braw, fine
—*in a braw wye o' deein'*,
  prospering
brawly, well
breeks, trousers
brither/breeder, brother
brocht, bought
brodmil, brood
brod, board
brook, endure
broon, brown
browster, brewer
buik, book
Burghers, sect of severely
  Calvinist seceeders
buzness, business
byous, extraordinary

cairry, carry, win
cam', came
can, responsibility
canna, cannot
cannas, canvas
—*winnow on 'er ain cannas*, fend
  for herself
cannier, more carefully
carline, old woman
castock, cabbage stalk
catechees, cross-examine
catechis
—*say yer catechis*, say your piece
caul', cold
caup, bowl
ceevil, polite
chairge, charge
chap, knock
cheelie, small or young man
cheir, chair
chiel, man
chowk, jowel
chyne, chain
claes, clothes
claik, gossip
clype, malicious tale
concurrent, assistant
condeschen', condescend

conneckit, connected
convainience, convenience
coo, cow
coonsel, advice
coont, count
—*count and reckoning*, enforced
  settlement of accounts
coorse, course
coort, court
cottar, married farm labourer
countra, country
covenanter, religious reformer
crap, crop, throat
—*craw i' their craps*, be to their
  disadvantage
—*shak' their crap*, air grievances
creatur, creature
creel, basket
creesis, crisis
crook
—*links o' the crook*, pothook
  chain
cud, could
cudna, could not
cutty, mischevious young girl

daachter, daughter
dask, desk
daun'er, stroll
daur, dare
daurna, dare not
daursay, dare say
dee, do
deed, indeed
deein', doing
defen', defend
deid, dead
deidly, deadly
deith, death
denner, dinner
depairt, depart
depen', depend
deteen, detain
dicht, wipe
didna, did not
dight, clad
ding, cast
dischairge, discharge
disna, does not
disobleege, disoblige

disregaird, disregard
div, do
dizzen, dozen
doesna, does not
dominie, schoolmaster
donald, measure of spirits
dooble, double
doon, down
doot, doubt
dootfu', doubtful
dootless, doubtless
dootna, doubt not
draigl't, tatterdemalion
dree, suffer
dung, knocked
dunshoch, large bunch

edicatit, educated
een, eyes
eenoo, just now
ees't, used
eese, use
eesfu', useful
en', end
enteetl't, entitled
enterteen, entertain
erran', errand
ettle, aim
expec', expect
expeckit, expected

fa, who
fac', fact
fac't, faced
fae, from
faever, whoever
fain, keen
—*wud fain hae*, would like
 to have
far'est, furthest
farrer, further
fash, bother
fat, what
fatever, whatever
fauldet, folded
faur, where
faut, fault
fawvourable, favourable
fearna, do not fear
fecht, fight

feck, most
feenally, finally
feerious, extremely
fence, formally open
fen'less, lacking in robustness
ferlie, wonder
fernyear, last year
fest, fast
fite, white
flawvour, favour
 Forbes Mackenzie Act limited
 opening hours in Scottish pubs
forby/forbye, as well
forehan'it, advance
forenent, against
forgie, forgive
forhoo, abandon
forrat/forrit, forward
four hours, tea
fowk, people
frae, from
freely, completely
freen/frien', friend
freuchle, frail
furth, out
fyou, few

gabbin', talking idly
gae, go
gaein/gaen, going
gane, gone
gar, make
gat, got
gey, very
gie, give
giein', giving
gin, if
glaid, glad
gloam't, become dusk
gloamin', dusk
goin', going
gowd, gold
graiff, grave
graip, grope
greetin', crying
grun, ground
gryte
—*gryte lawvyer*, expert lawyer
gweed, good
gweeshtie, exclamation

gya, gave
gyang, go

haar, sea fog
—*ha' bible*, large family bible
hadna, had not
hae, have
haena, have not
haibits, habits
haill, whole
hain, save
hairst, harvest
haiver, talk nonsesne
hame, home
han', hand
—*tak' in han'*, undertake
hasna, has not
haud, hold
haumer, clatter
hed, had
hedna, had not
heid, head
—*heid-speed*, head man
heilan', highland
hen
—*hen't it*, absconded
heritable subjects, properties
herriet, reduced to poverty
hert, heart
het, hot
hirplin', limping
hizzie, trollop
hoast, cough
hodden grey, coarse homespun
  cloth
hoo, how
hooever, however
hoord, hoard
hoor, hour
hoose, house
hoot fie, exclamation
horning, enforced payment
  of debt
houp, hope
howff, place of resort
howk, dig
hurley, barrow
huz, us

ilka, every

ill ee, evil eye
—*ill upon't*, badly placed
'im, him
'imsel', himself
insnorlt, entangled
interpone, intervene
isna/isnin', is not
ither, other

jeestin', jesting
jist, just
joost, just
joostice, justice
jougs, pillory

keil mark, brand
ken, know
kennin', knowing
kin', kind
kirkit, formally received in
  church
kittle, difficult, abrupt
knap
– *bit knap o' a laddie*, sprig
  of a lad
knowe, hillock

laddikie, little boy
lade, load
lair, grave
lairge, large
lairstane, gravestone
laitin, latin
lan', land
lang, long
langer, longer
lassikie, little girl
lat, let
lattin', letting
lave, rest
lawvyer, lawyer
leems
– *aye shavin' or*
sharpin yer leems, indulging in
  sarcasm
licht, light
lickly, likely
likein', maybe
lippen to, rely on
lochie, small lake

lood, loud
loon, boy
loonie, boy
lows, loose, unyoke
lug, ear
luik, look

maijesty, majesty
mainner, manner
mainteen, maintain
mair, more
mairgin, margin
mairry, marry
maist, most
maister, master
maistly, mostly
maitter, matter
marriet, married
maun, must
mauna, must not
mayna, may not
meith, landmark
mengyie, group
merchan', merchant
mervel, marvel
micht, might
michtna, might not
mim, quiet
min, man
min', mind
misfit, displease
mith, might
mitha, might have
mither, mother
mithna/mithnin, might not
morn, tomorrow
mou', mouth
muckle, big
mull, mill
muv, move

na, no
naar
– *naar-han'*, nearly
nackit, titch
nae, not, no
nain, own
nairrow, narrow
naitral, natural
nane, none

nateevity, nativity
necessar, necessary
neebour, neighbour
needna, need not
neist, next
nevvy, nephew
nicht, night
nickum, rascal
nit, nut
nown, own
nyeuk, corner

obleege, oblige
ocht, ought
offisher, officer
'oman, woman
onbeen, without being
onwal, interest, rent
ony, any
onyhoo, anyhow
onything, anything
onywye, anyway
oondependent, independent
oonder, under
oonhandy, unhandy
oonkent, unknown
oonweel, unwell
oor, our
oorlich, miserable
oorsel's, ourselves
oot, out
ootward, outward
ordeen, ordain
orra, vulgar
ou, oh
ouk, week
ower/owre, over, too

painch, paunch
paip, pope
pairis'/pairish, parish
pairt, part, district
pairts, ability
pairty, party
pass, passage
pawrent, parent
peertith, poverty
persuaad, persuade
pitten, put
pleesure, pleasure

poin'et, have property seized for debt
pooer/poo'er, power
poopit, pulpit
pow, head
preevacy, privacy
prent, print
preses, chairman
priveleege, privilege
prood, proud
prove, test
prov't, proved
puckle, lot
puddock, frog
pumphel, cattle pen

quaen, girl
queel, cool

rael/raelly, really
rape
– *trailin' the rape*, cursing with ill luck
red, rode
– *redd up*, put in order
refees, refuse
regaird, regard
requare, require
richt, right
rin, run
roch, rough
roup, sale by auction

sacrifeece, sacrifice
sae, so
saft, soft
sainior, senior
sair, painful, painfully; serve
sairin', serving
sairious, serious
sall, shall
sanctifiet, sanctified
satisfeet/satisfiet, satisfied
sattl'/sattle, settle
sauchen, willow
sax, six
schaime, scheme
scran, pickings
scrub, mean grasping person
seelence, silence

seener, sooner
seerly, surely
seleckit, selected
sen', send
set, suit
shaidow, shadow
shak', shake
shaltie, pony
shargarin', stunting
shavin', joking
shirra, sheriff
sib, related
siccar, secure
sicht, sight
siclike, suchlike
sid, should
siller, money
sindoon, sundown
sin'er, sunder
sizie, small size
sizzon
—*oot o' sizzon*, overcooked
skail, spill
'Skairey', Alexander Henderson, the Warlock of Wartle
slap, interval
slicht, slight
—*slicht han'it*, careless
sma', small
smairt, smart
sneck, latch
sneeshin, snuff
snell, cold
snifterin', snuffling
sobereeze, render sober
socht, sought
solemneese, solemnify
soliteed, solidity
sookin', novice
soosh, punish severely
soun', sound
souter, cobbler
spak', spoke
speer, ask
spen', spend
stan', stand
stane, stone
starn, a little
—*still an' on*, yet
stoot, vigorous